LATE AND SOON

D0993356

LATE AND SOON

E. M. DELAFIELD

PAN BOOKS LTD : LONDON

First published 1943 by Macmillan and Co. Ltd.
This edition published 1948 by Pan Books Ltd.,
8 Headfort Place, London, S.W.1

FOR

KATE O'BRIEN

I

THE rain, slanting and silver, drove lightly across the terrace and down the grassy hollows of the park where nettles and docks and bramble bushes grew freely amongst the clumps of yellow gorse.

General Levallois stood leaning on his two sticks under the portico that jutted out beyond the garden door of Coombe and spoke to his sister, although gazing away from her as he did so.

"Better have the tennis-court dug over, I suppose."

"I thought we wouldn't, Reggie. We've dug up the paddock, and the top field, and those other two and the old rose garden. Surely we can keep the tennis-court."

"My dear girl, who do you think is ever going to play tennis here again?"

"The children," said Valentine Arbell.

Her voice died away into silence, as though she foresaw the General's reply before he spoke it.

"What children?" he demanded derisively.

What children indeed.

Primrose was three-and-twenty and even before the war had never, once her school-days were over, wished to spend her time at home.

Jessica was seventeen and a half and was waiting to be called up for the W.A.A.F.

She would be gone long before summer came again.

Valentine Arbell had never had a son.

"I suppose you're right," she acknowledged with the gentle Edwardian courtesy of tone and manner that betrayed her years far more surely than did her appearance. "It would hardly be worth while to keep up the poor old tennis-court for one's possible grandchildren."

She smiled as she spoke and it would have taken someone more observant, and far more interested in

5

human reactions, than was the General to notice the real gravity—a kind of permanent, incredulous sadness—of her face.

"Grandchildren!" ejaculated the General. "You aren't counting on anything of that sort from Primrose, I imagine, and as for young Jess, I hope she's a long way from thinking of such nonsense as marriage with any of those shockin' fellers she romps round with."

"I'm sure she is, Reggie. Anyhow, none of them are in earnest. They're all much too young to marry."

"That doesn't stop 'em, nowadays. And they aren't necessarily thinking of marrying either, but I suppose Jess knows what's what, like the rest of the girls. What about coming in, old girl? It's turning wet."

It had turned wet long ago. Small puddles had formed on the gravel beneath their feet, and the blue distant hills and the square tower of St. Martin's church rising from the town in the valley below were all obscured by mist.

"Come on in," repeated the General, shuffling slowly round on his sticks.

"I must see to the hens. I'll come through the house and get my gum-boots."

They went in at the garden door that was placed in direct line with the big front double-doors of the house affording a view straight across the outer and inner halls to the terrace.

Valentine adjusted her pace to that of her brother which might have belonged to a very old man, although he was in reality only fifty-six—twelve years her senior. He was the eldest, and she the youngest, of a large family of Huguenot descent, long established in England.

General Levallois had come to Coombe soon after the death of Valentine's husband, twelve years earlier, and had remained there, without any formal discussion on either side, ever since.

The house was large enough to accommodate many more people than were likely to live there again—until it should be sold and turned into a school or an institution.

They crossed the inner hall that was coconut-matted, and very dark, with glass cases filled with stuffed fish and birds on every side, and passed into the hall proper.

6

This was large, furnished with comfortable, ancient armchairs and sofas covered in shabby, old-fashioned rose-patterned chintzes.

It lay under a glass cupola that had been painted a sinister dark blue in an effort to conform to the black-out regulations.

In January, nineteen hundred and forty-two, the paint had already begun to look thin and scratchy.

Out of the inner hall led half a dozen doors, each one badly in need of a fresh coat of cream-coloured paint—except one that was inadequately covered with shredded patches of red baize and obviously led to the domestic offices. The other doors led respectively into drawing-room, dining-room, library, billiard-room and a small sitting-room that was still traditionally called the breakfast-room. Of these, only the dining-room and the library were now in use. The hall had a large open fireplace and it was there that Valentine had long ago established her writing-desk and there that she sat when she was not out of doors.

The General lowered himself into the largest armchair, nearest the fire, with his habitual hissing sound as of indrawn breath, long since become automatic.

He let both his sticks fall clattering to the floor as he always did, although it would subsequently cause him considerable discomfort to reach for them again, and he would be annoyed if anybody picked them up unasked and would probably enquire whether he was supposed to be a damned cripple.

Valentine went on, through the glass doors at the end of the room that opened into a small lobby where coats and mackintoshes and hats hung, walking-sticks and umbrellas stood in a huge and hideous blue china receptacle, and an oak chest held old tennis racquets, old balls, still older croquet mallets and cricket-bats.

She remembered them, as she pulled a tall pair of gum-boots out of a corner and worked her slim legs and feet into them. Reggie was quite right.

The children were no more.

For twenty years her life had been conditioned by the existence of Primrose, and later on by that of Jess as well.

7

It had been so even in her husband's lifetime. She had loved Humphrey, but had put the children first—the child really, since Primrose had been the only one for six years.

When she and Humphrey had married, whilst he was on sick leave in nineteen hundred and seventeen, they had both been in love—Valentine imaginatively and Humphrey physically.

It had lasted longer with him than with her.

Wrestling with the slippery boots, Valentine thought back across the years as she so often did.

She had been thirty-two when Humphrey was killed out hunting and, whatever anybody might say, she knew that nothing in her had been destroyed by that shock and sadness.

Destruction, if there were any, had been accomplished during the placid, matter-of-fact years of her married life.

The romantic impulse that had once been the moving-spring of her nature moved her no longer. At Humphrey's death the strong strain of realism that is the concomitant of true romanticism had told her that she had nothing to gain by changing her way of life.

Coombe was her own, it was home, changeless and unchangeable to Primrose and Jess, and at Coombe she had remained, the months and the years divided into school terms, Christmas holidays, Easter holidays, the long summer holidays, the visits that she had paid to the children at their school on the East Coast.

Suddenly, as it seemed, all that was over. But it wasn't really sudden.

Primrose had left school at eighteen and said that she wanted to go to College and had been sent there—with difficulty, for there was hardly any money. Had she been happy there?

Valentine felt that she would never know. When once she asked the question Primrose had said: It's all right, thanks—with a slightly more discontented expression than usual on her always discontented face.

No one had expected her to take more than a pass degree, nor did she.

8

Since then, Primrose had spent most of her time in London, sometimes picking up a job, more often without one. She stayed with College friends or, very occasionally, with one of the Levallois' relations.

When she came home it was to sleep until luncheon-time every morning, strew soiled and torn underwear all over the bathroom and ask why one of the maids couldn't attend to it, and engage in endless and unexplained telephone calls that occupied her most of every evening.

With the outbreak of war Primrose had gone straight back to London. She had done a variety of war jobs, had scarcely been home at all, and now was driving a Mobile Canteen.

Primrose was gone—gone beyond recall, and it wasn't the war that had taken her.

Jess had come home when her school had been evacuated into Wales, begging and imploring to be allowed to volunteer for the W.A.A.F.

She was gay and eager and full of enthusiasm, and had declared candidly that there wouldn't be anything whatever to do at home, now that there was nothing to ride, and that she'd be wretched there—simply wretched. Any day, now, Jess might be called up.

Meanwhile she worked nearly every afternoon and evening at the Canteen in the village, and made friends with very young soldiers and asked them to Coombe.

When they came, she introduced them as Bill or Michael or Tony, and they had tea downstairs and then went up to the schoolroom with her or, more occasionally, played romping games in the hall.

Jess was only waiting for the moment when she should join up.

Come back she might or might not, but the words "the children" held no more meaning at Coombe, or for its mistress.

She stood up, fastened her tweed coat and went out, followed by Jessica's puppy—a leggy mongrel—and General Levallois' fat spaniel.

The hens, who should have been in the orchard, were straggling, wet and shabby-looking, on the oval grass plot before the house.

9

She made an encouraging sound and they lurched along behind her, squawking and clucking, as she walked to the stable yard that stood a little way off, built at right angles to the house.

Regardless of the rain, and with deliberation, Valentine fed them and shut them up in their dilapidated coops.

Then she went slowly back to the house.

Coombe was an old house, that had been often added to—three-storied, slate-roofed and stone-built. An open-sided lichen-spattered tower rose above all the irregular and numerous chimney-stacks, and in it hung a large bell, cast in the reign of Elizabeth.

Stone pillars, moss-grown and out of the true, supported, over the double-doors of entrance, a lead roofing shaped like an inverted V.

Against one of the pillars now leant a dripping bicycle, and Valentine saw a tall youthful-looking figure in battle dress reaching out to pull at the rusty iron chain that hung beside the door. She hastened her step, although knowing that she could not get to him soon enough to avert the minor disaster that experience warned her to expect.

As she had foreseen, the chain immediately broke in the young officer's hand and he was looking at the detached length of rusty links with some dismay when she reached his side.

"It's quite all right—it's been done before. It doesn't matter at all."

"I'm terribly sorry," said the young man. "I can't imagine how it happened. I didn't think I'd been so violent."

"I'm sure you weren't. The chain is very old, and every time it breaks somebody hooks it on again without mending it properly. Is there anything I can do for you? Won't you come in?"

"Thanks very much. I wondered if I could see Lady Arbell for a few minutes?"

He looked at her questioningly.

"I am Lady Arbell. Do come in."

The officer, who was apparently shy, muttered something about being very wet and scraped his boots with prolonged violence on the iron scraper at the door.

Valentine stepped inside, giving him time, and pulled off her own gum-boots. Then she turned round again.

"I'm afraid I don't know your name," she said apologetically.

At the same time she remembered, with a little inward flash of amusement, her daughter Jessica's repeated assurances that *no one*, no one in the world, ever asked anybody's name now. It just wasn't ever done.

But Valentine knew that she would continue to do it.

"Cyril Banks," said the young man. "Lieutenant Banks—1st Battalion——" And he added the name of his regiment.

As if fearing that he might have been guilty of a too great formality he finished with a thoughtfully-spoken pronouncement:

"I'm usually—in fact always—called Buster."

"Do come in," said Valentine.

With a final scrape, and a final mutter that denoted apology but was indistinguishable, Lieutenant Banks came in.

The General was still sitting by the fire and Valentine introduced the young man to him. She knew that her brother would be very slightly pleased and stimulated by the presence of any visitor, even one whom he would neither see, nor wish to see, ever again.

Perhaps, however, they would see Lieutenant Banks again. He had come to enquire, with diffidence and apologies, whether Lady Arbell would consider the billeting of two officers. One of them was his own Colonel, the other one he could not as yet indicate.

"It's just a case of morning and evening," he said, as though in explanation. "I mean, they'd be out all day and they'd probably be away quite a lot, too, on various exercises and things. I don't know whether all your rooms are full up?"

"No, not now. We've got three evacuee children, but they're in a wing at the back. There are three empty rooms in the front of the house, though I do try to keep one in case any relation who's been bombed out of London should want to come here."

"Oh, rather," said Banks. "Well, of course, two rooms would be perfectly okay."

"This house hasn't got nearly as many bedrooms as you might suppose, from the look of it," General Levallois observed. "And only one bathroom."

"Really, sir," respectfully returned Lieutenant Banks.

He sounded sympathetically dismayed, but Valentine guessed that he had not expected more than one bathroom. If he knew anything at all about houses like Coombe, he knew that they never did have more than one bathroom and that one a converted dressing-room, very cold and with an inadequate supply of hot water.

"Would you like to see the rooms?" she asked.

Lieutenant Banks wouldn't dream of troubling her. He was certain the rooms would be marvellous.

Looking shyer than ever—he was a very fair youth and blushed conspicuously—he made a number of statements regarding the conditions of the billeting of officers and their batmen.

Valentine listened with as much attention as though she had not heard exactly the same thing before, from representatives of the three different regiments that had previously been stationed in the neighbourhood and then sent elsewhere.

In each case they had said that she would be notified within the week of a decision, and in each case she had heard not another word on the subject. To the earnest and innocent Lieutenant Banks, who looked scarcely more than twenty years old, Valentine gave no hint of these previous experiences.

General Levallois was asking the Colonel's name.

"Lonergan, sir."

"Irish," said the General, without inflection.

"Yes, sir."

The General said coldly that he should hope to have the pleasure of meeting Colonel Lonergan one of these days.

There was a pause.

Valentine began to talk about the neighbourhood, to ask whether Lieutenant Banks knew Devon already, to ascertain from him that his own part of the world was

Northampton, and that before the war he had worked for one year in his father's insurance office.

She knew that he wished to go, but was finding it impossible to get up and take his leave.

She offered him a cigarette from a box on the table.

Lieutenant Banks thanked her very much, said that he didn't smoke, and talked for several minutes about the cigarette shortage, and also told a story of an uncle who had visited the East Coast and found all the shops full of cigarettes, matches, sweets and chocolates with nobody to buy them.

Valentine made the rejoinders long grown familiar and the General contributed an occasional observation. Lieutenant Banks, looking disturbed and uneasy, still sat on.

Suddenly there sounded an outburst of barking from both the dogs. The spaniel subsided at a ferocious-sounding order from General Levallois, but the pup dashed forward excitedly, springing from side to side and making a deafening clamour.

The glass doors were pushed open and left swinging as Jess came in.

Her first greeting was for her dog.

"Hullo, aunt Sophy! Down, like a good dog, down! Darling little dog! Get down."

The puppy leapt upon her, trying to lick her face, and Jess picked it up and carried it bodily across the hall.

"Hallo!"

"This is Lieutenant Banks—my daughter Jessica."

Banks stood up and Jess said "Hallo" again and shifted the wriggling dog underneath one arm.

"Sorry about the awful row, uncle Reggie. Hallo, Sally!"

The spaniel's tail flumped upon the floor in acknowledgment.

"I say, *what* do you call your dog?" the young soldier demanded—speaking in a quite new, much more natural and animated voice.

"Aunt Sophy. Actually, she's the exact image of an aunt I have, called Sophy. Even mummie admits that. It isn't her sister, or anything like that. In fact she's a great-aunt."

13

"Does she know?"

"We don't think so. She's only once been here since I had the puppy and of course I said I hadn't yet decided on a name. Actually, she kept on making rather dim suggestions, like Rover and Tray and Faithful."

Lieutenant Banks began to laugh, and Jess laughed too.

Valentine felt relieved.

She leant back in her chair and looked at her younger daughter.

Primrose resented being looked at so intensely that her mother could hardly ever bear to do so, although no single word had passed between them on the subject.

Jess was not only quite unself-conscious, but she was scarcely sufficiently interested in people to notice whether they looked at her or whether they didn't. She was tall and slight, much fairer than Valentine had ever been, and with exactly Humphrey's squarely-shaped, open face, with a well-cut, firm, insensitive mouth, rather thick snub nose and big, straight-gazing brown eyes.

She looked her best in the clothes that she most often wore, riding-breeches and a high-necked wool jumper, under an open tweed riding-coat.

Her head was bare and her hair, which was flaxen and very pretty, was just shoulder-length and attractively curled at the ends.

Valentine wondered, as she wondered almost every day of her life, what Humphrey would think if he could suddenly walk into Coombe now, after twelve years.

Supposing he were able to come back?

The place was hardly altered at all. There was a painting of himself, that his mother had insisted upon having done from a photograph after his death and that now hung above Valentine's desk.

She had never liked it, and thought it a bad painting—shrill and crude in colouring and with only a superficial resemblance to the original. But she had never had it moved, even after the death of her mother-in-law.

It was almost the only new thing in the room except for the rose-patterned chintzes. The year before Humphrey died, and for several years afterwards, the covers had been blue, with a violet stripe.

Valentine remembered them clearly.

Humphrey, if he could come back, would expect to see that familiar colouring. And the Spanish leather screen that now stood opposite to where she was sitting had been in one of the spare bedrooms in Humphrey's day. It had been moved to its now permanent station in the hall when the General complained of a draught behind his habitual armchair.

The spaniel, Sally, had grown old and fat. She was nearly fourteen.

Humphrey had probably never seen her at all. But he had had two spaniels himself—both of them dead, now.

It was the people over whom Humphrey might well hesitate longest.

Jess, when he saw her last, had been a baby of five years old, backward of speech and not particularly pretty. He had not taken a great deal of notice of her, perhaps because he was disappointed that she had not been a boy.

Impossible that he should ever recognize that baby in the tall, sprawling, graceful figure of the seventeen-year-old Jess, whose artless use of a candidly vermilion lipstick only served to emphasize her appearance of young, open-air innocence.

Humphrey would wonder who the officer was and would dismiss him with a phrase, "Not one of us, what."

Reggie? He'd know Reggie, of course, but the arthritis had only begun a year or two before Humphrey's death. Reggie hadn't been a cripple on two sticks before that. Seated, though, as he was now, he wouldn't have changed so very much. Humphrey would think he was on a visit. It wouldn't cross his mind that Reggie could be living at Coombe, paying a very small contribution to the household expenses and bringing with him his dog.

And then, thought Valentine as she had often thought before, there was herself. Humphrey would look first of all at her. She was the person he had cared for most in his life.

He had left her with brown hair—now it was heavily

streaked with a silvery grey. There were lines round her eyes and her mouth, and she had lost her colour. She used a pale-rose lip-stick, whereas she had used none at all in his lifetime. Her figure had not altered: she was as slim as she had been at twenty. And yet there was a difference. It was a soft, pliant slimness still but it was, indefinably, not that of youth. One realized that, looking at Primrose or Jessica.

All the same, Humphrey would know her immediately. He would find her altered only in the sense of having grown older. To this conclusion Valentine always came, in her habitual fantasy of Humphrey's return to the home from which he had been carried, in his coffin, twelve years earlier.

Long ago she had been startled by, and had subsequently answered, the question with which her own heart had confronted her.

If that impossible return could take place, if Humphrey could come back, a living man, from the grave, would it awaken happiness in her? Valentine knew without any doubt that the answer was No.

Humphrey had never given her either happiness or unhappiness. At best, their relationship had achieved a little pleasure, at most, some discontent.

Valentine, having known both happiness and unhappiness in her earliest youth, could still, at moments, vividly recall either.

"Oh, that'll be absolutely wizard!" cried Jess in her high, gay voice. "I don't suppose I shall be here myself much longer, I'm expecting to join up any minute practically—but it'll cheer up poor darling aunt Sophy like anything. She adores soldiers. D'you suppose they'll ever take her for a walk?"

"The Colonel's a terrific walker."

"Gosh!" said Jess thoughtfully. "Fancy a colonel."

She did not elucidate the exact grounds of the passing sensation of awe that had evidently prompted the exclamation.

It might have been the thought of the Colonel's rank, or his probable age, or his walking proclivities.

16

Lieutenant Banks said:

"The Colonel's the most marvellous man that ever lived," in quite inexpressive tones. Then at last he got up.

"Well, thanks frightfully, Lady Arbell."

"Must you go? Why don't you stay to tea?" Jess asked.

"It's terribly kind of you but I can't. I'm supposed to be back at three o'clock and it's ten minutes past four."

"Come on Sunday then. I expect I'll still be here. You could have a bath if you liked, and then tea, and then supper."

The young man's eyes turned towards Valentine.

She ratified Jessica's invitation.

"Thanks frightfully, Lady Arbell."

"Bring one or two other chaps with you, and we might play games or something," cried Jess.

"Yes, do," Valentine said.

Lieutenant Banks said that this was simply terrific, and absolutely marvellously kind, and completely okay so far as he knew but might he ring up?

Jess picked up aunt Sophy, holding her under her arm so that the puppy's legs all dangled in the air, and conducted Banks to the glass doors and through them.

There they remained, silhouetted against the light, and there they could be heard from time to time in apparently animated discussion punctuated by peals of laughter.

Valentine smiled involuntarily, exhilarated by the spontaneity of the sounds.

She looked at the same time rather apologetically towards her brother who was never in the least exhilarated by the behaviour of very young people, but quite the contrary.

General Levallois, however, was apparently not thinking about Jess and the officer.

He met his sister's eyes meditatively.

"Lonergan," he said. "Wasn't that the name of that feller in Rome?"

"Yes."

"Funny thing, if it should turn out to be the same one."

"It isn't an uncommon name, in Ireland."

"There aren't any uncommon names in Ireland," said the General.

"How did you remember, Reggie? You were in India at the time."

"Mother wrote reams, as she always did. Anyway, I never forget a name. You've never seen or heard of him since, have you?"

"Never," said Valentine.

She smiled.

"It was only a week, you know."

"What was only a week?" demanded Jess from behind her.

"A very silly business," declared the General.

"That happened more than twenty-five years ago," added Valentine gently.

"Mummie! Were you mixed up in it?"

"Yes. I was younger than you are now."

Jess gave her mother an affectionate, amused, incredulous look, before dropping on the floor beside her dog.

"Fancy you being mixed up in any very silly business!" she ejaculated.

Leaving them in the hall Valentine went up the steep, curving staircase with its worn carpet, almost threadbare, to her bedroom, shivering as she moved out of the range of the fire.

The stairs, the large circular-railed landing above and the bedrooms were all unheated, and their temperature seemed lower than that of the wet, mild January afternoon out of doors.

Valentine's room was a large, high one with two big windows that looked over the drive and the front of the park.

The furniture was shabby, of mixed periods, and there was not very much of it in proportion to the size of the room.

The walnut double-bed had already been in place, facing the windows, when Humphrey Arbell's mother had come to Coombe as a bride.

18

Valentine slowly changed her shoes, looked at her face and hair in the looking-glass without much attention and automatically pushed the loose silvery wave over her forehead into position.

She felt faintly disturbed.

It was not that she was afraid of meeting Rory Lonergan —if it should be Rory Lonergan.

On the contrary, she'd be disappointed if it *wasn't* Rory Lonergan. The idea of seeing him again brought with it a curious emotional excitement, partly amused and partly sentimental.

Her perturbation, Valentine found, arose from a faint sense of remorse that she had, by implication, accepted her brother's trivial estimate of the "very silly business" of twenty-five years earlier.

Reggie would necessarily see it like that—would have seen it like that even if he'd known far more about it than he ever had known.

But Valentine was clearly aware that what had happened that week in Rome in the spring of nineteen hundred and fourteen had held for her a reality that she had never found since.

II

THE evening meal at Coombe was still called dinner. It was announced, in a breathless and inaudible manner, by a fifteen-year-old parlour-maid.

The General nightly struggled into a patched and faded smoking-jacket of maroon velvet. Valentine Arbell—shuddering with cold—put on a three-year-old black chiffon afternoon dress and a thick Chinese shawl of embroidered silk of which the fringes caught in every available piece of furniture whenever she moved.

Jess, under violent protest, still obeyed the rule that compelled her to exchange warm and comfortable breeches or a tweed skirt and wool jumper for an outgrown silk or cotton frock from the previous summer.

19

"But once I've gone into uniform, mummie, never again," she said.

Valentine believed her.

As it was, she was always rather surprised that Jess should still do as she was told about changing for dinner when Primrose, at an earlier age, had flatly refused to do so.

"Come on, aunt Sophy," cried Jess hilariously as the mongrel rushed, falling over its own paws, at the young parlour-maid standing in the doorway.

Jess dashed at aunt Sophy, picked her up and allowed her face to be licked all over.

"Don't!" said Valentine involuntarily.

"Put the thing down, Jess," commanded the General. "Carting it about like that!"

Jess ignored them both, without ill-will but from sheer absorption in her dog and her own preoccupations.

Valentine sometimes wondered what those preoccupations were. Jess appeared so artless, so outspoken—yet never did she give one the slightest clue as to what her inmost thoughts might be.

She stood back now, politely, to let her mother precede her into the dining-room. The General shuffled along at his own pace with Sally, the spaniel, morosely crawling at his heels. She was old and fat, and hated leaving the fire in the hall for the unwarmed dining-room.

It was another large room and although shutters protected the three French windows behind their faded blue brocade curtains, a piercing draught always came from beneath the service door at the far end of the room.

It was impossible not to shudder, at the temperature of the dining-room.

The General made his nightly observation:

"This room is like an ice-house."

The oval walnut table, looking not unlike a desert island in the middle of an arctic sea, was laid with wine-glasses that were scarcely ever used, silver that required daily polishing, and a centrepiece of a Paul Lamerie silver rose-bowl.

Valentine disentangled the fringe of her shawl from

the arm of her chair and sat down at the head of the table, and General Levallois placed himself at the other end.

Jess shrieked directions to the dogs, knocked over a glass, laughed, and took her place facing the windows.

The conversation, which consisted of isolated observations and uninspired rejoinders, was spaced across long intervals of silence, and the first word was uttered by the General after Ivy, the maid, had left the room.

"These plates are stone-cold, as usual."

"I've told her, Reggie, but you know it's only Mrs. Ditchley. It's not as though she was a proper cook."

"Shall we ever have a proper cook again, mummie?"

"I don't think so, darling. It seems extremely unlikely that anybody will have one, at least until the war's over."

"And then we'll all be Communists, under Stalin, and there'll *be* no servants," said Jess. She glanced at her uncle out of the corners of her eyes.

"I'm not going to rise, Jessica."

Jess and Valentine both laughed, and the General looked pleased with himself.

When the few spoonfuls of thin potato soup were finished, Jess got up, pretended to fall over aunt Sophy and played with her for a moment, and then went and jerked the old-fashioned china bell-handle, painted with roses and pansies, at the side of the empty fireplace.

The harsh, metallic clanging that ensued could be heard in the distance.

Jess sat down again.

She talked to the dogs in an undertone. The General put on his glasses and read the little white menu-card, in its silver holder, that he always expected to find on the table in front of him in the evenings, and that Valentine always wrote out for him. He inspected it without exhilaration, and pushed it away again.

Ivy came in again, changed the plates, and handed round first a silver entrée dish, and then two vegetable dishes.

"Do we *have* to have baked cod every single day?" Jess asked plaintively.

"It was all I could get."

Much later on, General Levallois addressed his sister.

"I thought we'd agreed not to have the potatoes boiled every time they appear."

"I don't suppose Mrs. Ditchley has many ideas beyond boiling them. And it's not easy to spare any fat for frying them or doing anything amusing. I'll speak to her to-morrow."

Valentine made these rejoinders almost as she might have spoken them in her sleep, so familiar were they.

She knew that the food was uninteresting, ill-prepared, and lacking in variety, and she regretted it, mildly, on her brother's account, rather more on Jessica's.

Both Primrose and Jess had taken a Domestic Science course at school: on Primrose it had apparently made no impression whatever. Jess had acquired some skill at laundry-work and sometimes washed and ironed her own clothes. She said that she hated cooking, house-work and sewing, and never intended to do any of them.

Valentine rather wonderingly remembered her own education, in the various capitals of Europe into which her father's diplomatic career had taken him.

She had learnt two languages besides her own, and knew the rules of precedence at a dinner-party, and she had been a beautiful ballroom dancer and had had a good seat on a horse.

She could think of nothing else that she had ever acquired.

Certainly not the art of housekeeping in England on an inadequate income. She had never done it well, even in Humphrey's lifetime.

Contrary to what a good many people had repeatedly told her, Valentine did not really believe that she could have learned. She disliked everything that she did know about housekeeping and could not persuade herself that it was of sufficiently intrinsic importance to justify the expenditure of time, money and nervous energy that it seemed to require.

"Mummie, d'you think those officers will really be billeted here, this time?"

"They might be, Jess. But we never heard any more of the other ones who said they were coming."

"Still, a *Colonel*. They can't go chopping and changing about with *him*. I hope he'll come and I hope Buster'll be the other one."

"Buster?"

"Lieutenant Banks is always called Buster. He told me so himself. I thought he was divine. Mummie! D'you mean to say we're having a savoury *again*, instead of a sweet?"

Jess picked up, and then threw down, the small knife and fork that had led her to this deduction.

"My dear, it's almost impossible to get anything to make a sweet of, nowadays. And you know, we did have a pudding at lunch."

"Well, God help this poor Colonel person, that's all, if he comes here expecting to be fed."

Jessica's lamentations were seldom meant to be taken seriously.

When Ivy handed round the dish where sardines lay upon dark and brittle fragments of toast, it was not Jess but General Levallois who complained.

"I thought we'd just been eating fish, Val?"

"I know we have. Really and truly, Reggie, we've got to take what we can get nowadays."

"Certainly we have. But I don't think this woman has much idea of what's what. *Surely* she can arrange things so that we don't have two fish courses one on top of the other."

"She can't, but I suppose I could," said Valentine. "I must try and manage better another time."

The gentle politeness of this phrase, in return for a stricture that she thought both graceless and unreasonable, was quite automatic.

For more than twenty years now Valentine had been answering with gentle and polite phrases that meant nothing at all, most of the remarks addressed to her. She had been trained from babyhood to think politeness of the utmost importance, and she had never outgrown, nor sought to outgrow, the habit of it. But she was sometimes conscious that her own good manners afforded her a sense of superiority and of that she was slightly ashamed.

She knew that it had annoyed Humphrey, for the

Arbell tradition was the blunter, more outspoken one of the British squirearchy. He had once accused her of never losing her temper.

Valentine could not remember what reply she had made to that.

The true answer, she thought, was that it had never been worth while.

"There's another sardine left, mummie. Do have it."

"No thank you, darling."

"Uncle Reggie? Aren't you going to have it?"

"It doesn't sound as though I were, Jess."

"No truly—*please* do."

"Go on. Take it. I don't want it."

"It would be quite possible to have another tin of sardines opened," said Valentine. "We've really got plenty of those in the store cupboard."

"I'm glad we're not reduced to splitting the last sardine," Jess declared. "Well, if nobody wants it——"

She got up and helped herself from the dish left on the sideboard.

"Shall I ring, now I'm up? I'll have finished long before she gets here."

Ivy's final appearance was for the purpose of clearing everything off the table, sweeping up the crumbs onto a silver salver, and then putting down three Wedgwood dessert plates each with its glass finger-bowl, a decanter with a very little port in it before the General, and a dish of small red apples.

Jess ate one of the apples and the General made his customary gesture of passing round the decanter, from which no one—not even himself—ever poured out a drink.

"You know," said Jess, "I often think this house is a bit like a madhouse. The way we sit here, and let Ivy wait on us, and all that business of clearing away for dessert when there isn't any dessert—honestly, it's bats, isn't it?"

"Must behave like civilized beings," suggested General Levallois, rather wearily and without much conviction.

"Nobody else does. Really and truly. I mean the people at school's houses that I've stayed at, everybody

24

waits on themselves, and it's practically always supper, not dinner, and nobody *dreams* of changing their clothes. And at Rockingham, which is the only grand place I ever go to, there's a butler and a proper dinner. I don't mean that we don't get proper food here, mummie, but it isn't exactly dinner, is it? I mean, not compared to aunt Venetia's."

"Your aunt Venetia's husband is a rich man—or at least he was once. He won't be now," said the General, not without an underlying note of satisfaction.

"I bet you, however poor they get, aunt Venetia and uncle Charlie will go on having salmon and roast duck and pheasants and things. Isn't it awful how one never thinks about anything except food nowadays? Come on, dogs! It's time you thought about food, too."

Jess went out, preceded by the dogs, to feed them in the lobby.

Valentine and the General followed, Valentine disentangling the fringes of her shawl from a chair-back.

In the hall she threw another log on the fire, shook up the cushions and emptied an ash-tray. General Levallois remarked, as she had known that he would:

"Can't the housemaid or one of 'em do that while we're in the dining-room?"

"I could tell her about it."

The child of fourteen who, with Ivy and the cook, completed the indoor staff at Coombe had plenty to do already, and did it sufficiently badly. It would be useless to impose fresh duties on her.

Valentine, however, followed her usual appeasement methods almost without knowing that she did so.

"I should, if I were you," the General assented, as he had done two nights earlier and would do again on the morrow.

"Could you bear it, Reggie, if when Jess has been called up and we're all by ourselves, we had something more like—well, more like high tea? I don't mean at five o'clock, but perhaps at half-past six. It would simplify things, and as Jess says, it's what everybody's doing—except, apparently, Venetia and Charlie."

"I suppose we must give up whatever's necessary and

I'm the last man on earth to complain, but is that really going to make so much difference? I should have thought we'd done plenty as it was. Where's my whiskey, where's my tobacco, where's my after-dinner coffee?" enquired the General rather piteously. "All given up."

"I know. Well, perhaps we can manage."

"If we're to have two soldiers billeted on us, we shall have to. I'm not going to ask any Army man—even an Irishman—to sit down to high tea."

"I don't suppose they'll come."

The telephone bell rang from the inconvenient and draughty corner, exactly outside the door of the downstairs lavatory, where Humphrey's father had installed it.

"I'll go," shouted Jess from the lobby.

They heard her rushing to it, and the puppy barking.

"There's no such tearing hurry," muttered the General. "Come here, Sally!" he shouted. The old dog ambled up and settled down at his feet.

He slowly put on his spectacles and started work on the crossword puzzle in *The Times*.

Valentine took up her knitting.

She could hear, without distinguishing any words, one side of the telephone conversation. It was evidently someone wanting to talk to Jess. A contemporary, because she was screaming freely and every now and then emitting a shriek of laughter.

Perhaps it was Primrose, speaking from London.

Primrose and Jess often quarrelled when they were together, but they would sometimes hold long, expensive, seemingly friendly talks over the telephone.

Primrose never wrote, unless she wanted something sent from home, and then it was usually on a postcard.

Valentine evaded, as usual, dwelling on the thought of her elder daughter. She reminded herself of the next monthly meeting of the Women's Institute, of which she was President, and she tried to remember what had been planned for the evening's programme.

General Levallois asked her help over an elusive clue in his puzzle: she gave it tentatively and unsuccessfully.

"Isn't it about time to switch on for the news?" he asked suspiciously.

26

They never missed listening to the Nine O'Clock News, but General Levallois seemed always afraid lest they might do so.

Valentine glanced at the clock, saw that it was only ten minutes to nine, and obediently got up and turned on the wireless.

She shivered as she moved away from the small area of space warmed by the fire. The fringe of her shawl caught in a piece of furniture and she released it.

Jess came plunging back to them, the pup at her heels.

"That was Primrose, and she's got a week's leave from Saturday and we're to expect her when we see her."

"Is she going to spend the whole week here?" cried Valentine, the blood rushing into her face.

For a moment she felt as she had felt long ago when the children were coming home for their holidays and plans for treats and pleasures for them had thronged her mind.

"She says so. She must be frightfully tired," said Jess naïvely.

"Did she say how she was? Is she all right?"

"Everything seemed okay. And mummie—this is a frightfully funny thing—what do you think?"

"What?" asked Valentine apprehensively.

She was nearly always afraid now, at the announcement of any news that concerned Primrose.

"She says she knows this Colonel—the Irish one— and he's a friend of hers. And she's pretty certain he *will* come here."

"That explains her condescending to spend a week in her own home, then," remarked General Levallois.

"Fancy you thinking of that, uncle Reggie! I wouldn't know. I suppose he's one of her boy friends, though I should have thought he was much too old."

"Did she tell you his name?" asked Valentine. "I mean his Christian name?"

Jess nodded.

"She calls him Rory. Fancy calling a Colonel Rory!"

Valentine was aware that her brother was looking at her, probably with the raised eyebrows of an unspoken question.

27

It was quite true that he scarcely ever forgot a name, but all the same, he'd want to make certain.

She gave him his answer, but without turning towards him and with her eyes on the fire.

"If his name's Rory Lonergan, he's the man I knew years ago, when we were in Rome. Only of course he wasn't a soldier, then."

"What was he?" asked Jess.

"A painter."

"Gosh! Fancy a painter. He must have done jolly well in the war to have been made a Colonel. I shouldn't have thought a painter would be a scrap of use in the Army, except to paint camouflage or something."

"He went through the last war, and I believe he did rather well."

"Is he nice?"

"I haven't seen him for—let me see—about twenty-eight years."

"Gosh! You won't recognize each other. I suppose he's married and with masses of children."

"I don't know," said Valentine.

"So long as he doesn't bring any of his wives and children here," Jessica said. "Actually, Primrose didn't *sound* as if he was married. But he must be miles too old for her."

"Damned nonsense you sometimes talk, Jess," the General remarked. "Shut up, now! The news is just coming on."

"It'll be Bruce," said Jess, and she threw herself down on the floor beside the two dogs.

The strokes of Big Ben, followed by the voice of the announcer, filled the room.

Valentine, not listening, continued to gaze into the fire. It really was Rory Lonergan.

She was not surprised. She had felt certain, on first hearing the name of Colonel Lonergan, that it was Rory and that she was going to see him again.

In all the years that had gone by since the summer of nineteen hundred and fourteen, Valentine had thought of Rory Lonergan often but not, after those first few, long-ago months, with any wish or expectation of seeing him.

28

It was a most innocent story.

She had met him at a *petite soirée* in the most Catholic circle in Roman society, ten days before her seventeenth birthday. He had fallen in love with her and she with him, and they had met daily, in secret, under the olive tree in a remote corner of the Pincio Gardens near a broken fountain—and Valentine's mademoiselle had found them out within a fortnight and had told her mother.

Valentine's mother had told her father and both of them had interviewed the young Lonergan—that raffish-looking, beggarly art student of an Irishman, as her father had described him—and Val had been sent for—she had always been Val, in those days.

She saw again the high room with its painted ceiling and formal decorative plaster mouldings, and her father, very stern and handsome, sitting at a big table that had a lot of gilding about it.

Her mother, who was not stern or handsome but of a tense, nervous, neurotic type far more difficult to resist, had been there too. And Rory had gone.

Instantly, she had thought that they had sent him away for ever and had felt a rush of wild, uncontrollable horror and despair. And at once the romantic, fairy-tale hope had followed that he would come back for her and they would go away together and belong to one another for ever and ever.

But none of it had followed the fairy-tale tradition.

Val's father and mother had scarcely even been angry with her: her father had spoken with cold, rather amused, contempt of young Lonergan, and her mother had said that silly, underhand schoolgirl ways naturally led inexperienced boys to suppose that they might behave as they chose.

In future, had said Lady Levallois, Mademoiselle would exercise a much closer supervision over a girl so little to be trusted.

Almost at once Val had understood that it was over and that there was no hope—but she had made her stand.

"Where is he?"

"Never mind.'

"But he can't have gone without saying goodbye to me!"

Looking back she could realize the appeal in that childlike wail of despair and she could see why her mother, arbitrary woman that she was of violent, incalculable moods that were a terror alike to herself and others, had suddenly and for a moment softened.

"You may have five minutes to say goodbye. He's waiting outside."

No need to ask where.

Lady Levallois' eyes had turned to the window over-looking the Pincio Gardens, and Valentine had fled.

Fled to the broken fountain, where Rory Lonergan was.

Oddly enough, she could remember very little of their last interview except that he had kissed her in a way in which he had never kissed her before and that she had been frightened and, at the bottom of her heart, shocked.

Whether they had been five minutes together or half an hour, she had never known. It was the kind Made-leine, her mother's French maid, who had been sent out to fetch her back to the house.

Val had gone, obediently.

Rory Lonergan hadn't asked her to come away with him.

Indeed, thought Valentine Arbell, looking back at Valentine Levallois in her seventeenth year, nothing could have been less possible than that any penniless youth with his living to earn should make such a suggestion.

In time, the certainty that he couldn't even have entertained a serious wish to do so became part of her acceptance of the whole episode.

It had been, as Reggie had said, a very silly business, from every point of view except one, and that one was known only to Valentine.

Those innocent and rapturous hours of love-making that she had shared through that brief fortnight with Rory Lonergan, with the hot May sunlight thrusting through the grey-green olive trees, had taught her the meaning of happiness, pure and complete. Never since had she found it.

In the years that had followed, and beneath which youth lay so deeply buried, Valentine had forgotten a great deal: emotionally, she had long forgotten almost everything about Rory Lonergan.

She had only not forgotten what happiness was, nor mistaken for it any lesser experience.

"The damned Japanese . . ." said the General. "The damned Americans . . . the damned fools we've got in the Cabinet . . ."

He was meditative, rather than annoyed. Jess said that President Roosevelt was a divine man, and she adored him. She scrambled to her feet and announced that she was going to say good-night to Madeleine, who had a small sitting-room of her own on the second floor.

Valentine knew that Jess would turn on Madeleine's radio and that together they would listen to the light-hearted and noisy programmes they both enjoyed and that the General would never tolerate downstairs.

In the summer, they would open up the schoolroom again and Jess should have friends to stay and have a little fun. . . .

But before the summer came, Jess would be gone.

"Shall I come and say good-night to you presently?"

"Okay," said Jess.

She picked up the puppy.

"That dog will lose the use of its legs."

"Poor darling aunt Sophy! Shall I have to get you a little pair of crutches?" crooned Jess to the puppy.

She sketched a salute in the direction of the General— her usual fashion of evading any good-night formula— and went away.

General Levallois gave renewed attention to his puzzle and Valentine took up a book. She was glad to read, but she scarcely ever did so before Jess went upstairs from an obscure feeling that Jess might, one evening, want to claim her mother's attention, and hesitate to interrupt her.

This evening she was paying no heed to her book.

31

She was thinking, in a strange medley of thoughts, about Primrose's arrival for her week's leave and whether there was any way in which it would be possible to make her enjoy it, and about Rory Lonergan whom one might be going to see again—and as Jess had said, they certainly wouldn't recognize one another—and about Jessica's announcement, that seemed to Valentine almost fantastically unreal, that Primrose—so emphatically belonging to the present—should claim as a friend of her own the man who had for so long belonged to Valentine's own far-away past.

Perhaps she was in love with him.

But he was too old. Rory Lonergan must be forty-seven or forty-eight, and Primrose was twenty-four.

Besides, he had probably married long ago. And although, one had to admit, that wouldn't prevent Primrose from starting what Jess called "quite a thing," it might well prevent Rory Lonergan from doing so.

The General threw down the newspaper and took off his spectacles, exchanging them for another pair.

That meant that he had failed to finish his crossword puzzle successfully.

"Anything happening to-morrow?"

"It's Sunday. On Monday I shall be going to the Red Cross work-party in the afternoon, and up to the village in the evening."

"Another Committee?"

"No. It's the Monthly Meeting of the Women's Institute."

The General made his unfailing rejoinder.

"I suppose you and Mrs. Ditchley will settle the affairs of the nation."

Valentine gave the polite, unmeaning smile with which she, as unfailingly, received the remark.

She was thinking how very much she wished that she could do more, and more important, war work.

Yet, if Coombe was to remain her home and that of the children, it seemed necessary that she should stay there. Her brother had told her flatly, months ago, that it was the only place in which she could be of the slightest real use.

Primrose had declared that women over thirty-five weren't wanted anywhere.

"Especially untrained ones," she had added—and if the first observation hadn't been specially meant for her, Valentine knew that the second one had.

She sat silent, waiting for the hands of the clock to reach half-past ten when she would go, shivering, up the stairs and along the passage to Jessica's room, the fringes of her shawl catching here and there as she moved.

III

THE rain had turned to an icy sleet and the temperature dropped many degrees, when Primrose Arbell, two days later, travelled down to Devonshire in a crowded third-class railway carriage.

Everyone in the carriage had gazed at her with a varying degree of attention and Primrose had looked at no one at all, according to her wont.

She endeavoured and expected to attract notice, although not necessarily admiration, for she was under no illusions as to her looks.

Yet she was arresting, aristocratic-looking and, to many men, alluring.

The opinion of women did not interest her.

Primrose was tall, slight and with long and very beautiful lines from shoulder to ankle. She did not always choose her clothes well, but she put them on and carried them, whatever they were, with an insolent, triumphant success. Her face was long and narrow with a long, pointed chin, a high-bridged, arrogant and finely-cut nose and rather large mouth with a curious downward twist at one corner whenever she spoke or—infrequently enough—laughed.

Her most arresting features were her eyes and eyebrows. The brows were dark and thick, in astonishing contrast to her naturally blonde hair, forming arches that suggested a perpetual expression of scornful surprise.

The eyes, deeply set, were not large but of a dense, blue-green colour, set in thick black lashes.

She affected a heavy, carefully applied make-up of which the tawny smoothness entirely concealed the natural texture of her skin. The deep, reddish-orange colour of her mouth was painted on sharply and boldly.

The station nearest to Coombe was on a small branch line, and when the train stopped at Exeter, Primrose pulled down her blue suitcase from the rack, pushed her way along the carriage and got out.

She neither joined the jostling crowd of people slowly moving towards the barrier nor did she make her way to the siding where the stopping train was presumably waiting. She stood near the shelter of the bookstall, not appearing to look for anyone, with her suitcase at her feet.

She was wearing a dark-blue wool dress with a coat of which the up-turned collar stood out round her long neck and threw up the pale colour of her uncovered fair hair gummed into elaborate and deliberately artificial-looking small curls, laid flat all round her narrow head like a coronal.

She had pulled on a short camel-hair coat and thrust both hands into the deep pockets.

Gazing downward, apparently at the suitcase, Primrose never raised her eyes until Colonel Lonergan, coming to a standstill directly in front of her, said:

"So there you are. Do you know it's the purest chance I was able to come and get you?"

Primrose gave him her one-sided smile and he picked up the suitcase and shouldered a way out through the crowd to where a very shabby and mud-bespattered car stood waiting.

"God, it's cold," muttered Primrose.

They were the first words she had spoken.

"Are you frozen, poor child? There's a rug."

Lonergan threw the case into the back of the car and wrapped the rug round Primrose as she settled down into the seat beside the driver's.

"Would you like to stop somewhere and have some hot coffee or some brandy or something before we start?"

34

"The pubs aren't open yet. We'll stop on the way, and have a drink. There's quite a decent pub about twelve miles out. Probably you've discovered it: *The Two Throstles.*"

"I have."

He got in beside her and started the car.

"Are you glad to see me, darling?"

"Fearfully," said Primrose. "If you hadn't turned up I should have had to take a slow train and then telephone from the station for a car."

Lonergan gave a short laugh that sounded as though it had been unwillingly jerked out of him.

"You aren't going to turn my head with your flattery, are you, darling? Still in love with me?"

Primrose made no reply.

Lonergan took one hand off the wheel and sought hers.

She pulled off her loose glove with her teeth, keeping her left hand beneath the warmth of the rug, and gave him the right one. Its pressure responded to his touch immediately and electrically.

"That's my girl," said Lonergan.

He sounded content.

Primrose, without moving her head, slewed her gaze round so as to see his profile. Rory Lonergan carried his forty-eight years lightly. He was unmistakably an Irishman—not much above medium height, large-boned and heavily-built but without superfluous flesh. His dark, intelligent face had the characteristics of his race: clearly-defined black eyebrows and blue eyes, long, straight, clean-shaven upper lip and protruding under jaw. His voice was an Irish voice, deep and with odd, melancholy cadences, a naturally beautiful voice that betrayed the speaker's nationality at once by its un-English inflections, as well as by his choice of idiom.

"It's a sheer miracle that I was able to get away at all. And you didn't give me much notice, did you?"

"Are you staying at Coombe?"

He nodded.

"Luck's with us, darling. At least, I suppose it's luck. I'm moving up there to-night, with a lad called Sedgewick."

"You're moving up there now," remarked Primrose. "I suppose you're taking me there. Have you seen my family yet?"

"No. Hadn't you better give me the dope? I know nothing whatever about them. Young Banks made the arrangements."

Primrose, in an accentuated drawl, began to speak.

"I get pretty bloody-minded, I must say, on the subject of my family. That's why I never talk about them if I can avoid it. However, if you're going to be billeted there, all concealment is at an end, as they say. To begin with, Coombe is about the most uncomfortable house on God's earth—rather large, with big rooms for the family and dog-holes for the servants, no heating and the absolute minimum of electric light, one bathroom and never anything like enough hot water. It's idiotically run—feeble, incompetent little village girls taught to do a lot of useless, silly jobs that mean nothing, and cursed at when they want their evenings to themselves like other human beings."

"Who curses them?"

"Mostly my uncle, who lives with us, but my mama does the actual transmitting of the curses and doesn't even do that properly. She's afraid of servants."

The corner of Primrose's mouth twisted downwards contemptuously and her voice was coldly savage.

"Why do you hate your mother?" demanded Lonergan abruptly.

She took the question calmly.

"I'm not sure that I do hate her, though I despise her pretty thoroughly. If I hate her at all, it's reaction from having adored her as a small child. I was the only one for six years, and she used me as an emotional outlet, I suppose. It makes me sick to think of it. I had the guts to kick loose when I was, mercifully, sent to school."

"I thought girls of your class never did go to school."

"They do nowadays. I wish you wouldn't talk about class. It's a bloody word, denoting a bloody state of affairs that we're out to abolish."

"No one'll ever do that. Privilege may be abolished. Class distinctions won't, in England. They're ingrain."

36

"I couldn't disagree with you more than I do," said Primrose vehemently.

"Only the intensely class-conscious—like yourself, darling—would become so frantic on the subject. Go on about your relations. What did your mother do when you kicked loose?"

"What her kind always does. Looked more and more wistful and tried having heart-to-hearts that never came off because I wouldn't, and then got afraid of me. She's actually terrified of me."

"Of what you can do to hurt her," suggested Lonergan.

"I suppose so. Honestly, Rory, I don't set out to give her hell or anything like that, but I just come over utterly unnatural whenever we're within a mile of one another, and I hear myself saying the most brutal things and just can't stop. She embarrasses me so frightfully that I'm simply incapable of even looking at her, quite often."

"How is she embarrassing?"

"I don't know. She shows her feelings, for one thing. Or at least, she makes one know they're there. And she's so utterly incompetent—even more so th most of the women who were brought up the way she was. My grandfather was in the Diplomatic Service and she lived abroad till she married. I suppose that's helped to make her the dim kind of person she is—that and having a certain amount of French blood. Her name was Levallois. Mercifully both my sister and I take completely after the Arbell side of the family."

Lonergan kept silence.

After a minute Primrose said sharply:

"What is it?"

He gave her a look of appraisement.

"You're quick, aren't you. I was only thinking that I'd heard that name—your mother's name—Levallois —years and years ago, when I was an art student in Rome."

"That's right. They were there. Did you ever know them?" Her voice sounded incredulous.

"Embassies weren't precisely up my street—even less so then than they are now. But one remembers the name."

37

"It was before the last war. You must have been frightfully young."

"Twenty—as a very simple calculation ought to show you, since you know perfectly well that I'm twenty-four years older than you are."

"You're terribly age-conscious, aren't you? I think it's silly, especially in a man," Primrose observed coldly.

"I agree. I wasn't thinking of my age, particularly, especially as I seem much younger to myself than I doubtless do to you."

"What were you thinking of then?"

"Temporarily viewing the situation through your eyes: that a lover of yours should have been a young man, already twenty years old, when your mother was a girl. It's an odd, unflattering sort of link with the past."

"The past doesn't mean a thing to me. Why should it? My mother, of course, lives in it. That'd be enough, in itself, to put me off."

"How vicious you are, about her."

"I don't think so. I just happen to dislike everything she stands for. Though I've got personal grievances against her, too. She made a complete mess of me, with the best intentions. Apparently most mothers do that."

"Did she do it to your sister, too?"

"I'm not sure about that. On the whole I think not. Jess is terribly normal and rather stupid, and as she was only born six years after I was, the first force of this awful maternal egotism had all been spent on me."

"You're sure it was egotism?"

"Rory, don't be such a fool. Nine women out of ten compensate themselves for the emotional disappointments of marriage by concentrating on their wretched children."

"But there must be other forms of compensation, Taking a lover, for instance."

"For some women, of course I don't think mummie was that sort, even when she was younger Otherwise why didn't she marry again? She wasn't much over thirty when my father died."

"Was she very young when she married him? She must have been."

"Nineteen. An idiotic age, but it was during the last war when people seem to have lost their heads pretty badly. It made a hash of her life, I imagine."

"Weren't they happy?"

"I shouldn't think so. I remember him perfectly, and he was very dull and completely inarticulate. He couldn't have suited the sentimentalist that mummie is. She's the kind of woman who'd always think of herself as a *femme incomprise*."

She paused for a minute.

"Rory, I believe I'm shocking you."

"I think you are," he agreed dispassionately.

"My God, don't tell me you've got a mother-fixation. Did you like yours?"

"Oh yes. But then the middle classes almost always do. It's part of their tradition."

"Shut up about classes. It makes me sick."

"You'll feel better when you've had a drink," said Lonergan smoothly.

"That's another thing I'd better warn you about at Coombe. You'll never get a drink, unless you can provide your own."

"I probably can. What about the uncle?"

"He's given up whiskey for the duration, and I don't think there's anything in the cellar worth speaking of. A bottle of port or sherry is brought up about once a year, and there's supposed to be some champagne waiting to celebrate the peace. Uncle Reggie's called General Levallois. He was invalided out of the Army and he's practically a cripple. Arthritis. He hasn't got a bean, except for some semi-invisible pension, and he's lived with us since I was twelve."

"Anybody else?"

"Only Jess. She's volunteered for the W.A.A.F. and is waiting to be called up. There are some evacuee kids from London, but I need hardly tell you that, in our democratic way, we make them use the top floor, and the kitchen stairs, and the back entrance. One practically doesn't know they're there at all."

"Then who looks after them?"

"The housemaid, I suppose," said Primrose indiffer-

39

ently. "*I* shouldn't know. I'm practically never at Coombe. I shouldn't be coming now if it wasn't for you."

"Angel," said Lonergan, in a voice as uninflected and meaningless as her own had been.

He had loosed her hand in order to replace his on the wheel but presently he sought it again, and when he next spoke his voice was warmer and more eager.

"You haven't yet told me if you're still in love with me."

"I haven't fallen for anybody else. Have you?"

"No."

They both laughed.

"Primrose—about this business of being at Coombe together. Is it going to work?"

"Of course it is. Otherwise I shouldn't have suggested it. I needn't have taken my leave now. I only decided to when I knew you'd been sent here and it seemed obvious that you'd be billeted at Coombe. Personally, I think it's an absolutely heaven-sent chance."

"I know, darling. Of course it is. Only—in your own home—and with your family there——"

"It's a largish house," Primrose observed coolly. "You won't have to behave like the lover in a French farce, if that's what you're afraid of."

"Thank God for that, anyway. Do they know already—of course they do—that I'm a friend of yours?"

"Yes. I told Jess on the telephone. What I *did* say," Primrose elaborated, in a tone of careful candour, "was that we'd met in London at a sherry-party—which is true—and that you quite frequently took me out to dinner. What I, naturally, didn't say, was that I'd only known you a fortnight."

"Then, officially, how long are we supposed to have known one another?"

"Better make it a few months. But as a matter of fact, they probably won't ask. I've trained them not to ask me questions."

"It doesn't follow that they won't ask me any."

"You can cope with them, if they do. Don't pretend you haven't had practice enough, Rory. And mummie's not at all a difficult person to side-track."

Lonergan drove on in silence until he presently enquired:
"Are we stopping at *The Two Throstles?*"

"Aren't we?"

He laughed and turned the car into the gravelled sweep before the white stucco building, low and long, with fumed oak doors and window frames.

Little plaques above the doors on either side of the entrance bore respectively the words "Lounge" and "Drawing-room" but a painted board leaning against the wall pointed the way: *To American Cocktail Bar.*

Primrose walked straight to it, her long, flexible fingers pinching and pressing at the flat curls of her hair.

Rory Lonergan hung up his cap and overcoat and followed her.

The place was hot, crowded and thick with smoke. Every high stool at the bar was occupied, but a man and a girl, both in Air Force uniform, were just leaving a table and Primrose, pushing her way past two women who also were evidently making for it, flung herself into one of the vacant chairs and threw her bag on the other.

Lonergan said to the defeated ladies, neither of whom was either young or smart:

"I'm so sorry. Won't you take the other chair?"

They looked confused and abashed, murmuring thanks and disclaimers, and at that moment a party of young officers moved away from the bar.

"Ah, that's better. Will I get you two of the stools?" said Lonergan, and he allowed an exaggeratedly Irish intonation to sound in the words, knowing that this would somehow reassure them and cause them to think of him, not as a strange man who had spoken to them without an introduction, but merely as "an Irish officer."

As he had expected, they smiled and looked happier, and he pulled out two of the vacated stools and saw them perched, one on each, like elderly and rather battered birds on over-small gate-posts.

Then he joined Primrose.

"What the hell——?"

"You were damned rude, as you always are. We could have waited. The poor old girls had spotted these chairs before you did."

41

"I hate waiting."

"And I hate bad manners."

"In that case, I don't really see why you ever took up with me."

Lonergan looked her up and down.

"As I've told you before, I liked your looks. You've got the most marvellous line I've ever seen."

"Is that all?"

"Not quite all—though nearly," said Lonergan. "What are you going to drink?"

"Gin and vermouth."

He ordered the drinks.

"Why have you got such an obsession about manners?" Primrose enquired out of a long silence, after her second drink.

"It's just another middle-class characteristic."

"It isn't. My aristocratic parent is the same."

"Is she now! Diplomatic circles and all. Why didn't she succeed in bringing you up better?"

"Because what makes sense in one generation doesn't in the next, obviously."

"Well," said Lonergan, "of course she and I belong to one generation and you to another. That's clear as crystal. Have another drink?"

"Okay. Same again."

The third round was consumed in silence, but Primrose, sprawling in her chair, pushed out one long slim leg and pressed it hard against Lonergan's thigh.

It was he who eventually moved, suggesting that they had better be going on.

"Okay," said Primrose indifferently.

She got up and threaded her way past the tables and chairs, moving with her characteristic effect of ruthless, effortless poise. But when they were in the hall Lonergan saw that her eyes were glazed and she remarked in her most indistinct drawl:

"You all right for driving? I'm slightly—very slightly—tight."

"Well, I'm not. Come on."

He took her by the elbow and steered her out into the darkness.

"God, I can't see a thing in this damned black-out."

"You'll be all right in a second. Stand still on the step and don't move while I get the car round."

When they were on the road again Lonergan said:

"You can't possibly be tight on three small drinks. I suppose you haven't had anything to eat all day."

"Not a thing, except one cup of utterly filthy coffee for breakfast. I'll be all right, directly."

She slumped down in her seat, leaning her head against his shoulder.

Lonergan, driving slowly, partly because he was careful in the black-out and partly because he wanted to give her time to recover herself before they arrived, thought that, so long as she remained silent and rather movingly helpless, he could almost make himself imagine that he loved her a little.

The car was turning into the lane that led to Coombe before Primrose spoke.

"I wish we were staying at *The Two Throstles* to-night."

"So do I," Lonergan answered automatically, and wishing nothing of the kind since he was perfectly well-known at *The Two Throstles* and so, certainly, was she.

"When you get to the gate, which you'll have to get out and open, I'll tidy up a bit."

"Right."

A moment later he stopped the car and, before getting out, pulled her towards him and kissed her.

Primrose returned the kiss fiercely and he felt her hands clutching at him.

She was both exciting and easily excited, but already he wished that he had never embarked on the affair.

The idea of carrying it on in the girl's own home was idiotic, tasteless, and repellent to him. He was angry and disgusted with himself for having lacked the courage to tell her so when she had first suggested the plan.

As usual, he had been afraid of hurting her. As though a girl like that, whose affairs were as numerous as they were short-lived, was ever going to be hurt by any man! Least of all, he unsparingly added, a man twenty-

43

four years older than herself at whom she had only made a pass on a meaningless impulse, at a dull party.

Instinctively he released his hold of her.

"What's the matter?" asked Primrose.

"Nothing. Hadn't we better go on?"

Primrose gave her short, unamused laugh.

"I suppose so."

She had taken his words in a sense far other than that in which he had meant them.

Lonergan got out and opened the gate, drove through and then got out to shut it again.

When he returned Primrose had switched on the light in the roof and was making up her face. Her gummed-looking curls were perfectly in place.

"Ready, Primrose?"

"Not yet."

He sat without moving, his eyes fixed upon her, but neither seeing her nor thinking of her.

In a few minutes now they would reach the house.

Had Primrose Arbell's mother, more than a quarter of a century ago, been that touching child to whom he had made most innocent and idyllic love for a few breathless afternoons in a Roman garden, before—like the catastrophe in a Victorian novel—her parents had sent him to the right-about?

If so, she might well have forgotten the whole episode, his name included. Perhaps he'd have forgotten, too, if it hadn't been for that startlingly unforeseen interview—again, like the Victorian novel—with her parents, and for the odd, rather charming artificiality of such a name as Valentine Levallois. Yet some romantic certainty in him repudiated that idea, even as he formulated it. At all events, he wouldn't now recognize her, any more than she him. And it would be for her to decide whether or no she remembered his name. Whatever Primrose might say of her mother's incompetence Lonergan felt quite convinced that, socially, she was not likely to be anything less than wholly competent.

"Okay now, darling."

"Right."

He drove on.

44

The house, like all houses now, stood in utter darkness.

He drew up in front of the stone pillars with the lead-roofed portico above the door.

"Ring," directed Primrose. "There's a chain affair, to the left of the door."

Lonergan, leaving her seated in the car, got out and after some trouble found the chain, which seemed unduly high above his head. When he grasped it, he could tell that it had been broken off and not repaired. His vigorous pull resulted in a prolonged mournful, jangling sound, a long way off, that reminded him of country houses in Ireland where there lived, for years and years, elderly and impoverished people.

An outburst of barking followed from within the house, and he could hear someone approaching.

"They're coming, Primrose."

Lonergan stepped back to the car and put out a hand to help her out. He had no intention of walking into the house without her.

"Are you all right, now?"

"I'm okay," said Primrose.

Her voice sounded sullen as though she had dropped her words from one corner of her closed mouth, as she did when she was either out of temper or seeking to make an impression. He guessed that both states of mind might be hers just then.

A young girl in a cap and apron opened the door, very gingerly so as to avoid showing any light, and Primrose—ignoring her—walked in.

Lonergan followed.

He said "Good-evening" to the maid and she answered "Good-evening, sir" in pert, cheerful tones. He wondered what she thought of Primrose.

They went through glass-panelled swing-doors and were met by a renewed outburst of barking.

"Hallo!" said a girl's voice, and he saw the speaker scramble up from the floor in front of the fire, gathering against her the barking puppy, its awkward legs and large paws dangling.

"Hallo," said Primrose, and she swung round to face Lonergan immediately behind her.

45

"Meet my sister Jess," she muttered. "Colonel Lonergan—Jess."

Jess shook hands.

He was surprised to see how young and school-girlish she looked.

"Sorry about all the noise," she cried, slapping the head of the barking, wriggling pup. "Shut up, aunt Sophy. Look, Primrose, don't you agree that she's the *exact* image of aunt Sophy?"

"She is, a bit."

"Aunt Sophy," began Jess, turning to Lonergan, and then she broke off, and exclaimed: "Here's mummie."

He watched her coming through some further door, crossing the hall towards them.

Prepared as he was in advance for the meeting, it yet astonished him profoundly to see, in that first instant, that he could perfectly recognize in this woman of his own age the young nymph of the Pincio Gardens.

She wasn't, of course, a young nymph now. Time had washed the colour from her brown hair—the wave in front was entirely silver—and from her face. Only the dense blue-green of her eyes remained. It flashed across his mind that he had never seen eyes of quite that colour since, and it did not occur to him until long afterwards that the eyes of Primrose were of exactly the same arresting, unusual shade.

The very shape of her face—a short oval, with the beautifully-defined line of the jaw still unmarred—brought back to him the sheer sensation of pleasure that, as a draughtsman, he had before experienced at the sight of its sharply cut purity of outline.

He moved towards her and she held out her hand, smiling.

"Colonel Lonergan? How do you do?"

Curiously taken aback, although for what reason he had no idea, Lonergan shook hands and repeated her conventional greeting.

"Oh! I remember your voice," she most unexpectedly exclaimed—and he was not sure that the unexpectedness had not struck herself as well as him.

"And I remember your face," he answered, and

46

for an instant they seemed to stare at one another. "Hallo, mummie," said Primrose. She stood by the fire without moving, and her mother, after a tiny hesitation, went to her, and putting an arm round her shoulders, kissed her in greeting.

IV

THE house, the large front bedroom assigned to Lonergan, even the water in the chipped white enamel water-can standing in the flowered china basin on the old-fashioned washstand, were all as cold as Primrose had foretold. He was glad to hurry downstairs but he felt that the evening was likely to prove a strange one.

That past and present should so overlap was disconcerting enough, but Rory Lonergan, who had regretfully and at the same time competently deceived a great many people, had never yet seriously deceived himself and he was already aware of a sense of tension, almost of foreboding, that came from within himself and threatened others as much as himself.

He was oddly relieved to find no one downstairs except Jessica, still playing with her dog.

It was easy to make friends with Jess, and for her, as for the elderly ladies in the cocktail-bar, he deliberately accentuated Irish tone and idiom, in order to amuse her.

He took notice of the puppy, and listened to the explanation of why she had been so oddly named.

"Ah, the little poor dog! Isn't that a shame, now!"

"What a frightfully good point of view. Most people think it's awful for old aunt Sophy—or would be, if she knew about it. Nobody has ever said it's a shame for a poor darling little puppy to be called after a cross old lady."

"Have they not?"

"Not they," said Jess. "Actually, I shall probably change her name later on or perhaps just call her Sophy.

47

Otherwise it's a bit like those dim parents who give their children idiotic pet-names and will keep on with them for ever. I knew a person whose life at school was practically ruined because her mother came to see her and called her Tiddles. I ask you—Tiddles."

Lonergan expressed appropriate disapproval. He thought of asking her about her school but decided that she had too recently ceased to be a schoolgirl and said instead:

"I hear you're waiting to be called up for the W.A.A.F.?"

"That is correct. Did Primrose tell you?"

"She did."

"I wouldn't have thought she'd be enough interested. It's funny, you knowing her first, and then coming down here."

"Well, I was down here first, you know, for a few days and then I had to go to London for a special job and met her again," said Lonergan, adding the last word as he remembered that Primrose had decided to credit them with an acquaintanceship of some months.

"And it's *much* odder," said Jess, "that you should have met mummie all those thousands of years ago. She said she wondered if you were the same person when Buster—Lieutenant Banks—told us your name. And that reminds me, where's the other one?"

In spite of his preoccupation with the earlier part of her speech, Lonergan found that he understood to what she was so elliptically referring.

"Captain Sedgewick? He'll arrive after dinner, I expect. He had to go to Plymouth. Did he not let you know?"

"Oh, I expect so. I just hadn't heard, that's all. What's he like?"

"About twenty-three, with red hair, comes from somewhere outside London. He's said to be a very good dancer."

"Gosh, that's wizard," thoughtfully returned Jess.

She gazed up at him with ingenuous admiration.

"You're frightfully good at describing people, aren't you?"

48

Lonergan laughed and was aware that her childlike praise had pleased his vanity.

Extraordinary, he reflected dispassionately, how he had never outgrown the desire to be liked. Sometimes he thought that this pressing need was so urgent within him that, on a final analysis, it provided the motive spring for his whole conduct of life.

Jess chattered on, cheerful and at ease.

The tap of the General's crutches and his shuffling step sounded from behind Lonergan and he rose, and Jess reared herself to her feet in what seemed to be one supple, unbroken movement.

Valentine was with her brother.

She was in black and Lonergan noticed that the long fringes of the embroidered Chinese shawl round her shoulders became continually entangled in pieces of furniture as she moved. He saw the unhurried gestures with which she patiently disentangled them, again and again.

General Levallois, in whom Lonergan had immediately detected an emphatic but quite fundamental hostility directed against his nationality rather than against himself, made stilted conversation.

Jess said:

"Gosh, I'd better wash. Fancy, that makes poetry. Fancy me being a poet!"

As she dashed her way upstairs, the eyes of Rory Lonergan and Valentine Arbell met, and they both laughed.

He told himself that he had never seen any woman's face alter so completely as hers did when she was really amused. Already, he felt, he knew that her pretty, not infrequent smile had nothing to do with amusement and was one of her many unconscious concessions to the traditions of her upbringing.

"I know that much about her," thought Lonergan, assenting aloud to a proposition of the General's. And immediately another thought followed.

"I know that, and how much more!"

The watcher in him, that was never off guard and could never be silenced, added the note that carried to him a

49

familiar, never-to-be-mistaken warning, terrifying in its very brevity.

"*I'm sunk.*"

" . . . though mind you, I'm not denying that the feller had some reason on his side, up to a point," said the General.

And Lonergan, unaware of having heard the beginning of the phrase, found that he knew it was de Valera of whom the General was talking.

He had heard far too many Englishmen launch themselves, with an ignorance almost sublime in its unconsciousness, upon the subject of Irish politics to feel any dismay.

He was quite prepared to let General Levallois have his head.

But Valentine, it seemed, was not.

"Where is your home, in Ireland?" she enquired, shelving de Valera and the General alike, by the directness of the enquiry and of the look that she turned on her guest.

"My home, for a good many years past, has been in Paris. I came over here two years before the war and lived in a flat in Fitzroy Square."

"With a studio," said Valentine, and he admired the deftness with which she was making his exact standing in the London world clear to General Levallois, to whom such classification would obviously be of relative, although in this case not intrinsic, importance.

"How you must have hated leaving Paris. Though, two year before the war, one didn't imagine what was going t' happen too France."

"It's an extraordinary thing about the French——" said the General.

The French, so gently introduced by Valentine, slid into the place of the Southern Irish.

Lonergan assented, dissented where it woud osbviously be easy for the General to prove that his dissent was founded on inadequate knowledge, and felt that he had known Coombe, and all that made up existence there, for years.

It actually gave him a sense of shock when Primrose

came into the hall, at her most slouching pace, three minutes after dinner had been announced.

What had she to do, he almost asked himself, with these surroundings?

She belonged to a background of Bloomsbury flats, always untidy and generally dirty, hot and crowded bars —parties that reeked of smoke, intellect, blasphemy, love-making—and the dark interiors of rattling taxis and motor-cars.

Yet, except for her make-up, she did not really look out of place at Coombe, he had to acknowledge it.

She still wore her dark-blue travelling-dress and, divorced from the blue coat, it revealed itself as straight and simply-cut, with sleeves that stopped short above the elbows and a collar of which she had pulled down the zip fastener so as to show her long neck and small, delicate collar-bones.

She looked once at Lonergan—it was a look that revealed nothing at all beyond forcing him to observe that she never looked directly at anybody else—and did not speak until they were seated, cold, and apprehensive of further cold, in the dining-room.

"I thought there was a Captain Sedgewick," she said.

"Captain Sedgewick telephoned to say he wouldn't arrive much before nine o'clock," Valentine said.

"He's gone to Plymouth," announced Jess. "Sorry I'm late." She slid into her seat. "What were all those special exercises and things that ally our men were doing yesterday?" she asked Lonergan.

He replied, with a number of reservations, and was surprised by the extent of her knowledge and understanding of the activities of some portion at least of the British Army in war-time.

He liked Jess, and was pleased that she presently subsided and left the conversation to her elders, with an absence of self-assertion that Lonergan thought well suited to her youth. General Levallois looked at the menu-card,—Good God, a menu-card, thought Lonergan, whose views of the catering at Coombe were already of the lowest description—muttered something that was inaudible but clearly and deservedly uncomplimentary

51

about the cooking—and talked, to himself rather than to anybody else, about the state of agriculture.

Lonergan was prepared to look as though he were wftening and to make all the necessary rejoinders, but he found that Valentine could give what he recognized lisith some astonishment as being a genuine attention to the General's monologue although from sheer lack of imagination he made whatever he talked about seem uninteresting.

Once or twice Valentine appealed to Primrose, and once she brought the conversation round to the London background with a direct question, but she got no response.

Primrose let fall some sounds—they seemed hardly even to be recognizable syllables—from the corner o her mouth and pushed her plate away, the food on it left almost untouched.

"I can't hear a word you're saying, Primrose," remarked the General. "Why don't you speak up?"

Primrose made no reply whatever and Valentine, speaking gaily, said:

"You're very difficult, Reggie dear. You tell Jess not to scream because you can't hear a word she's saying, and now you tell poor Primrose to speak up, for the same reason."

At that Primrose, for the first time, looked her mother full in the face.

"For God's sake don't start standing up for me, there's nothing I loathe more, or need less."

The sense of shock imposed by the tone in which she spoke, no less than by the words themselves, kept them all silent for an ice-cold second.

Then Jess, in a high key, began an exclamatory "I must say——" checked by her mother's low, distinct voice.

"Very well, Primrose darling," said Valentine—and there was even something in her tone that hinted at a smile. "I won't stand up for you if you'd rather I didn't." She turned her head towards Lonergan and went on with exactly the same placidity.

"Why does one generation always accuse the next one

of speaking indistinctly? An ear-trumpet can't be the sole solution."

"I'd be sorry to think so," he agreed, with such lightness of tone as her own had been. "Otherwise I'd be looking for an ear-trumpet myself. Not that I believe people use them now, unless it's on the stage. My poor sister Nellie, who's very deaf indeed, has a most peculiar little invention."

He went on to describe it.

Valentine listened, commented. General Levallois asked in what part of Ireland Lonergan's sister lived, and, on being told that it was in the South, was immediately moved to put what he described as a question but what was, in reality, an embittered series of condemnations.

The bad moment was over—averted. Lonergan could have told the precise instant at which Valentine, gently unplaiting the fringes of her shawl from the arm of her chair, let the tide of pain that Primrose had loosed, rise within her. It was not a sharp, violent pain, he felt it must be too familiar for that. Rather must it be the recurrence of some deep-rooted misery that twisted in her heart and against which she had long ceased to rebel because rebellion was so useless.

He wondered very much at the skill with which she had handled that brief, intolerable minute of tension.

Was it just part of a social training that instinctively served her and would always serve her, or was it one way of protecting herself from facing a bitter truth? Did she always oppose the smooth, unreal self-effacement of the super-civilized to the onslaught of real emotion?

"There's a great deal in what you say, sir," he assured the General. "At the same time, Dev has done quite a lot for his own people according to his lights. I could tell you of instances——"

He noticed, with a pleasure that he felt to be rather irrational, that Valentine was not now seeking, as she had sought earlier in the evening, to avert the General's foolish spate of assertions and counter-assertions on the subject of Ireland.

She was leaving Lonergan to deal with them, taking for granted his ability to do so without discomfiture to

53

himself—for she would never, he felt certain, run the risk of allowing a stranger to endure discomfiture.

He and she, however, were most certainly not strangers.

On that conviction, Lonergan let his analysis of the situation rest temporarily.

When dinner was over, and they had moved out of the cold dining-room to the comparative warmth of the hall, Primrose said to him curtly:

"Have you seen the room that's supposed to be your office?"

"Yes. I saw it for a minute before dinner. It seems charming."

"The fire is laid there," said Valentine, "if you'd like to use it to-night. Please do, if you want to."

"Thank you very much. Perhaps later on."

He found himself looking at her, gravely and with attention, and averted his gaze with a conscious effort.

It met, for once squarely and fully, a look from Primrose who was standing behind her mother.

She signalled to him, briefly and competently with a backward jerk of the head, that he should seek the little breakfast-room now to be his office, and that she would join him there.

Lonergan slightly shook his head. He gave her at the same time what he himself had candidly described to more than one lady of his intimate acquaintance as "a look that's as good as a declaration," with narrowed, smiling eyes and an almost imperceptible movement of the lips.

He wished, at the moment, neither to humiliate her nor to let her think that he had been antagonized by her behaviour at dinner.

It was not possible to tell how she reacted inwardly to his refusal. Her face remained a mask, with its look of embittered discontent that gave the impression of having been painted on.

But Primrose, he reflected, had the hard, genuine shrewdness of disillusioned youth and showed sometimes an unexpected and disconcerting degree of intuition.

". . . late for the news," General Levallois was saying.

As Lonergan glanced at his watch, sure that it was a

quarter of an hour too early for the Nine O'Clock News, the old spaniel and the puppy both broke into vehement barking, drowning the far-away jangle of the bell just as it became audible.

The General shouted a command at the dogs and Jess, shouting also, dominated all the clamour.

"I'll go!"

The spaniel flopped to the floor again, and the puppy pranced after Jessica to the front door.

"It must be Captain Sedgewick," said Valentine, and she stood up.

Lonergan, rising also, saw rather than heard the words "My God!" forming themselves on Primrose's lips.

She turned away and went through the door behind which, Lonergan knew already, was the telephone.

He heard the faint tinkle indicating that she had lifted off the receiver.

Valentine moved forward to meet the arrival. Jess could be heard talking to him with friendly, effortless enthusiasm.

"What the devil makes people turn up just when one wants to be listening to the news? Ought to have more sense," grumbled the General.

He looked across at Lonergan, who could almost see the thought rising slowly in his mind that, give the devil his due, this Irish fellow hadn't done *that*.

With the nearest approach to cordiality that he had yet shown, General Levallois remarked:

"I think I'll listen to it in my own den. I don't know whether you'd care to come along—get out of this racket."

"Thanks very much indeed, sir, but I think perhaps, as Sedgewick knows I'm here——"

"Ah," said the General, "there's something in that, I daresay."

He reached for his sticks and hobbled off, with a not unfriendly "Good-night. Shan't be coming down again," and disappeared as the others returned.

Captain Sedgewick, whose physical type so unfailingly suggested a fox to Lonergan's imagination, was as cool, as unembarrassed and completely self-assured as his superior officer had always seen him.

55

He was an excellent soldier, better liked by his men than by his brother officers who knew him for a social climber.

A general conversation, polite and insignificant, followed.

Primrose made no return, until Valentine had offered to show Captain Sedgewick his room.

"I had four hours' sleep last night, and none the night before," he admitted, "so if I may, I'll say good-night. That is to say, unless you wanted me for anything to-night, sir," he added, addressing Lonergan. "I understand your office is here."

"I do not indeed. Th office is still in the town; this is only an unofficial office, so to say, that Lady Arbell has been kind enough to put at my disposal up here."

The formality of his own speech rather amused Lonergan, inwardly. He knew that had he been either alone with Sedgewick, or alone with Valentine, he would have worded the phrase quite differently.

Unexpectedly, out of the blue, he felt himself seized by a sick impatience, directed against himself and his eternal readiness to say and to do the thing that was appropriate to the situation.

He wanted, suddenly and imperatively, simply to ask Valentine if she wouldn't come downstairs again and talk to him.

"Jess, if you're going up to see Madeleine, darling, ask her if she'll be kind and go through all Primrose's things to-morrow."

Valentine turned to Lonergan.

"I'll be down again presently, but you'll do just as you prefer about going up to bed, or writing or anything, won't you?"

"Thank you."

Jess said okay, cried a general good-night to everyone and stopped to pick up her dog.

It took her a long while to adjust aunt Sophy to any degree of submissive tranquillity and Lonergan watched her with unreflective amusement.

When at last she went up the curving stairway, he took out a cigarette and stood looking round for a spill.

56

Primrose, with her thick coat drawn on over her blue frock, was suddenly there, coming towards him—and Lonergan was actually startled as though she were someone from another world.

So, indeed, she was, but on the heels of that thought there came, clear and complete as the statement of a mathematical problem, his realization of the inevitable, complicated and difficult adjustment towards which they were moving.

The sound of her very first words told him that she was angry.

"It's been one hell of a lovely evening, hasn't it? What the devil's the matter with you, Rory?"

"I'm not sure."

If she wants a show-down, let her have it, he thought, making himself deliberately callous.

"Well, if you're not, I am. You're shocked, like the sentimentalist you are, because I'm what I really feel with mummie instead of putting on an act for your benefit."

"I don't want you to put on an act for my benefit, and you know it. The best thing about you is that you're honest, as I've told you before."

"Then what's the matter? What did you come here for, if you don't want to spend the time with me when we've got the chance?"

"I don't see how I'm to make love to you, under your mother's own roof, when I'm here as her guest."

He felt ashamed of himself as he put forward his excuse, factually so well grounded and in reality so false.

"My God, Rory, you didn't say that in London. Things haven't changed, since then."

But they had—only he couldn't tell her so.

"Primrose," he said slowly, "obviously you think I'm the world's cad, and I'm fairly sure you're right."

He stopped, for once uncertain how to continue. She looked at him scornfully.

"I see. You've found somebody else. It would have been more decent to say so before you brought me down here on a fool's errand. However, you needn't worry, I can take it."

He noticed, with a horrid compunction, that two dark

57

shadows had suddenly sprung into life beneath her angry, contemptuous eyes and that behind the contempt there was real pain.

"Oh, God—Primrose!"

Unable to bear it, he pulled her into his arms.

She pressed against him, her anger disappeared.

"Darling, don't be such a fool. Why, in God's name, wil you always mix up love with all this sentimental, romantic bloody nonsense of yours?"

He could have answered that—had, indeed, answered it before—but it would be of no use.

Instead, he made the only answer she wanted or would understand and kissed her hard and passionately, giving her love as she knew and desired it and himself moved by the instantaneousness of her response.

"I don't give a darhn, really, if you have got another girl," she muttered. "This is all that matters."

Lonergan held her close and kissed her again, hating and despising himself.

"Was that why you wouldn't come into the breakfast-room this evening?"

"What?"

"Because you've started a thing with somebody else?"

"I haven't."

She drew back, honestly bewildered.

"Then what the hell——"

"What I said. I don't see how I can make love to you here," he repeated doggedly.

"But I've *told* you it's all right! No one's going to worry. My room is at the far end of the passage from yours—the last door on the left—and there's no one anywhere near. Anyhow, nobody dreams of stirring out of their rooms after eleven o'clock in this house."

He stared at her without finding a word to utter.

"Rory—my sweet——"

"In the name of God, child, don't go on like that! It's no good. I ought never to have come here."

He found the sweat breaking out on his forehead as he loosed his hold of her.

Primrose said incredulously:

"D'you mean you're not coming to me to-night?"

58

"I've told you I'm not."

Primrose was silent for a moment, looking at him, then she said, in the curt, slashing tones that she affected under the stress of anger or disconcertment:

"Thanks for the flowers, darling. And next time, when you've got over your panic, don't bother to come and explain things to me, because you won't find me."

There was the sound of footfalls coming down the stairs.

"Primrose—will you please let me talk to you to-morrow?"

"I shouldn't think so."

"Please, darling."

"I'm not like you. I think all this talking is idiotic and gets people just nowhere."

Valentine reached the bottom step.

"Jess and Madeleine are listening-in to a dance band in Madeleine's room. Madeleine was my mother's French maid, years ago," Valentine said, addressing Lonergan.

"So what?" drawled Primrose, and without further word she, in her turn, went up the stairs, leaving Valentine and Rory Lonergan alone by the fire in the hall.

They were both silent, Valentine stirring a log on the hearth with her foot, Lonergan motionless, seeking to fight down the sense of extreme discomfiture left by his scene with Primrose, and to establish within himself some kind of mental and emotional equilibrium.

He could not have told how long they had stood, speechless, when it occurred to him that Valentine, too, had found readjustment necessary. The atmosphere of hostility that Primrose's last words had created could hardly have failed to move her mother painfully.

Lonergan felt very sorry. On an impulse to do something for her, he pushed one of the armchairs nearer the fire.

"Will you not sit down and stay for a little while?" he asked gently.

She smiled and seated herself, and Lonergan took the chair opposite.

He was taken by surprise when she said with a simplicity that added dignity to her directness:

59

"Did you know that we were going to meet again?"

"Not until this evening, just before I got here. I'd only heard your married name and it didn't convey anything to me. Did you know?"

"When I heard that an Irish colonel called Lonergan might be coming, I felt that it might probably be you. And then Jess heard your first name, and I knew."

"It's curious."

"Very," she assented.

"Do you know that you've altered very little?" he said. "I don't mean that I'd have known you anywhere, as the saying goes, but that, essentially, you've kept so much of the girl I used to see in the Pincio Gardens."

"Essentially, I suppose I have. I often feel that I'm still almost as immature as I was then. It's a silly thing to say about a woman of forty-four, but it's true, I think."

"Yes," said Lonergan. "It's what I meant. Is that impertinent of me?"

She shook her head.

"Tell me about yourself. You've not stayed immature, at all events, although in appearance you've altered less than I have. That's astonishing. Did you go on painting?"

"I did, after a fashion. But the war of 1914 was an interruption, and then I went home to Ireland for a bit and did no good there, and after my mother died I left my sister Nellie—who was predestined for an old maid—to look after my father, and went to Paris. I'm just not good enough, you know, though I've been able to make a living with illustration work, and drawing for various papers, and an occasional portrait."

"And now you're in the Army again."

"Believe you me, that's no hardship. The war came at the very moment when I was sick of Paris, sick of France, sick of myself—only looking for an excuse to turn my back on the whole thing."

"So it came when you needed it."

"It did."

Lonergan allowed no hesitation to interfere with the sound of finality in his short answer, yet he felt himself to be on the verge of adding to it with an admission as unnecessary as it might prove unwise.

He had decided on silence when Valentine's next words shattered his determination.

"Have you ever married?"

"I have not. But it came to the same thing. We lived together for ten years, till she died, in 1934. She was French."

Having said it, Lonergan felt apprehensive. What comment could she conceivably make on so extraordinary, so premature a confidence? Almost anything she said must be wrong, and it would be he who had forced inadequacy upon her.

Valentine spoke.

"Were they terribly happy years?"

"Ah, you're wonderful! That was the one right thing you could have said!" he exclaimed with a rush of spontaneous delight that gave him no time to choose his words. "They were happy. She was very lovely. We used to fight, and have terrible rows, but it was a good relationship, and she was perfect in so many ways."

"I'd like you to tell me," said Valentine.

She sat leaning forward, her serious face, with its curiously childlike look of innocence, supported on her hand.

Lonergan caught his breath.

"I'd like to tell you," he said.

V

LOOKING into the fire away from Valentine, he spoke, hesitatingly at first.

"It's difficult to begin. You see, it's hard to make you understand what she was like. (Her name was Laurence, by the way.) I should imagine that you've never come very much across the kind of French people that she belonged to, however much you've lived abroad. French provincial *bourgeoisie*, keeping themselves to themselves, in a little close circle of relations and old family friends. . . .

61

The father had a job with one of those big firms that used to import wines. He wasn't a partner, nor anything like that, but he was important, in his own way. They'd a house at Saumur—one of those tall, pink, narrow houses with a garden at the back that ran down to the river and a *tonnelle* where they always had their meals in summer."

Lonergan paused; conscious of confusion, laughing a little.

"The way I'm going on—it's because I'm finding it difficult to describe Laurence to you."

Valentine helped him.

"Where did you meet her?"

He threw her a look of gratitude.

"In her own home. It was when I was doing a whole lot of sketches of provincial France for a newspaper, and they sent me down to the Loire country. One of the introductions they gave me was to Monsieur Houlvain, and I went to his office in Saumur. He was a nice old friendly chap. I don't think he'd have asked me to the house, if I'd been an Englishman and a Protestant instead of an Irish Catholic. But he invited me there for a Sunday *déjeuner* and off I went, little knowing what awaited me."

He recaptured, for a fleeting, unexpected instant, the blinding heat-haze of the long-ago July morning when he had walked the streets of Saumur, looking for the house of Monsieur Houlvain—*le numéro dix-huit*.

"A holy show I made of myself, that day! For some reason I couldn't find the house, and it was a scorching hot morning and I arrived late, and then I was only wearing some old shabby clothes I'd been walking in, and Madame Houlvain was all in black satin and a white collar, and monsieur in a new alpaca coat. I don't suppose he'd put it on in my honour, but it made me feel what kind of a mannerless lout was I, not to have taken a bit more trouble to look decent. They were rather ceremonious, too, to start with. You know how French people are."

Valentine assented.

"Laurence didn't come in till the *déjeuner* was ready. I imagine she'd been cooking it, and a nice time of it she must have had with everything getting spoilt because I'd not arrived. I didn't fall for her straight away, though I thought her extraordinarily pretty—she'd dark hair and eyes, and that sort of dead-white skin, and she was slim and rather tall, with good bones. Her forehead was lovely—I honestly can only think of one word that could ever describe the kind of breadth and purity of it, with dark thin eyebrows and very deep dark eyes underneath—and that's luminous. She had that quality, and it was all in that beautiful wide brow."

"How old was she?"

"Twenty-one. Nine years younger than I was. Well, you know what it's like in a French family. She never batted an eyelid all through lunch. Monsieur laid down the law a bit about politics, and Madame asked questions about what I was doing, and told me which were the best restaurants in practically every town in the Loire country. And they asked about Ireland, and we agreed that the English were difficult for the more civilized races to understand. Am I being very rude?"

"I don't think so. We are uncivilized, compared with the French. I'm not quite so sure about the Irish, but then I've never been to Ireland."

"Well," said Lonergan, "I don't know that I'm quite so sure myself, nowadays. But anyway, I agreed with monsieur. I daresay I'd have agreed with whatever he said. It was my idea of the way to make myself agreeable, I suppose."

He broke off abruptly.

"I'm making this story too long. It was all very simple, really. I did the sketches, going down the river, and then I went back to Saumur to finish them off because I'd liked the town; and I wanted to see the *cadre noir*, and Monsieur Houlvain had said he could take me there.

"He and madame were very kind to me—I saw a lot of them, off and on—and Laurence and I fell in love. We thought it wouldn't be any use, I was a foreigner, and hadn't any money except what I earned, and anyway, who wants their daughter to marry an artist?"

Lonergan fell silent.

63

Valentine asked:

"Was she their only child?"

"There was a son, doing his *service militaire*, and an older daughter, married. And there was a *parti* being arranged for Laurence. They still do that, in provincial France—or they did then. No compulsion, exactly, but the whole of the families talking it over—uncles and aunts, and a couple of priests, and the married ones and their husbands and wives. Laurence told me she liked the boy, and she'd been quite ready to say she'd marry him until she met me. We were crazy about one another. I'd decided long ago I wasn't ever going to marry—domesticity has never appealed to me, nor fidelity either for that matter, and I knew I'd be no sort of a husband for any woman, let alone a girl of twenty-one. But I had to ask Laurence to marry me. I was mad about her, and I thought I'd never get her any other way."

Again Lonergan was silent, and this time it was a little while before he spoke again.

"It's hard to make the next bit clear. But what happened was that Laurence told me she'd come and live with me in Paris, and not marry me.

"She knew I didn't want marriage. That was the thing about Laurence—she understood and accepted things that were quite outside her own tradition.

"I didn't know what to do. Or perhaps I did, and couldn't bring myself to do it. There was a terrible, mad, muddled week when I told monsieur I'd fallen in love with his daughter and he assured me that he was very sorry but she was already promised, and madame gave me a lot of good advice of which the whole point was that I must go back to Paris at once and not see Laurence again, and Laurence and I said goodbye in the *tonnelle*, and I told her it wasn't any good, she was too young and I couldn't ruin her life for her. Even if we were to marry, it would mean breaking with her family—her mother'd made that quite clear—and I couldn't afford to keep a wife.

"I can see her now—the little, poor child—with the tears streaming down her face, telling me that she wasn't too young—she knew what she wanted. I don't know how I ever left her.

"I went back to Paris and I thought, God forgive me, I'd forget her in time, the way I'd forgotten other girls before. But I found I didn't. And one day, about two months after I got back, I had a telegram asking me to meet her train that same afternoon—she was coming to Paris.

"From their point of view monsieur and madame had made the most idiotic mistake they could have made. They'd tried to rush her into this marriage, and she'd got angry and told them she wouldn't be persecuted and there'd been some terrible rows and one day she couldn't bear it any more and just packed a bag and walked out of the house without a word to anyone. The trust she showed—the courage—coming to me like that, never having had a word or a line from me since I'd left Saumur —I'll never forget it."

A log, burnt through, fell with a soft crash into the bed of white ash on the hearth and Valentine stirred to replace it by another one.

Then she said:

"Go on."

"Will I? You've a lot of patience. We didn't ever marry—neither of us wanted it. We didn't want children, either. Does that seem to you extraordinary?"

He saw from her face that she was surprised, and wondered whether it was because she found such an attitude of mind regrettable, or incomprehensible, or because it surprised her that he should have put it into words.

When she spoke, slowly and as though she had never before expressed what she felt on this matter, he saw that he had been mistaken.

All that surprised her was they should think so much alike.

"It doesn't seem at all extraordinary. I don't know that I'd quite realized before—but I feel like that about it, too. I mean—a really perfect companionship would be interfered with, wouldn't it, if there were children?"

"Of course."

"For anything less than the best," she said, with a timidity that touched him deeply, "I think children

65

would be a great help. They take up such a lot of time and thought."

So that's been your life, thought Lonergan. Aloud he said:

"Laurence and I never meant to have Arlette. It was a mistake. She wanted to stop it, but I was afraid of the risk for her. We fought over that like blazes, and while we were still fighting, it was too late. It would have been too impossibly dangerous, even if we'd had the money."

"But did you have a child, then?"

"We did. Laurence was nearly as upset about it as I was and she swore it shouldn't ever make any difference."

"Did it?"

"It did, a little. That was inevitable, in a tiny *appartement* that had one and a half rooms and a studio. When I was making more money, and Arlette was old enough, she went to the convent every day and she was very good from the start, and didn't give us much trouble. She was eight when Laurence died, and the nuns took her as a boarder. They kept her through the holidays— it's quite often like that in France, as you probably know."

"Yes. Then where is Arlette now?"

"Well, she's in Ireland, of all things. I had to get her out of France somehow, when the war started. I don't need to tell you that my family never knew of her existence, and I'd the work of the world deciding what I'd tell my poor old sister Nellie. I wrote her a letter in the end, and asked her to talk it over with Father Conroy, her confessor, who has sense—and I said the child's mother was dead and that Arlette had been brought up by the holy nuns and I wanted her in a Catholic atmosphere where I knew she'd be taken care of. I put in a lot of old cod, too, about her being the innocent result of something that had happened long ago in my youth. I felt disloyal to Laurence when I said that, well knowing that Nellie would think it was a terrible mortal sin I'd committed and repented of, please God. She did, too. I'd pages from her afterwards. But she sent me a telegram, almost directly after she got my first letter, telling me I could

66

send Arlette to her. She's there still, the poor child, with Nellie and old Maggie Dolan, in the wilds of Roscommon."

"Is she happy there?"

"I think so. And poor old Nellie, who's been all by herself since father died, is devoted to her. I got over there once, in the beginning of nineteen forty, and saw them. It seemed to be working all right. When all this is over, if I'm still living, I'll have Arlette with me."

"Is she like Laurence?"

"Not a bit. She's like her grandmother—old Madame Houlvain. Tough and small and dark— you'd never mistake her for anything but what she is—a nice little girl of the French *bourgeoisie*. The only way she's different is in having a good brain. She's extremely intelligent. The funny thing is, I wasn't interested in her at all till the last year. And now I am. And I was touched, when I went over to Ireland, and she was so madly pleased to see me. Of course, she was in a nation of strangers and I was part of the only life she'd known. But I got a much deeper feeling of responsibility about her then. I'm afraid I'd never really felt it before— except that I'd got to make the money to pay her convent bills."

"I didn't think of you as having children, or a child. I thought you'd have married, though."

"To all intents and purposes Laurence and I were married. I felt the same obligations. I loved her—I wasn't always faithful to her, God forgive me—I could never have left her."

"I understand," Valentine said. "Why did she die? She must have been very young."

"She was thirty-one. It was in the autumn of nineteen thirty-four. She got pneumonia, and died in ten days."

"Perhaps," said Valentine slowly, "she'd known only the best things. I don't mean just happiness, but all the things—real pain, and hard work, and——" She stopped, and then went on speaking very diffidently. "You did say you and she had fought over things. I may be talking of what I know nothing about, but I've some-

67

times thought that to care enough to quarrel—not just bickering but a serious quarrel—and still want to stay together, must mean a really vital relationship."

"How right you are!"

Lonergan looked at her, drawn back from his world of Laurence and the Paris flat that was only one and a half rooms and a studio, and the pink house at Saumur, and even the little dark French girl over in Ireland. He was in the world to which Valentine belonged, and a strange survival of a world it seemed to him—an islet upon which the tide of destruction was swiftly and surely advancing, impelled now by the forces of war but inevitably due to come, war or no war.

His thoughts veered rapidly to Valentine herself.

"How good you are, to have let me go on and on, telling you all this! Have I tired you out?"

"No. I wanted to hear."

In the silence that followed Lonergan knew that, into her mind as into his, had come the remembrance of the two children they had once been, making love in the Pincio Gardens by a broken fountain.

"You didn't altogether forget, then. I mean that time in Rome?"

"I know what you mean. I did, and I didn't. There have been years during which I never thought about it at all, if that's forgetting—and yet every now and then I've got back the—the atmosphere of those afternoons and——"

She left a blank to complete the sentence, not, he thought, as though the word she wanted had eluded her but of deliberate intention. With all her poise, all the finished social technique that belonged to her class and her upbringing and was in her so highly developed, he found in Valentine the delicate shyness of a young—a very gracefully young—girl.

"It's been like that with me too," he told her. "I've forgotten for years at a time, and I've turned into quite another person since then, so that I can't even always remember what I was like, or what I thought I was like, in those days—but it used to come back to life with me too, sometimes. And when I saw you this afternoon,

I remembered you perfectly. I think that was a queer thing, too."

"Yes."

"How simply you say 'Yes' as though it didn't surprise you at all, and you'd felt just the same."

"Oh, but I did," Valentine answered.

The gentle, candid manner in which she made the admission dumbfounded him completely.

He thought: "It's no good. I'm in love with her. I adore her." And following on the conviction came its graceless, inevitable concomitant: "God, what a muddle! What a complicated, god-damned muddle!"

A clock chimed, startlingly audible in the silence, and Valentine said:

"It's late. Did you mean to do any work to-night?"

"No. I wanted to talk with you. When you went up to show Sedgewick his room, I was afraid you mightn't come down again. I was terrified you wouldn't."

"But I wanted to," returned Valentine, and he thought how far removed was the quiet, considered way in which she said it from the quality, to him detestable, implied in the odious word "coquettish."

"I've talked to you a lot about myself, and you've listened so graciously—won't you tell me a little about what's happened to you, since the time in Rome?"

"In terms of actual happening, very little, and what there was, all came quite close together—between the ages of seventeen and twenty-one, really. When the war started my father sent my mother and me back to London and we took a flat in Sloane Street. It seems absurd now, but in spite of the war I came out in the way girls did then—one had to be presented at a Royal garden-party instead of at a drawing-room and so on—and I did some very casual war work that really only meant getting to know other girls."

Lonergan noticed her old-fashioned, oddly elegant pronunciation of the word and smiled at it.

She smiled back, in a shy, friendly way as though she understood what had amused and perhaps pleased him.

"I think my mother was afraid of my being at a disadvantage, because of having lived abroad so much. But all our relations were very kind and everyone was giving informal dances and parties, that were supposed to be for men home on leave, from the Front. I expect I had more fun, really, than I should have had before the war, doing the London season properly. Every girl I ever knew seems to have hated her first season."

"You know," said Lonergan, "that you're talking about a world of which I know absolutely nothing whatever? I don't mean—I've no need to tell you—that I'm not interested. But my own origin is so completely different—middle-class Irish. I know nothing whatever about the kind of background you're describing. Forgive me. I didn't want to interrupt you. Please go on. Were you happy, going to the dances and parties?"

"I was very young for my age. I think perhaps very young people aren't really happy but they always think that one day they're going to be. I used to feel quite certain that happiness of some marvellous kind must be waiting for me just round the corner."

"Was it?"

"Well, no. I can't say that. I don't mean at all that my life has been an unhappy one."

She paused. Lonergan guessed that she was finding it difficult, for a moment, to go on.

He thought: "Give her time. She'll tell me," and he remained motionless.

"I suppose by happiness I really meant falling in love and getting married. And that's what happened."

Lonergan experienced the onslaught of a sharp, furious jealousy.

He had seen the portrait of Humphrey Arbell hanging in the hall, and he had—he now knew—assumed that Valentine had never been in love with him.

Keeping his voice carefully neutral, he said:

"You were very young, when you fell in love and married."

"Nineteen. I met Humphrey when I went to stay with his sister, Venetia Rockingham. Charlie—her husband—was in Palestine and she was using their house at Maidenhead as a convalescent home for officers. Humphrey was there. He was one of the wounded officers. There was a sort of glamour about them, you know——"

She broke off, and said with a kind of mirthful distress:

"What a thing to say! And yet it's perfectly true. That sort of glamour was responsible for a lot of love-affairs in the last war."

"Of course."

He would have liked to know whether it had been responsible for her marriage to Humphrey Arbell, but would assail her with no crude questions.

Presently she said:

"A week-end can be a very long while. Humphrey fell in love with me—and I thought about him a lot, and Venetia asked me to come back again the next week-end, and I did. It was really a very obvious and straight-forward affair, I suppose—only one never feels that about oneself. Humphrey and I were engaged three weeks after we first met, and then he was given sick leave and we got married. We thought he was going back to the Front, but he never did. The Medical Board wouldn't pass him."

Valentine stopped speaking, and again Lonergan refrained from breaking in on her train of thought.

When she turned towards him again it was, once more, to surprise him.

"Those are just facts, aren't they, and facts all by themselves convey so little. I could tell you that Hum-phrey and I came to live here when the war was over, and that I had two children—and you still wouldn't really know much about my life."

"Were you happy?" he asked.

Valentine smiled suddenly at that, as though he had pleased her unexpectedly.

"That's the question I always want to ask people myself. I don't think men do, as a rule—I mean, want to know about that. I wasn't unhappy but I didn't ever want to think about happiness. That's the nearest I can get to explaining."

"It's near enough," Lonergan told her.

"What I minded most, when I was younger, was that life seemed so very uninteresting. I thought it oughtn't to be like that. I liked living in the country, and we had just

71

enough money, and there were the children, and Humphrey and I got on together quite well. Perhaps that was really what was wrong. I thought—and I still think—it isn't nearly enough, just to get on quite well."

"It isn't."

"Humphrey was killed in a hunting accident, twelve years ago. Quite a lot of people told me I was sure to marry again. I used to think so, too. But no one ever asked me to and I stayed on here, and Reggie—my eldest brother—had to retire on half-pay, and came to live with me. And I thought it was important for the children that Coombe and I should always be there—something they could depend on, that didn't change. When I was a child I used to long for a settled home that would always be the same. But I don't know, really, that it made much difference to *them*. It seems to me now that I didn't realize they'd stop being children after a few years, and of course that's what has happened. Naturally. It would have happened anyway, only the war seems to have made it come suddenly. And even that's not really true. Primrose has lived away from home ever since she was eighteen, practically."

The mention of Primrose's name stabbed Lonergan with an acute discomfort. He moved quickly, noisily pushing apart the logs on the hearth with his boot.

Immediately, he was aware of a complete change in the atmosphere that had enveloped them all through their long conversation.

The logs, in falling apart, sent up a little volley of sparks of which one landed on the shabby, discoloured hearth-rug and Lonergan stamped it out.

The spell of the evening was broken.

"Good-night," said Valentine. "I do hope you'll ask for whatever you want. Please tell me, if there's anything, won't you?"

"I will. Thank you."

"I must go to bed. Good-night," repeated Valentine.

Lonergan said good-night, and as she moved away he added:

"I'm so glad we've met again."

She looked back at him and smiled, saying "I am

72

too" with a sound of shyness in her voice that made her, more than ever, seem strangely youthful. He was glad of the words and yet he felt as though a chill had fallen upon their evening so that her going-away left him with a sense of desolation.

VI

VALENTINE lay in bed, wakeful.

She felt stimulated as she had not felt for many years, and she was aware both of a new and precarious sense of happiness and of strange, inescapable pangs of pain related to all that Lonergan had told her about the house at Saumur, Laurence, who had come to him and lived with him in Paris, and their child Arlette.

Neither happiness nor pain owed anything to the early love of Rory Lonergan and Valentine Levallois. They had been two children, disappeared long ago into the lost world of childhood. Through half a lifetime they had all but forgotten one another. Neither had ever had any claim on the fidelity of the other.

So that it was, Valentine acknowledged to herself, on account of Lonergan as she had known him for the space of one evening that she lay awake now.

She recalled, word for word, things that they had said to one another, and she saw again certain expressions that had passed over his dark, intelligent face.

The look that had come into his eyes when he spoke of Laurence and said that only one word—luminous—could describe the quality of her beauty, was vividly before her in the darkness.

It brought with it the sharp, unpredictable and uncontrollable onslaught of jealousy.

Valentine thought, lucidly and with the realism that belonged to her: "I think I'm falling in love with him. Perhaps I am in love already," and she remembered with a kind of astonished awe that both she and Lonergan were free to love as they chose.

The romantic miracle, in which she had all her life secretly believed, might come to pass.

The fourteen-year-old village girl, Esther, who bounced through the duties of housemaid and supplementary parlour-maid at Coombe and was so evidently convinced that she had nothing left to learn concerning them, called Valentine at half-past seven.

She slammed down a tray with a tiny early-morning tea service on it, pulled at the curtains and rattled up the blinds with noisy exuberance, and banged the door smartly behind her.

Valentine felt glad that the competent Madeleine always performed these offices for the General, that two soldier servants were responsible for her visitors and that Primrose was never called at all in the mornings.

She wished, as often before, that Primrose would allow breakfast to be taken up to her room.

At least, she reflectively told herself, it was nowadays no longer possible for Primrose to substitute for breakfast, and frequently for other meals as well, a succession of bananas, of which the skins, curling and discoloured, seemed always to be left lying about on pieces of furniture, mantelshelves and the edges of the bath.

Even three years ago Primrose had been fairly ready to regard her trail of banana skins as a household joke. Valentine had always felt that, with occasional references and mild jibings about the banana skins, she could still share a look or a smile with Primrose that momentarily lessened the strain in their relationship. Now, nothing at all could do that.

She had been terribly conscious on the previous evening that Primrose's hostility towards her had hardened. She felt that it was now something which Primrose had acknowledged and justified to herself, and would take no further pains to hide. Accustomed to stifle a misery for which she could nowhere find alleviation, Valentine made the effort of turning her mind away from it.

She went from her cold bedroom to the still colder bathroom, dressed as quickly as possible in a dark-blue

74

knitted dress that she had always liked and went downstairs.

There she automatically noted the signs of Ivy's and Esther's light-hearted disregard of all but the more obvious of their morning duties: she straightened some of the chair-covers, turned off an electric light left burning unnecessarily, and pulled a leaf off the day-by-day almanack that stood on the desk.

It was Sunday morning.

Valentine remembered how punctually her father, as Sunday after Sunday came round, had quoted the line: "Sweet day, so cool, so calm, so bright."

She herself, with equal punctuality, had recollected the triviality once a week for more than twenty years.

She went into the dining-room, shivered, and began to make the coffee.

Presently Ivy brought in toast and the breakfast-tray that Madeleine was waiting to take up to the General.

Valentine added what was necessary to it and Ivy went out and a minute or two later sounded the gong in the hall.

In a few minutes, Valentine told herself, she would see Lonergan.

She suddenly felt very young and very happy.

Almost immediately Lonergan and Captain Sedgewick came in together.

Valentine smiled at them both, telling young Sedgewick with genuine concern that he should have slept longer.

"Thanks very much, Lady Arbell, but I had a marvellous night. I feel fine. I can't tell you what it's like to be in a civilized home again after being in camp."

The soldiers all said the same thing, and it always rang true.

She knew that both the men would be away from the house all day, but, remembering Jess, invited Sedgewick to join the tea and games that her younger daughter had projected for the evening.

"Mr. Banks, who was here the other day, is coming and he was to bring a friend with him."

"Good old Buster," said Sedgewick leniently.

75

"It's very kind of you to have them," Lonergan told her. "They'll love it, poor lads."

"Perhaps you'll be here, too?"

"In the office, I expect. Will you ever recognize that charming little sitting-room under the name of the office, I wonder?"

Jess with unwonted punctuality came into the dining-room before breakfast was over. She wore, as usual, her riding-clothes and Valentine noticed that she had taken a great deal of trouble with the management of her hair.

"Hallo! Good-morning," said Jess.

She went to the sideboard, forestalling both the men.

"Please don't do anything. If you're going to be billeted here we'd better begin as we mean to go on, hadn't we, and it'll be such a frightful bore for you if you once start waiting on me. You'll see, it'll be quite bad enough at cold Sunday supper to-night when we're supposed to wait on ourselves and everybody gets into a flat spin and no one can sit and eat in peace. In some ways, I think this house is frightfully like a madhouse."

"Will you shut the door, darling?"

"I can't, mummie. Aunt Sophy'll want to come in at any minute. Aunt Sophy! Good little dog!"

Jess whistled and called, dashed from the table to the door and back again, and when no puppy appeared, shut the door briskly.

"I'm training her," she said to Sedgewick.

The talk, from which Jessica had dispelled any possible constraint, circled round the dogs, the weather, Valentine's intention of going to church and Lonergan's assertion that it would be impossible for him to do so.

"Being Irish, are you a Catholic?" asked Jess.

"I am. Not a very good one, I'm afraid."

"Fancy the Pope," said Jess thoughtfully, and the eyes of Valentine and Rory Lonergan met in a swift look of shared amusement.

Aunt Sophy whined and scratched at the door, Sedgewick and Jess rose simultaneously and raced for it. Jess, slipping, caught hold of his arm to retrieve her balance, shrieked with laughter, and almost fell again, picking up her dog.

76

"I'm afraid you can see only too plainly why Jess thinks this house is like a madhouse," Valentine said, gently ironical, to Lonergan.

"She's a riot," he answered under his breath, and the mirthful exhilaration that lay beneath the odd little phrase communicated itself to her.

She felt gay and irresponsible, as she had not felt for years, when breakfast was over, the two officers gone and Jess had taken the puppy out into the garden.

The sensation remained with her all through the Sunday morning routine: Jess, bringing the car to the door and receiving without expostulation all assurances that if she didn't go and change at once she'd be late, General Levallois' appearance, in the weekly spruceness of a dark-blue suit, black tie and well-brushed hat, the triumphant return of Jess miraculously transfigured in Sunday clothes, and the familiar drive down the hill to the church.

Valentine liked going to church, but she was aware that her liking was based on sentimental and traditional feeling. It had nothing to do with faith, or even with religion.

The familiar and beautiful words of the Psalms always struck her afresh, the hymns, associated with childhood, gave her a faint nostalgic pleasure. She even found repose in listening to the sound, if not the actual words, of the elderly clergyman's gentle ramblings from the pulpit.

He had been already for some years at St. Martin's when she first came to live at Coombe.

Prayer was not a form of self-expression natural to Valentine. On her knees, she thought of Primrose, Jess, her own dead parents and her dead husband, as she did always in church yet with a conviction that prayer in the true sense of the word must mean something more impersonal and deeper than anything within her comprehension.

The congregation, a very small one, went out and Valentine exchanged greetings with her neighbours. Most of them were from farm or cottage homes, and most of them she had known ever since her marriage.

They made comments on the war situation, the weather or local village news. One or two women who served with Valentine on the Women's Institute Committee came up and spoke with her about past or future activities.

Jess let the dogs out of the car, talked to people—especially those, mostly farmers' sons, whom she met in the hunting-field—and held General Levallois' two sticks for him while he clambered painfully into the seat behind the driver's.

"Mummie, I'm going to walk home by the short-cut with the dogs."

"Very well."

"Hadn't you better start? Uncle Reggie is definitely frozen."

"Very well," said Valentine again.

She went back to the car.

"The distributor!" shrieked Jess, starting off with the dogs.

Of course. Jess never seemed to forget anything practical. Valentine did so frequently.

She replaced the distributor and turned the car.

Her brother, who seldom as a rule spoke to her when she was driving, leant forward from the back seat.

"Val, did you find out whether this feller—the Irish one—was the chap you knew in Rome?"

"Yes, Reggie. He is."

"Dam' cheek," said the General.

She laughed.

"How could he possibly help it?"

"I grant you he couldn't help being sent down here—that's obvious. But I can see that he's the kind who if you give him an inch will take an ell."

"I don't agree."

"He managed to get himself billeted here on account of Primrose, I suppose. Jess let out that they'd been seeing one another in London. Look out, Val! You should never take a corner like that."

"I'm sorry. If he's a friend of Primrose's, naturally she might easily have suggested his coming here."

"There's no if about it. What's he doing, meeting her

78

at Exeter and driving her out here with him, and what's *she* doing, if it comes to that, dashing down from London for a week all of a sudden just as he arrives?"

What indeed? Valentine felt as though she had been abruptly confronted by a quite new aspect of Rory Lonergan and his possible concern in her life.

Because she was hurt and acutely, suddenly unhappy, she said at once:

"But Reggie, it's all perfectly. all right. Primrose knows a great many men, and I think a lot of them admire her. Why shouldn't Colonel Lonergan? He's a good deal older than she is, but that's all."

"He's probably got a wife and half a dozen brats in that damned disloyal country of his."

"He's not married at all."

"Good God, Val, the rate women go on. I suppose you've already made up your mind what kind of wedding-dress Primrose is to wear. Let me tell you that in these days people go every kind of length and marriage doesn't enter into it at all. Not that I mean," the General conceded rather grudgingly, "that Primrose would go off the rails or anything like that. All I say is, you'll be a fool if you trust an Irishman. They're plausible, that's what they are. Plausible."

He went on repeating words to much the same effect until they reached Coombe.

Valentine paid little heed.

She was telling herself that she was forty-four, and Primrose twenty-four. That she knew nothing, in reality, of Primrose's life in London beyond assertions, general rather than particular, of her attraction for men— assertions that had travelled to Coombe for the most part by way of Venetia Rockingham. That Lonergan was a man susceptible to women, and himself likely to charm them.

Then, her thoughts coming round again in a circle, she let herself remember the previous evening and her own happiness of the morning.

She knew that she had not been mistaken as to the atmosphere of mutual understanding, and even tenderness, in which their long conversation had taken place.

79

But one might easily be mistaken as to its ultimate significance.

Rory Lonergan could have been rendered happy, as she had been herself, by the warmth of the sympathy between them and that faint, romantic, shared memory of the Pincio Gardens, and it might all have meant no more to him than that.

Valentine had never believed herself to be capable of inspiring passion, but she believed Primrose to be so. And Primrose was young, and men had thought her beautiful before—her arrogant self-assurance, so obviously based upon experiences of a rock-like reality, had long ago convinced her mother of that. She could not have said when nor even why she had first felt certain that Primrose was no longer inexperienced in the ways of passionate love—but the certainty was there.

Valentine drew up the car in front of the portico. She left it there for Jess to put away.

The General slowly climbed out backwards. In the hall, he rang the bell. If the weather made it in any way possible he always walked up and down the terrace, round the garden and into the walled kitchen garden every Sunday morning on his return from church, leaning on Madeleine's arm.

The bell was his summons to Madeleine.

Madeleine never grumbled or protested whatever the demands made upon her.

She loved them all, and she had lived with the Levallois family in the old days.

She must have grown used to it all, Valentine felt, even to her curious, recluse existence at Coombe where she would have nothing to do with the other servants, always declaring herself unable to understand a word of English, and carrying her own meals up to her sitting-room, to be eaten in solitude.

She came into the hall now, muffled as though for an Arctic expedition in black-and-white check coat, ancient feather boa, shiny kid gloves, pointed black boots in goloshes and black felt hat with the brim pulled down over her eyes.

The clumps of her thickly-henna'd hair were visible under the hat. For some reason that Valentine had never analysed, the artificial colour was not out of keeping with the shrewd kindliness of Madeleine's pale, round face and of her large brown eyes, brilliant as diamonds.

"Bonjour, Madeleine."

"Bonjour, madame."

Valentine and the General, Jess and Primrose, always talked with Madeleine in her own language.

She spoke eagerly now of *messieurs les officiers* and said that she had met Colonel Lonergan on the stairs and that he had spoken to her in French that she characterized as perfect.

She had also seen the young Captain, and thought him *très gentil*, although he had said nothing. He probably knew no French and was less *homme du monde* than his superior officer, said Madeleine, but she was glad of his presence, which would amuse Mademoiselle Jess.

"So long as she's here, but she may be called up any day."

"Alas, madame!"

The General enquired whether Primrose was down-stairs yet, and Madeleine, with a subtle change of tone to which Valentine was well accustomed, replied that she was not.

"Well, we don't wait luncheon for anyone," declared the General. "Come on, now, Madeleine—the best of the day'll be over."

Madeleine took one of his sticks—a privilege accorded to nobody else—and substituted her own sturdy arm.

They disappeared slowly through the garden door.

Valentine, moving scarcely less slowly, went over to the fire which the maids had as usual neglected to make up, so that it had sunk to red embers on a small bed of wood-ash.

She put on more logs and, kneeling down, began to blow upon the sparks with the bellows.

Her mind was dwelling once again on Lonergan's story of his life in France with Laurence, and on what he had said about Arlette.

". . . I wasn't interested in her at all till the last year.

81

And now I am. . . . When all this is over, if I'm still living, I'll have Arlette with me."

All the things that had conditioned his life were things of which she knew practically nothing—his work as an artist, his relationship to Laurence, his belated affection and sense of responsibility towards their child, even his Army career—at best, if he chose to talk to her of them she could enter into his descriptions sympathetically but that was all.

Other people, of whose very names she was ignorant, has shared his experiences with him and had helped to build up the background of past associations that made up so large a part of every life.

She turned her mind for a moment towards the future but, in the midst of war, there could be no escape there. To live from day to day was the only possibility, so far as personal problems were concerned. She reminded herself, without much sense of reality, that Rory Lonergan was as likely as any other man in the Forces to lose his life before the end of the war.

At length her thoughts stopped, where she had known they must, at the immediate present.

Was she to watch a love-affair develop between Primrose and Lonergan?

After all, Valentine told herself, it couldn't prove to be an unendurable situation. Her own romantic illusion had been based on a single evening and could have thrown out no indestructible roots.

Primrose was her child and she had always wanted, and still wanted, happiness for her. She had even believed that happiness might make Primrose normal and simple and kind, and it had seemed to her that no price could be too high to pay for that.

I never thought it might come like this though, Valentine reflected, and a dark shadow of misery and uncertainty seemed to settle down upon her spirit.

She started violently at the sudden noise made by Jess returned from her walk.

"Mummie, this is frightfully important. I want to ask you something."

"What, my precious?"

Jess, at least, never resented or sneered at terms of endearment even if she never made use of them herself.

"Well, look, we've got all these officers coming for tea and they'll be staying on for supper, and I don't suppose I'll be at home after about another week or something, for the rest of the duration, so couldn't we possibly, just for once, make a party of it and scrape up some drink for them? Isn't there anything at all in the cellar?"

"I think there must be," said Valentine, touched. "Anyhow, there's a bottle of sherry left in the wine cooler, and we'll open that, Jess, and have it in before supper."

"Gosh, that'll be Heaven. And I could not take any, if that'd make it go round better. Actually, I loathe the taste of it unless I mix it with water."

"I don't think you'd better let uncle Reggie see you mixing it with water."

"Would he go bats or something? It'd be rather fun to try, in a way. Thanks terrifically, mummie."

"Just tell me how many there'll be."

"Buster and a friend who I don't know the name of, and Captain Sedgewick—he definitely wants to be called Charles, by the way—and I suppose Colonel Lonergan if he's not too grand?"

"I'm sure he's not. Jess—do you like him?"

"Oh, I think he's divine. He's just Irish enough, isn't he? I mean, I'd have had a definite pain if he'd been after saying Begorrah all day long, like Irish people on the films."

Valentine laughed.

"I don't believe anybody ever says it at all, off the films."

"Oh, the films wouldn't have it unless *somebody* did. They're frightfully realistic and careful about things like that," Jess asserted. "Prob'ly it's said like anything in some part of Ireland that Colonel Lonergan doesn't come from. I'm glad he'll be here this evening. It'll suit Primrose fine."

"I suppose it will."

"Well, she's sure to despise all the others, isn't she?

83

I think Primrose is too terribly like a camel, when she pulls down the corner of her mouth. I wish I could do it. I've often tried, but I never can."

"My dear, do you really want to look like a camel?"

"Well, mummie, you can't say it doesn't get one somewhere. Look at Primrose! People ringing her up all the evening, and now a Colonel falling for her!"

Valentine gazed at Jess in silence.

"Mummie, you look awfully as if you thought I was the Brains Trust or something. Is there anything wrong with me?"

"No, darling. Nothing at all."

VII

CAPTAIN CHARLES SEDGEWICK, returning from Head-quarters four miles away in the market town late that afternoon, deduced from the battered motor-cycle stand-ing before the door of Coombe that Banks and his friend had arrived.

He went round the house and in at the garden door—that was, he had discovered, always left open—and up to his room without entering the hall.

He could hear the little girl, Jess, laughing.

He was a young man who tabulated his impressions of people carefully and he had summed Jess up as a nice kid, unaffected and a good sort, not likely to set the Thames on fire unless she made an unexpectedly brilliant marriage. She might do so, at that, thought Charles Sedgewick, slamming down the heavy window-sash in his unwarmed bedroom.

Where Jess fell in love, she would almost certainly marry, and where she fell in love would depend entirely on where she happened to be. He knew already that she was niece to Lady Rockingham, and "People of that sort," he said to himself, "are a regular trades union. Wherever she's stationed with the W.A.A.F., she'll get invitations to her own kind of house. I only hope, poor kid, they won't be as damned uncomfortable as this one is."

There was no rancour in the thought.

Charles Sedgewick despised dependence on creature comforts. He never smoked, seldom drank, and had won a mention in despatches on the beach at Dunkirk.

His widowed mother's suburban house had exactly the kind of cosiness that he most disliked and to which, before the war, he had so much preferred a dingy bedroom in the Strand from which he could daily walk to the Bank where he worked. His sentimental mother's plea that Charlie was all she had in the world and that they ought to make a home for one another until he should marry some nice girl, had not moved him the least.

He was kind and often affectionate to her, wrote to her frequently, had himself photographed in uniform to please her, and spent most of his leaves at *Dunroamin*, coldly civil to her circle of Bridge-playing, grievance-mongering and domestically-minded ladies of middle age.

As for the nice girl that his mother thought she wanted him to marry, Sedgewick had no intention whatever of getting married, least of all to the type of girl his mother called "nice."

It would be difficult enough to live at all after the war, should he survive it, without being saddled with a wife. With quiet regularity, when on leave he visited the more expensive of the London brothels.

Capable, energetic and with a cast-iron self-confidence, Sedgewick applied himself to his soldiering and made the most of every opportunity that came in his way.

He was pleased to be at Coombe, in the same billet as his Colonel and with a family that he had at once classified as "the real thing."

As he pulled off his boots, washed his hands and sleeked his smooth, straight red hair close to his narrow head, he wondered what the elder daughter was like.

He had guessed, from references made by Jess, that she was not of the unsophisticated "county" type. She was three- or four-and-twenty, and had been living an independent existence in London.

85

On Lady Arbell he wasted no thoughts at all. She was as completely unreal to him as he probably was to her.

They would merely exchange the polite spoken symbols of civilization current between two people belonging to different generations and, indeed, different worlds.

He went downstairs and found the two subalterns—Banks and a stocky North Country youth called Jack Olliver—playing spillikins at a round table in the hall with Jess, her mother and Colonel Lonergan.

Lady Arbell looked up at him and smiled, enquiring whether he had had any tea.

Jess and the subalterns, evidently on the friendliest terms already, were loudly disputing over the heaped-up slivers of white bone.

"I had a cup of tea in the town, thank you."

Sedgewick's extremely observant eye had already discerned that the other daughter, Primrose, was downstairs too. She was sitting in an armchair with her back to the players, and Sedgewick could only see the top of a pale blonde head and two long and well-shaped legs with sandalled feet resting on the hearth.

"Primrose, I don't think you've met Captain Sedgewick," said her mother.

The blonde head turned and Primrose, scarcely moving, looked round the chair-back.

Her mouth twisted to one side and she made a sound that scarcely amounted to a spoken word.

Sedgewick thought: "She's like someone on the stage, playing a Society girl."

He moved over and sat down opposite to her.

"Come in on the next game, Charles," amiably shouted Jessica.

"Okay. Thanks, I will."

"You don't have to," remarked Primrose—and this time he could hear what she said.

"I like spillikins. Don't you?"

"Not particularly. Why should one?"

"To test the steadiness of one's hand, perhaps," Sedgewick suggested.

He was not interested in what she might be saying, even as an indication of her personality. He was thinking of her looks, of her figure and her long legs and flat, narrow hips, and of her air of arrogant discontent.

She wasn't at all like Jess or her mother. Her bad manners, he decided, were just a pose, probably intended to show how different she was.

They neither pleased nor displeased him. So long as a girl had poise, and was well-turned-out and confident of her own power to attract men, Charles Sedgewick was perfectly ready to be attracted. He had hoped, from the beginning, that one or other of the girls at Coombe might interest him.

Cries and exclamations came from the players at the round table.

"Buster! The whole pile *rocked*! I saw it."

"Come on, then. See what you can do."

"Steady. . . . That little hooked one is your best chance. . . . The Colonel's left it all ready for you. . . . Look out—don't move——"

"You *blew* on it, you cad!"

"I swear I didn't."

Primrose said:

"How do you like being stationed down here?"

"It's okay. Devon's new to me."

"What's your own part of the world?"

"London."

"Me too."

"Now then, sir—you've a clear run."

"I have not, then. I'll need a hand like a rock."

"That one moved!"

"Two of them moved."

"Most of them did. Lady Arbell, I've done all the spade-work for you now."

"You drive a van or something, don't you?" Sedgewick asked Primrose.

"That's right. What I don't know about London Bridge in the blitz is nobody's business."

"One or two noisy moments, no doubt."

"I'll say so. Have you been mixed up in any of the bomb racket?"

87

"Not I. This is a civilians' war," Sedgewick answered carelessly.

He had no intention of telling her that he had been at the Dunkirk evacuation. For one thing he disliked talking about it, and for another he was perfectly well aware that she would neither be, nor pretend to be, in the least interested.

"Go for that one at the corner and you ought to get the lot."

"Keep your head, now, Jess."

"You're putting me off . . .!"

There was a shriek from Jess, and laughter and scuffling rom the subalterns.

"I *swear* I've won!" Jess cried earnestly. "Haven't I, Colonel Lonergan? Don't listen to Buster and Jack, they're not speaking the truth."

"The Children's Hour," said Primrose.

"Come on, Charles," Jess cried. "Or shall we try something else? I'll tell you what—let's play Racing Demon!"

Banks and Olliver were loud in their acclamations at this suggestion.

"This table won't be large enough, though. Shall we go into the dining-room?"

"No," said Lady Arbell, "it's too cold, and besides, I think Ivy laid the table before she went out. Four of you can play at this table all right."

She got up and moved towards the fire.

"Take my place, Captain Sedgewick. If you like Racing Demon?"

"It's my favourite sport."

"Play instead of me, Lady Arbell," urged Jack Olliver.

Jess interposed.

"It's all right. Mummie really isn't a Racing Demon fan. She almost always loses, because she has a complex about manners."

"You can't afford manners for Racing Demon," agreed Colonel Lonergan. He smiled at his hostess.

Jess went to a cupboard, pulled out a drawer and produced several battered packs of cards.

Sedgewick looked at Primrose.

"Playing?" he asked.

She shook her head.

He went over to the table, and Lonergan at the same moment got up from his chair.

Sedgewick sketched a polite protest.

"All right, Charles. You carry on."

The Colonel, like Lady Arbell, had moved over to the fire. He was standing, looking down at his hostess.

Jess and the subalterns were flicking over the cards, counting the number in each dog's-eared and discoloured pack, and explaining to one another the rules by which the game should be played.

Charles Sedgewick, lightly stroking his small red moustache, looked from Jess to her sister, from Primrose to the man and woman over the fire,—so much older— of whom one was his superior officer and the other a slender, faded creature with greying hair, into whose house the fortune of war had taken him.

He heard her say to the Colonel:

"Do go and write in peace in the breakfast-room, the noise in here will be ear-splitting in another minute."

"I've been writing most of the day. I was wondering if you'd care to come and listen to the Six O'Clock News. I've a grand fire in there."

Lady Arbell looked across at her daughter.

"I've one or two things to see to before supper. I think I'll wait for the news till nine. I daresay Primrose would find it warmer in there. Your batman makes a much better fire than my house-parlour-maid does."

Primrose remained without stirring.

Lonergan, after waiting a moment, went by himself into his new office.

"Ready?" cried Jess. "Does everybody understand everything? Charles, you'd better keep the score, and mind you don't cheat."

She thrust paper and pencil at him.

Primrose slouched out of the hall, up the stairs.

These people knew how to make one feel perfectly at home and natural. Sedgewick would hand them that, he told himself, grinning at the thought of the two delighted boys who had raced one another to the bath-room and whose loud, cheerful voices he had heard a moment ago on their way down to supper.

He thought of the painfully polite hospitality to wh:ch he was best accustomed—the obvious preparations, the apologies that deceived nobody, and—usually—the laboured nature of the conversation, taking the form of question and answer.

Charles Sedgewick was quite certain that houses like Coombe had long ago had their day—not many of them were left, he imagined, and a good thing too.

The privileged classes, amongst whom he unhesitat-ingly placed Lady Arbell and her family, were in the last ditch. Some of them would go down fighting, of course —but they were doomed, one and all.

Girls like Primrose and Jessica would either have to earn a living or, if they married, would have to work hard in their own homes instead of paying other people to do it all for them.

He hummed to himself "*I don't want to set the world on fire*" and went downstairs.

A decanter and glasses stood on a small table; the old gentleman—General Levallois—had come to life again and was sitting by the fire, wearing a curious old velveteen coat, and Lady Arbell and Jess were talking with Cyril Banks and Jack Olliver.

They were drinking sherry, and Sedgewick noticed with amusement the controlled expression of disgust with which Jess was sipping at hers.

"Have some sherry?" said the General.

Sedgewick thanked him and refused.

He joined the group.

A clock struck eight.

"Why isn't dinner ready?" instantly enquired the General.

"It's Sunday, Reggie, and Ivy's out. Supper is cold, nd it's quite ready. We're just waiting till we're all here."

"You're not going to wait for Primrose surely."

"Colonel Lonergan isn't here either," Jess pointed out. "We must wait for a Colonel."

"He won't mind if we don't," said Lady Arbell, smiling."

"Here is the Colonel," said Jack Olliver.

"I beg your pardon if I'm late. You shouldn't have waited."

"Primrose is later. Not that we ever wait for her," remarked Jess. "Take aunt Sophy, Buster! She gets under one's feet so."

The ungainly puppy changed hands.

The General was already heaving himself to his feet and adjusting his sticks.

"Can't wait for Primrose," he muttered. "Bring that decanter with you, Jess. Come along."

As they moved towards the dining-room Primrose joined them.

She had changed into a long, tightly-fitting house-coat of some thick material that looked like flannel. It was a hyacinth-blue colour, and made her hair look very light and her eyes very dark.

"Hey, what about my drink?" she asked.

"Have it in the dining-room," said her uncle.

Colonel Lonergan held out a glass to Jess, and she filled it from the decanter for her sister.

Sedgewick thought that Primrose seemed more natural, and certainly more cheerful, than she had been earlier in the evening.

"Please sit anywhere you like," Lady Arbell said in the dining-room. "And I think it'll be simplest if only two people change the plates and so on, and everybody else sits still. Jess, darling——"

"I knew it'd be me. Here, take aunt Sophy, someone."

"Put the dam' dog *down*!" said the General.

"Who else, mummie?"

"I think Captain Sedgewick, if he will."

"Mummie, he's asked to be called Charles."

Lady Arbell looked an enquiry.

"That is correct," said Sedgewick, smiling.

"Certainly. Then, Charles, would you mind helping her?"

"Charles is quite a good name for a footman, isn't it?" Jess observed. "Or James or William. Jack would have to be John, and Buster simply wouldn't exist."

"Not even as Cyril?" suggested Banks.

They laughed and talked.

Primrose was an exception. She sat next to Colonel Lonergan, but appeared to have little to say to him. When she did speak it was from one corner of her mouth, and it struck Sedgewick that she made no effort at all to join in the general conversation.

The Colonel did, though.

He kept on trying to include his hostess in whatever it was that Primrose was muttering—Sedgewick couldn't always hear her—but Lady Arbell, though she always answered, usually with simple, acquiescent phrases, didn't seem to want to be included.

She left the Colonel to her daughter, and talked to Jack Olliver, sitting beside her.

Sedgewick himself occupied the chair on her other side.

He tasted his soup—a thin, pale soup that was not even very hot. His mother would have seen to the soup herself, if the maid had been out, and it would have been hot, and strongly flavoured. On the other hand, she certainly wouldn't have entertained visitors at all, on her servant's evening out.

He glanced at the two subalterns, and saw how much at ease they were, although Jack Olliver at least, Sedgewick guessed, had never before sat at a table where the men waited on the women. His mother and sisters, if he had any, would always do the waiting and expect Jack and his father to sit still.

The General, at the other end of the table, was looking at a menu-card—good lord!—and not talking.

"That menu is for my brother's express benefit," said Lady Arbell's soft voice, sounding as though she were rather amused. "He knows, and we all know, that Sunday supper is always the same—soup, and cold meat and salad, and anything we can get, nowadays, for a cold sweet—but he likes to see it written down beforehand. I can't think why."

Sedgewick laughed. He was amused, and rather

impressed, that she should have guessed the trend of his thoughts. She was certainly a good hostess, in spite of having a bad cook and insufficient heating and an out-of-date bathroom.

She noticed things, even while she seemed to be giving her full attention to whoever was talking to her. And she talked very little herself, and what she did say was on the subjects chosen by her guests: seldom drawing attention to herself or her own opinions.

Sedgewick was dispassionately, consistently interested in every manifestation of what he always firmly described to himself by the out-moded expression: Class-distinctions.

He thought their importance overrated, nowadays, but he also thought it foolish to deny or to ignore their existence. They were there, they did create a barrier—of which the middle classes were more conscious than anybody else—and it would take generations to eliminate them. Unless, indeed, England caught the Russian infection and was swept into a bloody revolution, with the firing-squad for those whose ancestors had enjoyed privileges long since denied to their descendants.

Slightly to his own surprise, Captain Sedgewick found himself talking to his hostess on the subject.

She was a good listener, and presently he noticed that she had somehow caused young Banks to go and help Jess with the waiting instead of himself.

"I'm afraid I'm neglecting all my duties."

"No, you're not. It's your turn to sit still. Please go on talking to me. The English revolution is taking place now, all the time, isn't it?"

"I hope so. It's needed."

"I'm afraid it is. Though I still hope there's enough genuine democracy established in the country by now to prevent a revolution of the Bolshevik kind. But perhaps I'm wrong about that, and it's a kind of dreadful, necessary short cut?"

Lonergan joined in.

"A short cut to where? Not, I think, to freedom for the individual, or to the development of the creative spirit. I was in Russia for a month or two in '37 and from

93

the little that I was able to see, everything was harnessed to the State—family, individual and art."

"That's one reason why the Russians are doing so magnificently now, isn't it, sir?" Jack Olliver enquired. Only deference to his commanding officer, Sedgewick knew, had given that interrogative twist to the sentence.

Olliver was a convinced young Communist.

"No doubt it's one reason," Lonergan agreed. "It's also why their Moscow and Leningrad art galleries have the most superb Dégas hanging next to the most deplorable canvases on which ardent young propagandists ever splashed rivers of scarlet blood onto white snow."

"Does every picture tell a story?" asked Sedgewick, amused.

"It does. And it's always the same story. Either the soldiers shooting the peasantry, or the peasantry shooting the aristocracy. No, I'm wrong. Sometimes it's Lenin addressing the workers on his way to or from exile."

"Why not?" drawled Primrose. "I think that might make rather a good picture."

Lonergan laughed.

"Ah well, I'm prejudiced, you see. I think freedom of expression is essential to art, and that artists should have nothing to do with propaganda."

"You're only thinking of painting. What about the Russian ballet?" Primrose demanded.

"Quite right," said Lonergan. "I'll give you that. It's as good as ever it was."

"I'm glad they've kept something," Lady Arbell said.

"Perhaps when their new order is more firmly established the Russians won't feel it so necessary to sacrifice the individual to the State."

"Obvious," said Primrose, and her upper lip twisted contemptuously.

Lonergan turned.

"Obvious is exactly what it isn't," he said coolly. "The Soviet Government, for the past twenty years or so, has been bringing up a whole generation with a set of clearly defined ideals. They may be good ideals or they may be bad ones—either way they'll stick. Freedom of

94

expression, or even of thought, will have ceased to be looked upon as a right."

"How utterly tedious," said Primrose

Her tone was insolent and the subalterns exchanged glances.

Colonel Lonergan raised his eyebrows.

"Is it the Soviet system you're referring to or my, no doubt uninformed, views about it?"

"Both."

Sedgewick had no particular prejudice against rudeness—he thought it, in fact, rather smart and modern—but he objected strongly to it when directed against a senior officer in the presence of his juniors.

For a moment he felt horribly embarrassed.

"Do you know," said Lady Arbell, "that you've none of you got anything to drink? Beer is all I can suggest, except water. On the sideboard, Jess."

She had seemed not to raise her voice, but it carried clearly—and the conversation about Russia was over. The General began to speak about beer, Jess and young Banks were jumping up and fetching the beer bottles, the Colonel returning attentive-sounding comments to General Levallois' assertions.

So that was how one did it—and it worked.

It seemed to Sedgewick a characteristic evasion of a difficult moment—but he admired it all the same.

And one had to be fair. In a better assorted company the discussion, whether polite or impolite in its expression, might have been allowed to go on. This evening it could only have been disastrous.

Doubtless, too, in the eyes of Lady Arbell, Sedgewick himself, Banks and Olliver, Primrose and Jess, were all of them too young, and too completely lacking in social diplomacy, to be allowed their heads in a political debate amongst their seniors.

He glanced at the pale, defined profile of his hostess and noted her serious, attentive and yet withdrawn expression. It occurred to him that she must, years ago, have been pretty, although of a type that made no appeal to modern taste.

Most interesting, thought Charles Sedgewick—rather

pleased with his own capabilities for dispassionate observation—to meet a woman like this one—so evidently
intelligent without being intellectual, whose standards of
behaviour were still ruled by the careful, useless, utterly
obsolete training of a vanished social system.

VIII

"Gosh! That heavenly green liqueur! I didn't even
know we *had* any," cried Jess naïvely.

"Uncle Reggie did. He thought it was a good occasion
for producing a liqueur, after what I'm afraid was rather
a dull meal," said her mother.

She poured out the coffee, and the young soldiers made
polite protests in defence of the meal, just over.

"What's the other stuff?" asked Jess. "Is it
brandy?"

"Yes."

The crème-de-menthe and the liqueur brandy came
as an agreeable surprise after the indifferent coffee, and
Jess delightedly distributed glasses.

"I bet everyone except uncle Reggie and Colonel
Lonergan will choose crème-de-menthe."

Sedgewick nodded.

"As you say."

"Well, you're wrong. I hate that filthy, sticky, green
poison. Me for the brandy-bottle every time," Primrose
declared.

"Gosh! It always makes me think of being sick.
They gave me some once at Rockingham, when I had a
bilious attack," Jess remarked. "It was foul."

"This is probably not quite the same type of brandy,
my dear," the General informed her rather drily. "But
as I doubt whether you'd notice any difference, by all
means leave it for those who do."

Lonergan, smiling, accepted his glass from Jess.

"It is not, indeed," he appreciatively remarked.
"This is worth its weight in gold, nowadays. One

can't get the stuff in London, under a small fortune."

"The last brandy I had in London was one you bought me, as it happens, Rory my pet," said Primrose.

The casual term of endearment, to which she managed to give a contemptuous twang, came with a rather shocking effect, and again Banks and Olliver looked at one another, slightly aghast.

Jess and Sedgewick both stared openly at Lonergan.

His blue, angry eyes were gazing straight at Primrose. "*Last* is the word," he said.

For a split second the atmosphere in the hall was electric.

A tiny, clashing sound of tinkling glass broke into it sharply.

Valentine's liqueur-glass had slipped from her fingers and lay shattered against the hearth.

A small stream of green was slowly oozing its way towards her shoes.

"How careless—and what a waste of crème-de-menthe!" she said meditatively.

"Have mine, Lady Arbell," Sedgewick offered.

"Or mine, mummie. Only I've drunk half of it."

"Get your mother another glass from the pantry, Jess. Or ring for one of the damned servants."

The two subalterns were hastening to the rescue, Olliver with his handkerchief and Banks with a piece of blotting-paper snatched off the desk. The old spaniel, Sally, sniffed at the mess.

"Come off it, Sally!" cried Jess. "We can't have you taking to drink at your time of life."

The young men took up the joke enthusiastically, relieved from the strain of a moment earlier.

"Perhaps Sally's a secret addict."

"Her real name's Sarah, I expect. Sarah Gamp."

"Gosh, I shan't send this handkerchief to be washed for a month. The bouquet's marvellous!"

"Thank you so very much," Lady Arbell said. "I'm sorry to have given so much trouble."

"I'll fetch you another glass, mummie. Here, Jack, take aunt Sophy."

"You can bring two glasses, Jess," said her uncle. "We'll send one up to Madeleine."

4

"Okay. We'll *all* take it up to her. Madeleine's a pet," Jess informed the officers. "She's French, and she adores having visitors, especially soldiers."

"Here, can't I fetch those glasses for you?"

"You don't know where they're kept."

Jess raced for the red baize door, and the young men followed her, laughing and jostling one another.

The door was left swinging and banging as their voices echoed away down the distant, stone-floored passage.

Lonergan got up to shut it.

Primrose looked at her mother and said, speaking more inaudibly than ever:

"You needn't have wasted a glass, to say nothing of a drink. Rory and I understand one another okay, and we're neither of us in the least afraid of a scene, or of saying what we mean."

"Please say it somewhere else, then, Primrose, and not in front of Colonel Lonergan's own subalterns," Valentine answered quietly.

She received unexpected support.

"Damned bad form, the way you spoke just now," the General curtly told his niece.

Primrose stood up.

"I seem to be a bit unpopular."

She turned to Rory Lonergan, who had come back to the fire.

"My relations aren't liking me at all. They think I've insulted you or something."

Lonergan looked, not at her but at her mother. The look was a profoundly troubled one.

"We've been making a holy show of ourselves, no less, and vexed you. I'm terribly sorry."

Valentine shook her head, smiling very faintly.

"It's all right. Let's leave it."

"Why?" coldly asked Primrose. "I'm damned sick of all this pretending and keeping on the surface and *corps diplomatique* rubbish. Why shouldn't I be rude to Rory if I feel like it, and why shouldn't he answer back? I feel like having one hell of a row this evening."

General Levallois pulled himself up onto his feet and reached for his sticks.

"Well, I don't, and if your mother and Colonel Lonergan take my advice they'll leave you to have your row by yourself. Good-night, Val. You can send me up a glass of brandy with Madeleine's drink to the sitting-room. 'Night, Colonel."

"Good-night, sir."

The General stumped away upstairs.

Shrieks of laughter, subdued by distance, came from beyond the red baize door, and the barking of dogs.

"Well, that's that," said Primrose. "Frightfully characteristic and old-school-tie and everything, isn't he? Where do we go from here?"

Lonergan was still gazing at Valentine. Her eyes were quiet, and her hand covered her mouth.

"For God's sake, Primrose," he said, "you've no need to go on like this, girl. Why do you have to spoil the party for everyone?"

Primrose shrugged her shoulders.

"You're very social-minded all of a sudden. How about finishing the fight in your office, if you're so anxious not to upset anybody?"

Valentine rose.

"Is the fire still burning in there?"

Lonergan accepted her dismissal gravely.

"It should be. We can go there, if that's what you wish."

"It's what *I* wish," said Primrose.

She walked away into the breakfast-room and they heard the click of the electric light switch as she turned it on.

Lonergan remained behind.

He could see Valentine's mouth now, and the expression of it told him, as he had expected, more than her guarded eyes had done.

"What's the matter?" he asked bluntly.

"With Primrose? I don't know."

"Not Primrose. You."

She hesitated so long before speaking that he thought she was not going to reply at all.

At last she said:

"I'm sorry she's being so difficult. It's partly because

99

of me, I think. I mean—Primrose doesn't like me, and that shows her at her worst. I expect you know how very different the real Primrose can be."

"Damn Primrose," said Lonergan.

Her face, at that, showed nothing but pure astonishment.

The sound of loud, laughing young voices and rapidly approaching feet reached them.

"I *must* talk to you," Lonergan said wildly and urgently. "I don't know what it is you're thinking—it may have been true once but it isn't any longer—God, what a cad I sound!—but don't you see, it isn't Primrose that matters, in the very least? It's you."

Valentine flushed deeply, like a young girl.

"I thought——" she said, and stopped.

"They think the pantry's *marvellous*!" hilariously announced Jess, bursting in with her train. "Jack says his mother would *die* if she had such a frightful sink to wash up at!"

"It's enough to break any woman's back."

"Jack, where are your manners and who asked your opinion of the sink anyway?" shouted young Banks.

They were indeed feeling at home and happy. Sedgewick put down glasses.

"Who's this mysterious French Madeleine of yours?" he asked Jess.

Valentine answered him.

"Madeleine's an old French maid of my mother's. She's been with us for years. She's in her sitting-room upstairs. Jess, take the whole tray if you're all going. Uncle Reggie wants a glass of brandy."

"Mummie, do you *always* remember not to say 'another'? I never do. Shall we all have *a* drink upstairs?" asked Jess collectively of her escort.

Sedgewick picked up the tray.

"Isn't Primrose coming?"

"Not at the minute," Valentine said. "I daresay she'll come up later."

"No, I shan't," said the voice of Primrose from the doorway of the office. "You can bring me a brandy in here, Rory."

Silently Lonergan poured out brandy into two glasses.

He carried them into the other room and Primrose shut the door.

Lonergan placed his glasses carefully on the desk and then turned round.

They stood facing one another.

"Well?" asked Primrose. "Say it, for God's sake. Don't just look at me as if I were a cup of cold poison. If anyone's got a grievance, it's me—not you."

"What grievance?"

"What grievance!" she mimicked scornfully. "Come on, Rory, let's have it out. If we're going on like this, I may as well go back to London to-morrow. Give me that drink, will you?"

He handed her the glass.

"Why didn't you bring the decanter? One glass isn't any good to anybody in a crisis."

"We'll have to get through this crisis without drink, my girl. Drink never settled anything yet."

"I couldn't disagree more. What on earth's the matter, Rory?"

"Let's sit down to it," suggested Lonergan. He moved towards the swivel chair that stood in front of the desk.

"Here," said Primrose in a stifled voice. She pushed him into the big armchair near the fire and threw herself onto his knee, curling herself against him with a fluid, boneless ease that made her seem, for all her length of limb, small and supple as a child.

Instinctively his arms closed round her.

"That's better," muttered Primrose, her voice stifled against his shoulder.

"Darling, this isn't any use, you know. We aren't getting anywhere. And truly, I'm in a terrible jam and I'm hating myself for having got into it and, still more, for having got you into it."

"I'm in no jam whatever. You and I started a thing, and as far as I know we were both getting quite a lot of fun out of it till you arrived here, and came over all Sir Galahad or whatever his name was. Is it because I'm not at my best and brightest in the old home atmosphere? If you remember, I warned you I shouldn't be."

"You did."

"Do I turn your stomach all of a sudden or something?"

"No. I think you're damned attractive, sexually, just as I always have."

Primrose raised her mouth to his and kissed him long and hard.

Then she said, most unexpectedly:

"Look here—I'm sorry I was a pig to you at supper. I know I was, but this place gets on my nerves."

He was touched, as he always was by her shattering honesty.

"God, Primrose, you make me feel like the hound of all the ages when you say a generous thing like that. I don't care what dog's abuse you hand out to me, as well you know, when we're by ourselves. But with those lads there——"

"Oh, Lord, that's what mummie said. I could have screamed when she did that fool trick of dropping her glass accidentally-on-purpose in the hall. Like something in an Edwardian drawing-room comedy, being all diplomatic and saving-the-situation-like."

"She did save it."

"If you ask me, I think she made a complete fool of herself."

Lonergan moved involuntarily.

"All right, you needn't kick me into the fire. I suppose your mother-complex is too much for your common sense."

"I certainly don't admire the way you speak to, or of, your mother. In fact, I think the way you behave to her altogether is quite disgusting."

"Well, need it matter? I mean, I daresay there are lots of ways in which we don't admire one another—I don't mind telling you that you're far from perfect yourself—but I can't see that it need interfere with *us*."

"Darling, I'm afraid I can. You've always held it against me that I'm a sentimentalist, and you've been perfectly right. I'm too much of a sentimentalist not to want to love, as well as be *in* love."

Primrose sat upright and gazed at him incredulously.

Her dense, blue-green eyes expressed wrath and contempt rather than pain.

"You aren't trying to tell me that it's all off, I suppose?"

Lonergan drew a long breath and spoke with the courage of desperation. "I'm afraid that's exactly it, my dear. You can't hate me more than I hate myself."

"You'll have to give me a lot better reason," said Primrose slowly. "After all, I'm not a fool. We both knew perfectly well, when the whole thing started, that we weren't out for a *grande passion*. It's what I said in the car coming down, Rory. There's somebody else."

"Very well. There is. Only it's not the way you think."

"I don't know what I think. Look here, Rory, I'd a lot rather you came into the open about this."

She was being at her best—straightforward, adopting no pose, and ready to face anything. Lonergan recognized it instantly, and as instantly realized that nothing could make his own dilemma harder. Well, it was his own fault. He'd let himself be rushed into this affair with a girl young enough to be his daughter simply because she had appealed to his sensuality and he had lacked the moral courage to rebuff the blatant advances with which she had assaulted him.

At least, this time it was not he who had made the assault, who had pursued and persuaded and compelled into love a woman whom he had temporarily found seductive and from whom he had sought the romantically perfect relationship that he had only found with Laurence, and which, in the inmost depths of his heart, he never really expected to find again. It had always been he, unreasonably disappointed and nervously exasperated, who had broken up the relationship, unable to endure its falsity or to keep up its pretences.

With Primrose, he had felt secure because she openly derided romantic love and they had admittedly embarked on their affair without protestations of love or fidelity on either side. She had told him that he was not her first lover, and would certainly not be her last, and she had never wanted any but physical love-making with him.

Even now, he told himself with relief that it was her vanity she was trying to protect, not her heart.

She deserved the truth and he—in a different sense—deserved the pain and discomfiture of making her accept it.

"My dear, you've been wonderful to me and I'll never forget it. But I warned you what I was, at the very beginning. Utterly fickle and unreliable, always landing myself into caddish situations and—what you loathe most—an incurable sentimentalist. It's *got* to be more than just the physical relationship with me, if it's to last at all."

"You knew all that at the beginning, and so did I," Primrose remarked coldly. "You can't pull that stuff now, Rory. Besides, you've just told me there's somebody else. Who is she?"

"Does that matter?"

"Is she in love with you?"

"I don't know. I haven't asked her."

"But you're going to?"

"I am. Look, Primrose, you've told me you'd rather I came into the open. I'll try. This—thing—encounter—call it anything you like—is something that's almost impossible to explain. I can only say that I do honestly believe it's real, and important, and may alter the whole of life. I didn't know it was going to happen, and she didn't either. But it *has* happened, and if it's what I believe it to be—everything else is out."

It was said.

Sick with self-disgust, Lonergan stopped speaking.

Primrose hadn't moved.

Then she began to laugh, disconcerting him utterly.

"I suppose this is Keltic romance or something. Well, it leaves me stone cold, because I simply don't understand it. All it boils down to, so far as I can see, is that you've fallen for another woman and you want to persuade yourself that you've never really loved anybody else before, and never will again. But I should like to know how often you've said and thought that, in the last ten years? Or twenty, for all I know."

"All right. You're entitled to say all that. I'm not

going to argue. I can only tell you the thing as I see it."

"But Rory, it doesn't make sense! You've said yourself that nothing has happened, yet. I don't know what this girl can give you that I can't, but for the moment you're here, and I'm here, and—well, what's the odds anyway?"

He understood that she was prepared to overlook altogether what she took to be his imaginative interest in another woman, for the term of her stay at Coombe.

He shook his head.

"It's no good, Primrose."

He hoped she might be angered by his gracelessness, but instead she put her arms round his neck.

"You don't deserve it, but I've got fond of you," she said, low and indistinctly, her face against his.

"Primrose!"

Pity, remorse, affection, all seemed to be tearing him to pieces.

She pressed herself against him and he kissed her yellow curls and half-hidden face.

"Don't be a fool, Rory darling. We're in the middle of this god-awful war that may land any of us anywhere at any moment, and there honestly isn't time to throw fits about true love and all the rest of it. Let's take what we can while we can."

He had never felt her nearer to him, for he had never felt her to be more completely sincere. She was generous, too, for she might well have reproached him—as indeed he wished that she would. But she had accepted what he said, although without understanding it, and had not even pressed home the inevitable questions.

And she had, most uncharacteristically, admitted that she had grown fond of him.

Rory, in despair, could only groan "Primrose!" as he kissed her again and again.

"Is it all right, pet?" she muttered.

"No, darling, it is not. I think you're wonderful, but I can't be your lover any more."

Primrose disengaged herself and stood up.

"I think you're a dam' fool, that's all. I've told you

once, in plain English, that I'm ready to go on as we are for this week. After all, it's what I came down here for, isn't it? But I certainly shan't say it a second time. It's now or never, Rory."

"Then, my dear, it's never."

She turned rather white but answered coolly.

"Okay. Now we know where we are. I shall probably go back to London to-morrow as I suppose you're stuck here now—thanks to my own efforts, which seems a bit ironical—and I hope this marvellous new love of yours gives you the hell you deserve."

She turned and went to the door.

As she opened it the shrill note of the telephone-bell rang through the house.

They heard someone crossing the hall to go and answer it, and both automatically moved forward and then stood waiting, not looking at each other.

Valentine came towards them, from the door that concealed both the telephone and the entrance to the downstairs lavatory.

"It's a London call for you, Primrose."

"Okay."

Valentine pushed the silvered lock of hair away from her forehead. She looked tired and nervous and Lonergan felt a passionate desire to reassure and comfort her.

"What's Jess done with the British Army?" he asked, instinctively putting before her the recollection of so much youth and normality.

"They're still upstairs, I suppose, with Madeleine. Unless they've all gone to the schoolroom—but I hope not, it's so cold in there."

There was an unusual note of nervousness in her voice, and he saw her tired eyes and mouth.

"I'd like to talk to you, if I may," he said abruptly. "Are you too tired, now?"

"No, but haven't you and Primrose—aren't you talking to her?"

"We've said all we have to say. She was just going."

"I thought she came out because she heard the telephone. It's nearly always for her."

"Yes, I see."

The words fell from their lips, meaningless for both of them.

Other words were crowding Lonergan's mind and causing his heart to thud heavily against his side.

He could hear Valentine's quickly-drawn breathing.

"I think I must go," she said at last. "I ought to see about——"

Her voice trailed away into silence.

Lonergan stepped forward quickly and took both her hands.

"Ah, don't go. Valentine, don't ever go away. I love you so much."

He saw, with shattering clarity, the look of pure, incredulous happiness that illuminated her face on the instant as she gazed full at him.

"But do you?" she asked in a breathless, shaken voice. "Are you sure?"

Exultant joy and relief rushed over him.

"It's a pity I wouldn't be sure, when we fell in love all those years ago in the Pincio Gardens! Darling, darling—do you love me too?"

"Yes."

They looked at one another as though not daring to move for fear of breaking a spell.

Then she said his name, gently and lingeringly as if experimenting with her right to say it.

"Rory."

"Valentine! Love."

He drew her towards him, forgetting everything except her nearness, and said to her—reverting unaware to the long-disused idiom of his youth:

"Ah—c'mon while I tell you!"

IX

Sloping her length against the wall, a cigarette in one hand and the telephone-receiver in the other, Primrose drawled rejoinders into the mouthpiece, replying to the nervous, high-pitched tones that reached her from a disembodied masculine voice in London.

"Primrose, are you all right? Are you having a decent rest?"

"I'm okay."

"Are you—are you liking it better than you expected? Anyone with you besides family?"

Primrose knew what that too casual-seeming enquiry meant. Jealous fool, she thought, made furious as she always was at a hint that anyone—and in particular Hughie Spurway—had any claim upon her.

"We've got some Army chaps billeted here," she said coolly. "Colonels and what-have-you. So that's cheering things up a bit."

"Is Lonergan one of them?"

"He is, my pet. I'd forgotten you knew him."

"I met him when you did. Look here, Primrose, I really rang up—well, partly to hear your voice, and partly because I've got a man to see at Plymouth and I wondered if I could meet you anywhere. I could drive you back to London if you liked."

"When?"

"I can make my dates fit in with yours."

She could hear the hysterical eagerness in Hughie Spurway's voice. It irritated her, just as it had always irritated her ever since she had realized, nearly a year ago, that he had fallen frenziedly in love with her and that the worse she treated him, the more deeply fixed his infatuation became.

"Look here, Hughie, I'll have to let you know. 'S'matter of fact, I've rather been debating getting back to London."

"I can come and get you any day you like."

"For the matter of that, I can take a train."

"As you say, of course, but travelling's pretty foul, this weather. Primrose, have you had any letters from me?"

"Plenty."

"I know you loathe writing, my sweet, but you did say you would."

"Did I?"

"God, Primrose, why do you say you'll do a thing and then you never do? You don't know what it does to me."

"Don't be a fool. Look, I'm going to ring off. You'll be ruined."

"I'm ruined already. But it's as you say. Only let me know which day to come, because I must let the Plymouth people know."

"Okay. If you *don't* hear, you'll know I can't make it."

"Primrose, for God's sake—I've *got* to see you."

"You will, when I get back."

"When can you dine with me? Can't we fix an evening now? I want to talk to you. I can't go on like this."

His voice held the desperate note that Primrose at once dreaded and despised.

"Forget it, Hughie. I loathe hysterics, as you know —they make me sick. I'm going to ring off."

"No—wait. Don't. I've *got* to——"

"'Night, Hughie." She hesitated for a second and added: "Good-night, pet."

Then she quickly replaced the receiver.

Hughie had rung up for nothing really. He just wanted to make the same old scene, over and over again.

He couldn't understand, apparently, that when one was through with a thing, one was through with it. Nothing could bring it to life again.

God, thought Primrose wearily, I suppose that's what Rory feels about us—him and me. Funny, when you come to think of it, because I've always been the one who got sick of it first, before.

Her cigarette finished, she threw it on the tiled floor and stamped it out.

The telephone-bell rang again.

That was Hughie. He always did that. If she answered, he'd say that he'd simply got to hear her voice again—he couldn't leave it at that—he *must* speak to her.

But she wasn't going to answer.

Hughie was neurotic, and exacting and jealous, and hopelessly on her nerves. She wished she'd told him to get himself released from his B.B.C. job and go into one of the Servicees. If he did wangle a journey to Plymouth and she let him drive her back to London, she'd say just exactly that to him, thought Primrose savagely.

Weary, cold and exasperated she leaned against the wall, furious with herself as well as with Hughie Spurway, and anxious to believe that she was still more furious with Lonergan for letting her down.

And who the devil was this new girl of his?

Primrose recalled the names of girls whom they both knew, but her acquaintance with Lonergan was so recent that she could only think of one or two.

It's someone I don't know, she decided. Somebody either in Ploomsbury, who goes in for being artistic, or some awful woman in the suburbs that he's fallen for without any reason whatever. Just one of those *things*. And he's such a fool, he's gone off the deep end and taken it as deadly serious. God, he might even marry her— unless she's got a husband who won't divorce her. Though for all I know, he's married already—why not? He's exactly the kind of lunatic who'd marry at twenty and then walk out and never pull himself together and get rid of his wife. Artists and such. . . . I'm well out of it.

She knew she didn't believe that, even while she tried to think it. Rory Lonergan had attracted her at sight, and she found his intelligence in love-making agreeable and exciting. To her, it furnished quite a new experience. It pleased her, also, that he was articulate and told her things about herself that were never stereotyped and that made her, she thought, sound nicer than she really was.

She reflected drearily: If Rory isn't married, perhaps that's why he's dropped me. He wants to marry this bitch whoever she is. He said: If it's what I believe it to be—everything else is out. I wish I'd made him tell me. I still can. I needn't go back to London to-morrow. In fact, I don't actually want to, if he's here. I suppose I'm bats, but that's the way I feel.

Amazed, and angry with herself as well as with Lonergan, Primrose still stood in the cold little cupboard of a room, contemplating without seeing them the polished surfaces of her pointed nails.

She had never before felt so undecided, so profoundly at a loss.

She was unable even to decide whether she would or would not return to London next day.

At last she walked away, still undetermined, and went back to the hall.

Jess and the soldiers were there, Banks and Olliver regretfully protesting that the time had come for them to leave.

"They've thought up a lovely plan for keeping us all out of mischief to-morrow," explained Banks gloomily, "and it begins at five in the morning."

"We rely on you, Jess, to see that Charles leaves this house in good time," Jack Olliver added.

"Oh, is he in it too?"

"He's in it too."

"*It* being a sopping wet ditch on the moors, presumably," said Sedgewick.

"The moors! You'll have to go miles!"

"How right you are."

Jess took her two young men to the hall door, whistling to the puppy.

"Come on, aunt Sophy!"

Primrose saw that only Charles Sedgewick was really aware of her presence. He had looked once in her direction, quite expressionlessly, out of sharp, bright, red-brown eyes.

"Is Rory in his office?" she asked, instinctively showing him that she had another man in whom to be interested.

"Probably. He generally works late. But as a matter of fact I've not seen him since we came down."

"Where's mummie, Primrose? They want to say goodbye and thank you for having me, like they ought," Jess said.

"I haven't the slightest."

"I'll say it for you," Jess volunteered to the subalterns. "Or she may come when she hears the motor-bike starting up."

"We shall be half-way down the drive by then. We go like the wind."

Jess threw open the door and a gust of cold air swept in.

"Gosh! It's suddenly got freezing again. How utterly dim!"

"Dim is the word all right," called out the voice of Olliver, as they moved out into the darkness and Jess let the glass doors swing behind them.

They did not shut out the abrupt, volcanic noises of the motor-bicycle, as the engine started, stopped, started and stopped again.

"What a row," Primrose muttered.

Sedgewick said:

"Shall I go and give them a shove?" and looked again at Primrose.

The door of the little breakfast-room opened.

Primrose saw her mother come out as well as Lonergan.

"They wanted to say good-night, Lady Arbell," Sedgewick politely explained.

"I didn't know they were going so soon."

"They're not gone yet, by the sound of it," Lonergan observed.

He moved, just behind his hostess, to the front door.

"Keep the glass doors shut, Primrose," said her mother, "or the light will show when we open the hall door."

Primrose glanced at her quickly, catching a new note in her voice.

Mummie simply never *told* her to do things, like that— she knew better. One wasn't Jess, after all.

But she shut the glass doors, retiring into the hall, and found that Sedgewick had remained with her.

"A very jolly evening," said the Captain, pensively rather than enthusiastically.

"Oh yeah? Well, you've seen us all now. How do you think you'll be able to stand your new billet?"

"I think I'm lucky."

"That's frightfully polite. So long as you don't mind no heating, and bad cooking and uncle Reggie's grousing and grumbling, and mummie's generally dim outlook, you'll do fine. Jess will be off any day now and I'm probably going back to London to-morrow."

112

"For all I know we may all be off ourselves to-morrow," said Sedgewick imperturbably. "We get shoved around quite a lot."

"I'll say you do."

She knelt down to warm her hands at the fire.

"Have you really got to go out on exercise at five o'clock to-morrow morning?"

"Not quite as bad as that. I want to be in camp by seven, though."

"Is *he* going too?"

She indicated Lonergan with a backward jerk of the head.

"No."

Sedgewick, after pausing a minute, asked her:

"D'you know him terribly well?"

"Fairly. Do you?"

"Not awfully. I haven't been seconded very long. I think he's an unusual type, rather. One wouldn't expect an artist to make a good soldier, normally."

"He probably wasn't a good artist."

Sedgewick laughed.

"He much more probably was. He's perfectly well known as an illustrator, and I've seen some of his stuff. I'm no judge, but it looked okay to me."

"Is he like most artists, struggling to support a wife and family?" Primrose said, hoping that she wasn't over-doing the nonchalance.

"He's not married, is he?"

They were silent as the doors swung open again.

The roar of the motor-bicycle had become inaudible.

"What fun it was," cried Jess. "I think Buster and Jack are simply divine. Madeleine did, too. They were angelic to her."

Primrose did not move.

So Rory wasn't married. It was odd, because she'd have taken any bet that he was. And if not, how *had* he escaped it? Anyway—who cared?

She felt chilled, angry and dejected.

She fingered the stiff, tautly-twisted curls that stood out round her forehead and thought what a fool she'd been to put on that periwinkle-blue house-coat. Rory hadn't so much as spoken of it although he was usually good at noticing things like that.

Primrose furiously, and against her will, remembered things that he had said to her and that she had coldly told him were just so much Irish blarney, but that she had enjoyed, from their very dissimilarity to the brief, slang exchanges that passed for conversation amongst her own contemporaries.

Damn Rory. He had charm and he was frightfully articulate and intelligent, and one was going to miss it all quite a lot.

Especially, thought Primrose, if there wasn't anybody else to take his place. And there wasn't, unless she could get something going with Charles Sedgewick.

At the thought she slewed her eyes round without moving her head and looked at him.

He'd be all right, she supposed, and he'd already noticed her, quite definitely.

Anything would be better, thought Primrose drearily, than going back to London in the cold and with no one there whom she specially wanted to be with any more.

Valentine, overwhelmingly happy, stood in the shelter of the portico and said goodbye to the subalterns, and laughed at their difficulties with the motor-bicycle and, at Jessica's shouted request, held aunt Sophy out of the way of harm.

All the while her heart was singing and she felt light-headed, intoxicated with the suddenness of her joy, and hardly conscious of anything that was happening.

She did not realize that it was a cold night until Lonergan, standing behind her, put a cloak round her shoulders. Then, feeling his arm encircling her, she leant back against it and bliss flooded her.

"I love you. Darling, I love you. I adore you," he whispered, close to her ear.

"I love you, Rory."

The noise from the engine redoubled, aunt Sophy barked and struggled, and the motor-cycle rushed away into the darkness showing only a pin-prick of light.

"Gosh, what fun it was! Where's aunt Sophy?"

114

Without waiting for an answer Jess hauled the puppy towards her.

"I simply must take her for a run, black-out or no black-out. I'll just go as far as the gate."

Valentine felt Lonergan's hand clasping her own closely, as though to prevent her from moving, and she stood motionless.

They heard Jessica's footsteps on the gravel, and her voice talking to her dog, then dying away.

"My own love. Will we wait here for a little while, or is it too cold?"

"I'm not cold," said Valentine, and she turned towards him in the dark.

The kisses that he gave her restored to her all her youth, and it was with the untouched fervour and passion of youth that she returned them.

"Darling, you're crying!"

"I didn't know I was. It's because I'm so happy,—so terribly, terribly happy."

"My darling, lovely child. So am I. Terribly happy."

"Rory, I never knew it could be like this."

"Nor I. Believe you me, in all the years, and all the adventures I've deliberately sought out—God forgive me—it's never been like this. There's only been one real thing in my life, until now when I've found you."

"I know."

She felt his clasp upon her grow tighter.

"You mind. You're unhappy about that."

Valentine was amazed, as much by the quickness o his intuition as by the ease with which he put it into words.

It was true that a pang, startling in the intensity of its pain, had struck savagely at the very centre of her being, with the recollection of Laurence.

She could only say, helplessly:

"It's all right. I understand."

"Ah, it isn't all right. I know you understand, dearest —but it isn't all right. It makes you unhappy. We'll have to talk about it. Everything has got to be clear between us—always."

He bent his head and his mouth found hers again and they clung to one another.

"I want to hear everything about your life, and to tell you everything about mine. When will we be able to talk to one another, love? Can't you come and sit over the fire in the little office with me now?"

"I can do anything you like," said Valentine unhesitatingly.

She thought dazedly of the things that she wanted to hear from him and, in her turn, to say to him.

Jess came back through the darkness, and Lonergan pushed open the doors for her.

They all went in together.

Primrose was standing over the fire by herself.

"Where's Charles?" Jess demanded.

"Telephoning. Where on earth have you been? I shouldn't have thought it was a night for strolling in the park."

"Aunt Sophy and I strolled. We had to. I don't know what mummie and Colonel Lonergan did," returned Jess. "They just stayed in the porch."

Primrose, who as a rule never looked at her mother, suddenly turned and looked at her now with a hard, fixed stare. Their eyes met and Valentine, from old depths of pain thus reawakened, felt herself flushing deeply and uncontrollably.

"I'm afraid that was my fault," said Lonergan easily. "I kept your mother standing in the cold, when I should have had more sense."

As he spoke, he realized that neither Valentine nor Primrose had heard even the sound of his words.

They were only aware, for the moment, of themselves and of an unspoken revelation that hovered between them.

Lonergan ceased speaking abruptly and stood motionless, as though at attention.

For an instant the tension in the atmosphere seemed as if it might become unendurable. Jess, opening her mouth to speak, left whatever she had to say unuttered and her mouth still half open, and stared round at them with puzzled eyes.

Once again, the code that, so many years ago, had once and for all formed the standards of Valentine Levallois, held good.

"Colonel Lonergan and I have discovered that we really did meet, years and years ago in Rome, when I was a girl," she said calmly.

She turned to him and offered him the charming smile that curved her lips but did not reach her eyes.

"Of course I thought of it when I heard your name, but I wasn't absolutely sure until we spoke."

"I'd have known you anywhere," said Rory Lonergan.

He was far less calm than she, because he was far less certain of the importance of averting a scene.

Scenes were part of Rory Lonergan's national and personal tradition, whereas they were not part of Valentine Arbell's at all.

She's afraid of a show-down, flashed through Lonergan's mind with an extraordinary mingling of tenderness, amusement and pity for her, and of shame for himself.

The fatuity of it, standing there with the reluctant, inescapable conviction pressing upon him that, if there were to be a scene, it would have been brought about by his own presence at Coombe, and his relation with each of these two women!

Charles Sedgewick came back and, like everybody else who had been forced to spend any time at the Coombe telephone, he looked extremely cold and made straight for the fire.

"We're all fixed up for to-morrow morning, sir," he told his Colonel. "I've just confirmed it."

Lonergan nodded.

"Are you going on this bind too?" Jess asked him.

"I am not. I shall be at the Camp all day and back here some time in the evening."

He looked at Valentine and found in her eyes the look that he wanted to see there, that recalled the young girl of the Pincio Gardens with such astonishing clarity.

She said nothing, but their eyes held one another and he knew that in her surged the same almost unbearable excitement and happiness as now possessed him. He had so completely forgotten everything and everyone else in the world that it was with a kind of astonished shock that Primrose's indistinct drawl reached his hearing.

"I'm thinking of going back to London, myself, to-morrow. I don't seem to be particularly wanted here."

"But you've only just come!" cried Jess, scandalized.

"It's cold and dull, I'm afraid," Valentine said. Her voice was level, but the light had gone out of her face.

She looked her real age again.

"However, we can talk about it later, Primrose. I think it's bedtime now."

"Gosh, what a pity," Jess remarked. "We've had marvellous fun, haven't we?"

She gave her sketchy salute, that included them all, and picked up her dog.

"You ought to make aunt Sophy walk up the stairs," Lonergan told her. "The way you carry her about, you're just teaching her to make a show of herself, the wretched creature. Go on up to the landing and then cal h,er."

l,She won't come."

"She will."

All of them, except Primrose who never turned her head, fixed their attention on the puppy.

While the fat, ungainly creature scrambled up the flight of stairs the two men laughed and Jess screamed encouragement from above.

Valentine had moved to the foot of the stairs, and turned as though to say good-night, but Captain Sedgewick said it first and she answered him with automatic courtesy, as though she were speaking in a dream.

He went upstairs, two steps at a time, and they heard Jess laughing as he joined her on the landing.

Then Primrose did look round.

"Was that general exodus just tact, or a happy coincidence, or did you somehow organize it?" she asked Lonergan, unsmiling.

"Ah, you—cut it out!"

"I only wanted to know."

If Valentine looked her forty-odd years, Primrose, strangely, appeared far younger than her actual age.

118

She had become an angry, ill-behaved schoolgirl, anxious to hurt because she was herself being hurt and finding only the crudest means of retaliation.

"As it seems a bit late and cold to stand and talk in the porch, I suggest your office once more, Rory. You and I had a very good fire there a little while ago."

"As you say, Primrose. In fact, I've already asked your mother if she'll be good enough to let me sit and talk to her there."

"Then I'll leave you to it. Good-night."

Valentine and Lonergan both stood, silent and motionless, as Primrose—walking no faster than usual—moved away from them, picking up the long, periwinkle-blue skirt of her house-coat and holding the hampering folds away from her feet as she went up the stairs.

Lonergan turned towards Valentine, saw the stricken look on her face and caught her hand in his, moved by the sheer impulse to comfort her if he could.

"She knows," faltered Valentine.

Her fingers clung to his.

Lonergan signed his uncertainty, waiting to hear what she would say, that might give him the measure of her insight.

"I thought at first," said Valentine very slowly, "that it was Primrose who'd attracted you. And that seemed natural. She's young. But this evening, you told me it was me."

"And you know that's true."

"Yes, I know that's true. Only I think that, besides being angry, she's hurt. Were you in love with her, Rory?"

The simplicity and directness of the question moved him very deeply.

"Darling, I'll answer anything you want me to answer. There's going to be nothing hidden between us. There's only this: would you rather talk to Primrose first?"

Valentine shook her head, smiling painfully.

"She wouldn't let me. I think she hates me. I don't know when it all began, or even where I went wrong. When she was a little girl!——"

Her voice faltered and stopped.

Lonergan, in a passion of pity, took her into his arms. "Darling—my poor little love! It's hard for you."

She clung to him, and he could feel her slight body tensed against the threat of tears.

"Cry, if you want to," he whispered.

But he saw that she had already commanded herself and that this self-command had grown to be one of the strongest impulses of her nature. If she was to be hurt —and she had been hurt already—he would have to contend with the lifelong habit that would always lead her to conceal pain, perhaps even to deny it.

To Lonergan, an artist and an Irishman, himself emotional and supremely articulate, the thought brought nothing but dismay.

He took her into his office, where the fire still burnt redly, and made her sit in the armchair. Kneeling beside her, with his arm round her, he said gently:

"I'll tell you anything you like, sweetheart. It's going to hurt us both, but it had to come. Whatever it's going to mean, we've got to get everything clear between us. Our relationship is far too important for anything else to be possible."

"Yes," said Valentine without hesitation.

"You realize that I'll have to talk like the cad of all the ages, saying all the things that no decent man is ever supposed to put into words? Unless I do that, I'm simply not offering you the truth, as I see it, at all."

"I do understand."

"Val, you're perfect!"

She looked up, suddenly smiling.

"You called me Val!"

"It came very naturally. I called you Val in the Rome days."

"I know."

"Darling Val. D'you like me to call you that?"

"I love it."

The atmosphere was easier, lightened between them. Lonergan drew a long breath of relief.

He saw that Valentine, too, was more relaxed. It was she who spoke first:

"I know Primrose has had love affairs. I know that

several men have been in love with her, though I don't know if they've asked her to marry them. She's never told me anything, of course. But my sister-in-law, Venetia Rockingham, has. She doesn't like the men that Primrose knows, because they don't come from one particular set of people. And I think she's jealous, too. Venetia used to be a great beauty in Edwardian days."

Lonergan sat silent, holding her closely, knowing that she was gaining time in which to steady herself for the inevitable question.

She came to it at last.

"Rory, were you one of the men who fell in love with Primrose?"

"Yes, darling. That is to say I found her stimulating and physically desirable and my vanity was enormously flattered because she liked me, who am quite old enough to be her father."

He forced himself to look at her, terrified at the thought of the pain that he must see in her face.

She met his eyes and her own were quiet, but he saw the lines of her mouth, and leaned towards her and kissed it passionately.

"It's all right," she whispered, and the childish phrase touched him.

"Primrose is in love with you, isn't she?"

"Val, it isn't like that. It isn't being in love as you mean the words. Primrose isn't in the least romantic, and if she were—it wouldn't be about someone like me. She was attracted to me—God knows why—and then I think she liked it because I was more intelligent than most of the men she knows, and I think too, she liked, without knowing it, the fact that I'm of a different class and nationality and religion, and generation. It gives her what she'd call a kick."

"Have you ever wanted to marry her?"

"Never. It never crossed my mind for one single instant, nor hers either, I'll swear. I've never wanted to marry at all, and Primrose doesn't believe in marriage. She may outgrow that, of course, but even so I think she'd always view marriage realistically. More as the French see it—an affair to be decided upon reasonably and not on an emotional impulse."

"Will you tell me how it began, between you and Primrose? Has it been going on for a long while?"

"No. I met her at a party in London just after the battalion had been sent down here, and we found out at once that I was stationed here, of course, almost next door to her home, and I said something about finding billets, and then she suggested Coombe."

"Did you like her at once?"

"I admired her. I liked the contrast between her very aristocratic appearance and her extreme toughness—and there's a sort of hard realism about her that's unusual, and that appeals to me. And, as I've told you, my vanity was flattered. But Val—none of all that is love. I didn't love her, any more than she loved me."

"I know that. But you did—fall in love, I suppose?"

"I did, darling. I'm not going to deny it. I fell a little bit in love with her, as I've fallen in love scores of times, and when I saw, as I did, that she was attracted too, I tried to put more into the affair than was really there. It's always been like that—except with Laurence. Some of the times I've been far more in love than others, but even when I've gone all out after a woman, I've known in my heart that I was riding for a fall. That I wouldn't find the perfection I was mad enough to believe in, and that I'd only land myself and someone else in a relationship that was bound to end in disappointment and humiliation for both of us. Actually, with Primrose, I felt less of a blackguard than I've sometimes felt, because there was never any pretence between us of being out for anything serious or permanent."

"I think I see," slowly said Valentine. "But since you've been here, Rory?"

"Well, love, since we've been here, it's not been quite so straightforward. I'd only to see you, my girl of the Pincio Gardens, with your hair turned to silver, and I knew that *there* was the only reality for me. I'd like to say that I'd anyhow not have had the gracelessness to make love to Primrose under her mother's own roof, but it simply wouldn't be true. What stopped me was meeting you again."

"Have you told her that?"

"At first I told her a lot of old cod about behaving decently in the house I was billeted in and so on, that she didn't believe. And then this evening, no later, we came into the open, to the extent of my telling her I was seriously in love—God, is it serious!—and that everything else was out."

"Did she understand—no, she couldn't have understood—that you meant me?"

"She did not—then."

"Rory, what are we going to do? Primrose is my own child. I can't hurt her deliberately."

"Listen, Val. You saw her face to-night, when Jess said we'd been out together in the porch, and you and she suddenly looked at each other. You heard the way she spoke afterwards, about going back to London to-morrow. After she'd gone upstairs you said to me: 'She knows.' I think you may be right. She may have guessed."

Valentine hid her face in her hands.

Lonergan kept silence. He stroked her hair, drawing her head against his shoulder.

When she looked up again the colour seemed to have been drained from her face.

"I don't know what to do."

"God forgive me for breaking your sweet heart like this! But dearest, isn't it true that there's nothing you can do? Things had gone wrong between you and Primrose before any of this happened. I know she's angry—perhaps she has a right to be angry, at least with me—but she's not unhappy, in any way that matters."

"Why do you say that? She must care for you, at least a little, if you've made love to her."

"I have—but that doesn't mean she cares for me, in any lasting way."

"I don't see how she could help it," returned Valentine, simply and sadly.

"Val, darling—I love you so much. Can you forgive me for the muddle I've made of everything, for the difficulties I've involved you in?"

Valentine, with her characteristic gesture, pushed the hair back from her forehead.

She spoke slowly, but without any hesitation.

"Forgiveness doesn't come into it, Rory. I love you and nothing will ever alter that now. You say that Primrose doesn't love you. I don't know that even if she did I could give you up to her. That's what frightens me."

Stricken into silence by the utter candour with which she had told him the truth, Lonergan bent his black head over her two hands, kissing them whilst he forced back the tears he could feel rising into his eyes.

"You'll marry me, my darling?" he whispered, after a little while.

"Is that what you want?"

"With all my heart and soul."

"But you said you never wanted to marry anyone." And she added, with an effort that touched him deeply: "Except Laurence."

"It's different, now. This is war-time, darling, and there's no knowing what may happen. We've got to belong to each other in every possible way there is, for whatever time we have left."

"Yes. I think that too. Only there's Primrose."

"You've no need to feel that you're taking anything from Primrose, darling. What you've got to face is your own knowledge of the fact that I've been her lover."

He looked at her steadily and, for the second time that night, saw the slow, deep colour staining her face.

When she answered it was in a half-whisper.

"I wasn't perfectly sure."

"It's true."

There was silence again, for what seemed to Lonergan a long time.

At last she said:

"You know, I love you so much that I don't think anything makes any difference. I don't know whether that's right or wrong. I will marry you, Rory."

X

It was after one o'clock in the morning when Valentine, leaving Lonergan at the foot of the stairs, went quietly up to her own room.

She wanted nothing so much as to be alone with her joy and her sorrow, and she hoped that Madeleine would not be, as she so often was, waiting for her in her room. It was sometimes difficult to get rid of the devoted, tyrannical, affectionate creature, and her native shrewdness, backed by a relationship extending over almost the whole of Valentine's adult life, made it nearly impossible to keep anything from her.

But Valentine had, most unexpectedly, an encounter to face other than one with Madeleine.

As she moved across the landing, the General's door opened and the General, in a very ancient Jaegar dressing-gown and without his teeth, appeared.

"There you are," he mumbled.

"Did you want me, Reggie?"

"Wait a minute," he ordered, and Valentine waited obediently while he turned back into the room again, put in his teeth and then called to her to come in.

She went in, closing the door behind her.

Her brother stood, leaning on his stick, in the middle of the room.

"Look here, Val, do you know what time it is? Getting on for half-past one. What do you suppose servants and children are going to make of this sort of thing? In another five minutes, I may tell you, I was going to come down myself and get rid of that fellow for you."

"Thank you very much, Reggie, but that wouldn't have been in the least necessary."

"It's all very well to take that tone, but after all, you're not an old woman and this house is full of idiots who'll be only too ready to chatter. What does he *mean* by it?"

"If you're talking about Rory Lonergan—and I suppose you are—he and I have been sitting in the breakfast-room—I mean, his office. I wanted to talk to him."

"I don't know why on earth you should want to talk to him at all, but if you did, why should you have to choose the middle of the night? It looks bad, old girl—really it does. What are Primrose and Jessica going to make of it, I should like to know?"

The mixture of indignation and plaintiveness in the General's manner very nearly caused Valentine to laugh.

"Truly, Reggie, I don't think there's anything to worry about," she said. "And do remember how old I am—nearly forty-five."

"You don't look it," General Levallois rather grudgingly admitted. "I suppose you might tell me that it's none of my business, but after all, poor Humphrey's not here to look after you and, personally, I should never trust an Irishman."

"But I should," said Valentine.

The General gazed at her in astonishment.

"Val, d'you like this chap?"

"Yes."

"I thought he was after Primrose. And pretty good cheek if he were, a chap of his age, old enough to be her father. But I must say, I shouldn't have thought that even an Irishman would have had the nerve to come down here as a pal of Primrose's and then sit up half the night with her mother. Well, it's nothing to do with me but I felt bound to tell you what I thought about it. And unless I'm very much mistaken, other people will think the same."

"I don't know that I very much mind what other people think, Reggie, and I don't believe you do either."

"You don't want to upset Primrose."

Valentine shook her head, distress again waking within her.

"Then there's another thing," the General admonished her. "Now that I've gone so far, I may as well do the thing thoroughly. You've got to remember that once upon a time this fellow was, or thought he was, in love with you. You don't want to have any trouble of that kind cropping up now."

"Reggie, please don't go on."

"I don't want to upset you, old girl. It's the last thing I want. You'd better go and get some sleep. Only for the Lord's sake do have some sense, and realize that you're still an attractive woman and that a chap like Lonergan, if you don't keep him in his place, will make a nuisance of himself as soon as look at you. I know the type well."

Valentine gazed at her brother with a feeling that almost amounted to despair.

She knew that his mind, rigid and tenacious, was practically incapable of taking in a new point of view and that to try and force one upon him would be wasted effort. In his own way he was fond of her and of her children, and for that reason she could not wholly resent his interference. She could find nothing better to say than: "I'm sorry, dear, if you've felt worried. But truly you needn't."

It was not until they had exchanged good-nights and she was at the door of her own room that it occurred to Valentine how far removed from the truth her assurances really were, since there was, from the General's point of view, every reason for him to feel worried.

If only we could be left alone, Rory and I, she thought. If only we need consider nobody but ourselves. Is that ever possible, for any two people, or are there always responsibilities to take into account and other people to interfere? She felt suddenly very tired and her sense of grief overpowered her sense of happiness. Primrose— the memory of Laurence—the thought of Rory's daughter, Arlette—even the General's assumption that there could be nothing between them beyond indiscretion on her side and presumption on Lonergan's, filled her with fear for both the present and the future.

As she went to her own door, a distant sound made her pause.

Another door, some way off, had closed sharply. There had been no attempt at silence.

It could only be the door of Primrose's room.

So Primrose had been waiting to hear when her mother would come upstairs, and was making no secret of it.

The revelation appalled Valentine, with all its implications.

Her hand was shaking as she turned the handle of her own door and went into her room.

Madeleine, thank God, was not there.

Valentine pulled off her clothes, shivering as much from agitation as from cold, and in a very few minutes lay in bed in the dark.

She did not sleep before morning, and then only lightly so that she heard the careful creaking of Captain Sedgewick's boots as he came down soon after six, and the distant, muffled barking of old Sally as he unfastened the chain and bolt of the front door and let himself out.

There was no other movement for some time after that, and Valentine knew that the servants, as usual, were allowing themselves to oversleep.

She lay very still, again experiencing the strange mingling of pain and happiness that had assaulted her on the evening before.

Rory loved her, and wanted her to marry him, and she would see him to-day.

Primrose was unhappy, and angry, and had said that she was going back to London. What had she done to Primrose?

Her brother's interference came back to her mind, also. It was true that she was a woman of forty-four, accountable to no one but herself, yet how little that glib assertion really meant! How impossible it was, in actual fact, to disregard the people with whom one lived, who took for granted their right to question and to comment.

Perhaps if I were a braver woman—thought Valentine. It induced in her a sudden new sense of security to remember that she had given Rory Lonergan every right to protect and supplement her lack of courage, and that he was entirely capable of doing so.

Sudden crashing noises from downstairs, diminished by distance but so familiar that Valentine could identify them without difficulty, denoted that Esther and Ivy now believed themselves to be making up for lost time by rushing through such portions of their work as could not be omitted altogether.

She was not surprised when Madeleine came in and drew up her blinds, saying blandly that those miserable little girls were late again and deserved to be severely beaten.

"You don't say that about Jess, when she's late," observed Valentine, smiling.

"Mademoiselle Jess is not being paid good wages to come downstairs at a proper hour," said Madeleine.

Her brown, shrewd eyes travelled over Valentine's face as she gently put down the tea-tray by the bedside. "Madame is very tired this morning."

"A little, Madeleine."

"To-day we have the Red Cross sewing here and this evening there is the First-Aid class in the village. Perhaps monsieur le Colonel will run madame down in his car."

"He's much too busy for that. Yesterday was Sunday, but to-day he'll be out all the time and probably come back late."

Madeleine shook her head.

"He has no doubt many responsibilities and one sees that he takes them seriously—naturally, in war-time—but one knows men. He is happy to have met madame again." So Madeleine knew, also. She was, Valentine saw, signifying her approval.

Even as their eyes met, Madeleine nodded with an air of calm reassurance, and Valentine felt herself helpless before that penetrating kindliness.

She put out her hand to the portable wireless beside the bed. "It's time for the Eight O'Clock News."

They listened to it together in silence.

It amused, vexed, and yet rather touched Valentine that her brother, who often had his breakfast upstairs and when he did come down was usually late, should now exhibit a determined punctuality, designed, she well knew, to obviate the possibility of a tête-à-tête between herself and Lonergan.

The meal was over quickly, and passed almost in silence. But when Valentine left the room, Lonergan followed her and they stood together for a moment at the door of his office.

"Did you sleep, sweet?"

"Not very much."

"Neither did I. Listen, my darling, I shall be busy all day and probably not back here before ten o'clock to-night. Can you meet me in the town for lunch somewhere? I can take an hour or so off in the middle of the day."

Valentine, unreasonably startled by the suggestion, hesitated. He gave her his attractive smile.

"It's not really such a very daring suggestion, my sweet love. Is it?"

"It's only that I've not done anything like that for years—except with the children."

"You've promised to be my wife, and I don't know that I mayn't be sent away from here at a minute's notice, any day. We've a good deal to settle, love. I want you to tell me how soon we can get married."

Valentine said "Whenever you like, Rory," and knew instantly that she had given him, from the very depths of her heart, the only answer possible to either of them.

"Ah, God bless you. My own darling!"

He caught her hand in his. "I adore you, Val."

Clattering footsteps, that combined speed with lightness, announced the descent of Jess, and the tapping of the General's sticks approached, muted by the coconut matting.

"That hotel—what's it called—in the High Street. One o'clock?" said Lonergan.

"I'll be there. The Victoria Hotel."

They exchanged a smiling, intimate look that made her heart race. Then Lonergan went into his office and Valentine turned automatically to her writing-desk.

The telephone-bell rang, with its usual strident effect of urgency, and she went to answer it.

"London wants you. Hold the line, please."

"Thank you."

It would be for Primrose, probably. Jess could go up and fetch her, since no one who telephoned to Primrose ever seemed content to leave a message. Valentine was perfectly certain that she herself had no wish to go and confront her elder daughter. The encounter would have to come, but not at once, her shrinking soul cried to her. She wanted—temporizing, as cowards do—to put off that pain and humiliation for as long as might be.

"Is that Coombe? Lady Rockingham speaking."

"Venetia? This is Valentine."

"Hallo, my dear," said the clipped, distinct voice of Valentine's sister-in-law. "How are you, darling? Are your evacuees driving you quite bats? How are the girls and Reggie? Darling, I suppose you couldn't possibly give me a bed for two nights? To-night and to-morrow. I'm speaking at a meeting in Bristol this afternoon, and Charlie won't *hear* of my sleeping there. Too foolish, as I told him—you know what a complete fatalist one is—but of course it would be too lovely to see you and one needn't get back till Wednesday."

"Do come, of course. We should love to have you," said Valentine, aware that she was lying and that Venetia probably knew it, since beneath her habitual transparent affectation of silliness she was a woman of shrewd perceptions. "I suppose you're coming by car? We can easily find a bed for Taylor at the lodge."

"I shan't have Taylor or the car. Hughie Spurway— you know who I mean—has offered to drive one down —he's got to go to Plymouth, he says. How he found out I was going to Bristol, I can't tell you. Anyway, he'd adore to spend a night at Coombe, and so should I, if you can bear the thought. Do say, if the whole thing is too inconvenient for words."

"Hughie Spurway?" Valentine repeated, knowing from Venetia's tone, and from her own sense of familiarity with the name, that she was expected to identify its owner.

"Dorothy Spurway's eldest son. He's crackers about Primrose, darling, as you probably know already, and I'm sure the whole idea is a put-up job, don't you know what I mean. Still, of course, one would far rather be driven by him than by Taylor—but I simply couldn't bear to add to your difficulties, knowing what staff and rationing and one thing and another mean, nowadays, so if you can't bear the idea, just say so, don't you know what I mean. I couldn't understand more."

"Oh! no, Venetia. Do bring him, of course. It won't be very confortable, I'm afraid—I've got no proper cook —but we can manage perfectly, if you don't mind."

"Angel! I'll bring some bits and pieces with me, so don't worry about food. Had we better dine *en route*, as we can't arrive by daylight anyway?"

"Whatever you like. No—do come in time for dinner. You'll find two officers billeted here."

"Would I know them?"

"I don't think so. One is Colonel Lonergan, whom I knew years ago in Rome, and the other is a Captain Sedgewick."

"Darling, all one can say is that officers are far better than expectant mothers, or children, or school teachers. You know that Rockingham is filled, from attic to cellar, with odds and ends from Whitehall?"

"Yes, I know. What are you and Charlie doing?"

"Still putting up at the Dorchester till the bombs start falling again and then we shall probably suggest your taking us in as P.G.s, don't you know what I mean."

Valentine asked for news of her nephews, one of whom was in the Guards and the other in the Air Force.

"All is well, for the moment. We heard from Michael yesterday and Nicky last week. Of course, one lives on the edge of a volcano, day and night. My dear, one's always pitied you, as you know, for having no sons, and now one simply envies you. How are the girls? Is Primrose at home?"

"Yes. I'm not sure how many days she'll be here. Jess is waiting to be called up."

"I hear they've a waiting list and aren't calling up *anybody* for six months at least."

Venetia, thought her sister-in-law, was always hearing things of that sort, and retailing them to those who were likely to find them disconcerting. She would be certain to say something of the same kind to Jess.

"Well, I'll expect you and Hughie Spurway—is he in the Army?—some time before dinner," she said, with a feeling of helplessness.

"Darling, I thought you understood. He's something important with the B.B.C. Well, it's too angelic of you

132

to let us come. Bless you, and 'bysie-bye. *A ce soir.*"

Valentine replaced the receiver.

Jess was in the hall, dressed in her riding clothes and eating a slice of dry bread.

"Was that aunt Venetia?"

"Yes. Haven't you had breakfast?"

"This *is* my breakfast. Is she really coming here to-night, and who's Hughie Spurway? I could hear every word you said."

Valentine explained.

"Fancy aunt Venetia! Hughie Thing is one of Primrose's boy friends. He rang up every night, last time she was down here. What a terrific crowd we shall be. Almost a house-party. Were house-parties fun, mummie, in the old days? They always sound wizard in books."

"Yes. No—I don't know. I didn't go to very many."

"Will they be here for dinner?"

"They've got a meeting at Bristol this afternoon."

"What a pity Charles and the Colonel won't be back till late. Though I suppose you'd say, as usual, that it'd make too much work for the maids, with so many. Did Primrose really mean it, about going back to London at once?"

"I don't know, Jess."

"Well, she's not down yet, so she's missed the good train. Mummie, can I have the car to go and fetch the rations and could I take the evacuees? They do adore going out in the car."

"Yes, darling."

"That'll be marvellous," said Jess. "They start school again to-morrow. I'll take the dogs. They love squashing up in the car with the evacuees."

She went off, whistling cheerfully.

Valentine went to the kitchen. She found the domestic problems there, that struck her as being so tedious and so unnecessarily complicated, more endurable than they usually seemed. They don't really matter, she thought. Nothing matters now except ourselves.

She told Esther to get two bedrooms ready and went upstairs to help her with her work.

Trailing along the passage towards the bathroom was

Primrose. She wore an incredibly thin silk dressing-gown and nothing underneath it, her feet were bare and her yellow hair carefully set with little flat pins and confined in a net. Valentine's impulse to exclaim "Darling, you'll catch cold!" was checked instantly. Instead, she said good-morning.

"Why?" said Primrose—not aggressively, but as one offering some dreary pleasantry. Valentine, to whom every tone and overtone in her child's voice was familiar, recognized the intention and smiled, in what she felt was a crudely obvious attempt at conciliation.

"Why indeed. It's a nasty, raw morning. I suppose you don't want any tea or coffee or anything?"

Primrose shook her head. "What was that telephone call?" she asked suspiciously. "Was it for me?"

"No. It was Venetia. She's arriving this evening, for two nights, after doing a meeting at Bristol. She's coming with someone called Hughie Spurway who knows you."

"Is she coming by car? Because if so she can drive me back to London. I suppose she's going back there."

"Yes, she is but Mr. Spurway is going on to Plymouth, and I think it's his car. Who is he, Primrose?"

"Who is he?" echoed Primrose scornfully. "I suppose that means: who are his people? Well, I don't know or care. I daresay they're in Debrett okay."

"But that isn't what I asked you. I know that he's a son of Dorothy Spurway's, because Venetia said so. I meant what does he do and what is he like, and what kind of age is he?"

"Twenty-six-ish," said Primrose, "and as nearly bats as they come. One of these neurotics. Terrified of getting mixed up in the war, and terrified of being thought a shirker because he isn't in uniform."

"Is he a friend of yours?" ventured Valentine.

"He thinks he is," said Primrose, without emphasis. She pulled her skimpy silk garment round her.

"I suppose the bloody bath-water will be cold, as usual." She walked on.

She had been disagreeable, but not angry.

"I'm glad," thought Valentine without irony.

From the back-stairs at the end of the long passage in which she stood came the sound of high, childish voices as the Coombe evacuees, with cries of joyful excitement, hastened downstairs to their expedition with Jess.

For an instant Valentine was back in the past, some eighteen years ago, and heard the flying feet and the gay, excited voice of the child Primrose running to meet her on her return from some brief absence of an hour or two.

She saw, for that flash of time, the small, eager figure with yellow hair flying towards her, and all but held out her hand to steady the little form that must surely be about to fling itself against her, clasping her waist. The brief illusion fled. Primrose had long been grown-up, she hated and distrusted her mother now.

"And I shall never know", thought Valentine as so often before, "how it began—where it all went wrong." She went into the big, closed-up room that was called the Red Room, and began to take the dust-sheet off the bed.

Esther, singing shrilly, made her appearance, decorously hushing herself as she reached the open door.

Just before twelve o'clock Jess reappeared with the evacuees—hilarious and sticky with lemonade and cake —and dismissed them cheerfully to the society of Madeleine.

Val, sitting at her desk in the hall, nerved herself to carry out a resolution to which she had come in the course of the morning.

"Jess, will you look after uncle Reggie at lunch? I'm going to be out."

"Where are you going?" Jess asked, friendly and inquisitive.

"To the Victoria Hotel. Colonel Lonergan asked me to have lunch there with him."

"How perfectly wizard! I wish he'd ask me. Who else is going to be there?"

"He didn't say that anybody was."

"Not Primrose?"

"No."

Jess looked at her mother long and thoughtfully. Her young face was inexpressive of all but its smooth unsubtle innocence, yet Valentine knew that her mind was working, probably very clearly and dispassionately, on a new idea.

Jess was neither imaginative nor unduly sensitive, but she was not at all lacking in perception, and she had confidence in her own judgments.

"Mummie, quite personally speaking, I think it's a perfectly sound idea, you going to the Victoria Hotel for lunch with the Colonel. But you do realize that Primrose will think it's a bit lousy?"

"I'm afraid she will. But you see, darling, I knew Colonel Lonergan years and years ago in Rome, and when he came here we picked up that relationship again where we'd left it off. He and I are friends."

"I see." Jess was still thoughtful though not, Valentine felt, antagonistic.

"Well," she said at last, "it's okay by me, naturally, but do I have to tell Primrose?"

"No, darling. I only wanted you to understand."

"Oh, there isn't anything to understand," Jess declared, and Valentine felt that she was firmly, if kindly, repudiating any idea of a possible alliance between them. She might concede to her mother every right to an independent life, but she would never range herself beside her, least of all in opposition to a contemporary of her own.

"There isn't anything to understand," she repeated. "Why shouldn't you go out to lunch with the Colonel if he asks you? Besides, it isn't any business of mine, is it? But it's a bit different for Primrose, because she knew him in London and all that. She's sure to be ratty, but after all there's nothing new in that."

"Oh, Jess! I wish Primrose was happier. I wish we could do anything."

"Honestly, mummie, aren't you being rather sentimental? I mean, here's this war going on all over the place, and Poles and Jews being tortured, and babies being bombed, and families all broken up—I can't feel it matters a scrap whether Primrose is happy or not. Or anybody else, for that matter."

Valentine gazed at her, appalled.

"It's odds on we shan't have any kind of *happiness* in the world, even after the war's over—if it ever is over—

but probably happiness isn't as frightfully important as one thinks," Jess said. "I mean, honestly and truly, mummie, what do individual people matter?"

"Perhaps you're right," Valentine admitted sadly, "but I don't think one ever feels quite like that about one's children."

"Gosh, how funny. I mean," Jess explained carefully, "funny-peculiar. Shall you be back in time for the Red Cross meeting?"

"Yes, certainly."

"That'll be fine," Jess returned, rather absentmindedly. She never attended the Red Cross sewingparties herself, even when they were held in the drawingroom at Coombe.

"Would you see if you can find a few chrysanthemums for aunt Venetia's room?"

"Okay. And for the boy friend too?" Jess enquired blithely, and Valentine understood that their conversation was over. After Jess had gone, she sat on at her desk, not moving, thinking over what she had said: What *do* individual people matter?

Valentine had always thought that they did matter. She thought so still, and Jessica's point of view, so different, and so matter-of-factly expressed, saddened her deeply.

It surprised her, too, and made her understand afresh how little she knew about the real Jess. She almost felt now as though she knew more about Primrose than about Jess—but each, in their different ways, kept her at arm's length. Her sense of having completely failed as a mother was more overwhelming than it had ever been, although it was so often with her.

Suddenly and instinctively she raised her eyes to the portrait of Humphrey. The painting, hard and shallow as she thought it, gave her his blunt, rather arrogant features, his straight-gazing eyes that saw things so much more clearly than they had ever seen people, and for an instant—all her perceptions heightened and sharpened by her own new and vivid emotional experience—she realized to the full the utter unreality that their marriage had been.

"Val!" said her brother's voice, and he spoke irritably so that she started with a sense of guilt. "What's all this about Venetia coming here to-night?"

"She's got to be at Bristol this afternoon, and she's coming on here."

"What for?"

"To see us, I suppose," Valentine suggested, although she felt by no means certain that this was altogether true.

The General appeared to share her doubt.

"Doesn't sound like her. She'll give a hell of a lot of trouble, as usual, and she'll expect drink, and talk all through the News. And how's she going to like the Irishman?"

"He isn't coming back to dinner to-night—it'll probably be about ten o'clock when he gets back—so they won't see so very much of one another."

Valentine, as usual, had spoken to placate. But in her own mind the General's question woke echoes so that she, also, wondered how Venetia would like the Irishman.

XI

THE Victoria Hotel was as resolutely Victorian a period-piece as the conservative West of England could produce. Plush *portières*, enormous sea-scapes painted in oil and framed in gilt moulding, rose-patterned wall-paper, fret-work screens and brackets bearing Toby jugs, were all there. The furniture was dark and heavy, and there was a great deal of it.

Valentine, who had walked in from Coombe, saw Lonergan's car standing in the yard beside the hotel entrance when she arrived. She enjoyed walking, and the lanes, even in January, showed colour and beauty, and as she walked into the darkness of the hall, knowing that her lover was waiting for her, happiness came back to her in a rush.

Lonergan was standing before the steel-barred grate in which was glowing a coal fire. He came to meet her.

"Thank God you've come. I've been nearly out of my mind."

"Am I late?"

"Well, no. You're not. But every minute has seemed like an hour. I'd a wild hope you might be here when I arrived. Take off your little hat, darling—I want to see your pretty hair."

She pulled off her soft woollen cap and smiled at him.

"Ah, you're lovely, Val."

His voice, with its warm strength and tenderness, made her want to cry. Looking at her as though he knew and understood this, Lonergan pushed forward a deep chair, and then took one beside her.

"I've ordered sherry. It's coming now. I got through the morning's work quicker than I expected and I wanted to come and fetch you, but I thought perhaps you'd have started by some other way and we'd miss one another."

"I did come by a short cut—it saves over a mile."

"I'll be able to take you home, so that you'll be in time for your Red Cross meeting."

"How did you remember about that?"

"The way I'd remember anything that concerns you, my darling."

"Rory, you say all the things that no one has ever said to me, and that I've always known I should love to hear."

The elderly head waiter brought their sherry, and they drank, looking and smiling at one another.

There were other people in the hall, talking and smoking and drinking, and Valentine and Lonergan spoke together in low voices. The ardour and the directness of his love-making gave her a sense of enchantment. She could scarcely believe that she was awake and not somehow, strangely, reverting to romantic fantasies of her girlhood.

She had meant to speak of Primrose, to tell him that Venetia Rockingham, her competent, hard, rather alarming sister-in-law, was arriving that evening, that she felt afraid of Venetia's rapid, shallow judgments and unsparing tongue—but all these things fled from her mind.

They talked only about themselves.

In the dining-room, after ordering lunch, Lonergan said to her:

"I'd a letter from Arlette this morning. I've brought it, to show you."

Very simply, as though she had been his wife already, he handed to her across the table two thin sheets of ruled paper in a cheap blue envelope.

Valentine was unreasonably surprised to find the letter written in French, in a careful, sloping, characteristically French handwriting.

The Irish address at the head of the paper looked incongruous.

It was a lively, amusingly-written letter, showing originality and a certain precocity in the young writer. At the end of the letter she admitted candidly that she often felt lonely, and that her aunt Nellie was very kind to her but *"peu sympathique du côté intellectuel."* She asked whether there was any hope of seeing her father again soon, and said that anything else, the war excepted, had for her *"peu d'importance."*

"She's terribly fond of you, Rory."

"The poor child. I want to see her, too."

"Of course," said Valentine, the more gently because of the pain it caused her to realize anew the strength of the link that still bound him to Laurence and the long years that lay behind him—years in which she had no part.

"Could you get over there?"

"I doubt it. Unless we suddenly got some embarkation leave. I could manage it then."

Afraid that her face might betray her pain, Valentine laid her hand across her mouth and kept her eyes steadily fixed on Lonergan as she uttered her assent.

"Darling, what is it?" he asked instantly. "If I did go, I'd want you with me—as my wife."

She said nothing, knowing that her eyes answered him.

"Dearest, I was mad to think we could discuss marriage in a public place like this—but thank God I'm coming back to Coombe to-night. We'll talk then."

She handed him back Arlette's letter.

"Thank you for letting me see it. Rory, couldn't we possibly get her over here? She could come to Coombe, if you'd like it."

"Ah, you're sweet. But you don't understand. Arlette

140

wouldn't know what to make of a house like Coombe. She's just a little Parisian *bourgeoise*."

"But she's with your sister now."

"Nellie's a nice old middle-class Irishwoman, darling. She doesn't belong to your world, any more than I do. It wouldn't matter to her, living out of her class—though I doubt if she'd enjoy it—because she's elderly, and simple, and without very much imagination. But it wouldn't do with a sensitive young girl like Arlette. You'd both be embarrassed."

"Oh, Rory, no."

"I don't mean that you'd ever be anything but an angel to her—tolerant, and understanding."

"How could one be anything else, with a child—even if she wasn't your child? And after all, I've lived abroad, I've met French people."

"I know, darling."

He paused for a moment.

"It's like this, Val. We'll have to face it sooner or later, just as we'll have to face everything that's going to affect our future together. We can't ignore the fact that your relations won't know what to make of me—or rather, they'll think they know only too well—and they certainly wouldn't know what to make of my child. I don't mean her illegitimacy."

"I know you don't. I think you're exaggerating the importance of the old traditions now, Rory. Primrose and Jess, and all their generation, just ignore them."

"I'm not so sure. But anyway, love, it's not Primrose and Jess that matter now. It's you. Shall you mind that my background has just been Irish middle-class and French *bourgeoisie*, with a few years of second-rate artistic Bloomsbury thrown in?"

"Why should I?"

"Darling, because it'll mean that your friends won't have any use for me whatever, and that mine will probably seem to you a strange, rather squalid collection, if you ever meet them."

"Don't you want me to?"

He hesitated.

"Well, no. In a way I don't. I think you'd find them

141

impossible, and that it would distress you. Arlette, of course, is different. She'll always be a part of my life, and I want you to know each other."

"But you don't want her to come to Coombe?"

"I don't, sweetheart. If it was just you, it might be different. But you have people coming and going—and servants——"

"Oh, Rory! Those two little village girls?"

"They're nice little girls, I know," he conceded, "but English servants aren't like French ones, or Irish ones either. A real Irish servant is like one of the family. Old Maggie Dolan, who does all the work except what Nellie does herself, gives her opinion freely, I'd have you know, on anything and everybody. Nellie and Arlette very often sit with her, evenings, in the kitchen and she thinks nothing of bawling to Nellie up the stairs if she wants her for anything. It's a different sort of relation altogether."

"It's probably a much better one than ours, which is artificial. But think of Madeleine—*she's* not an English servant."

"Madeleine would be shocked, at your having Arlette as a step-daughter. She's a kind, nice woman—I can see that—and she'd like Arlette and understand her on her own merits—but not as one of your family."

Valentine reflected, grievedly and rather sadly, on what he was saying.

At last she asked:

"Does it matter much? Supposing that all you've just said is perfectly true, need it make any difference to us?"

"Not so long as we talk it out, and don't just shirk discussion, and ignore the whole problem. Does that frighten you, dearest?"

"I think it does, a little. You see, Rory, I've always lived amongst people who do, deliberately, ignore a great many things. I've taken it for granted that one should."

"You have," he agreed. "Just as you've taken it for granted, I think, that if anything hurts you or makes you unhappy, you mustn't show it."

Valentine smiled faintly.

"It's the conventional English tradition, isn't it?"

"It is, and I'm not saying there isn't something fine and good about it. But not between two people who love each other as you and I do, Val. We've *got* to be honest with one another. If I hurt you—God knows I won't want to, but I probably will—you'll have to let me talk it out with you."

"Do you mean, if you were ever unfaithful to me?"

"I don't, darling. I've no right to say it, but I believe I'll be faithful to you always. And that's a thing I've never felt about anybody else in the world."

She murmured her response in a word of endearment, and they were interrupted by the service.

"Tell me why you said you'd probably hurt me," she asked, a little later.

"Because we're human beings," Lonergan answered sadly. "Because it's like that. Even the people who love each other most are bound to hurt one another sometimes in little things. But it's all right—I mean, it doesn't spoil anything really—if they're always able to talk it out together."

Valentine thought of her own instinctive reaction to pain. Even in the last forty-eight hours she had experienced it consciously—in the pangs of acute jealousy that she suffered in thinking not only of Arlette, but of Arlette's dead mother—and had hidden it.

Quite suddenly, she found that she was smiling.

"We ought never to have been separated, that time in Rome. We ought to have been together ever since our youth, Rory."

"Ah, how right you are!"

It startled her when she found that they had almost finished their luncheon and that Lonergan was telling the waiter to bring coffee to the table.

"It's better than the hall, or lounge, or whatever they call it," he explained. "Though it's absurd that I should be trying to tell you how I adore you, here, in public, and in these surroundings. Tell me, love, will we be able to be somewhere this evening, by ourselves?"

"Oh, Rory, I forgot to tell you. My sister-in-law— Humphrey's sister Venetia—has telephoned and she wants to come to Coombe for to-night and to-morrow.

She's bringing a young man called Spurway with her. He knows Primrose, I think."

"They'll be there when I get back, then?"

"I'm afraid so, yes."

Lonergan emitted a thoughtful, ejaculatory Damn! but that he was also preoccupied with another idea was evident and he added immediately:

"Have you seen Primrose this morning?"

Valentine told him that she had, and that Primrose had spoken to her without any unkindness.

"But I think she wants to go back to London. She doesn't want to stay on at home."

"Will you and Primrose say anything to one another before she goes?"

"It will depend on her," said Valentine rather faintly. "I don't really know how much she realizes what's happened to us. Last night I thought she did."

"So did I."

"Rory, why don't I mind more that you've been in love with Primrose? I ought to feel it a most terrible thing, that would put a barrier between us for ever. But I can't feel that. I suppose it would be different if I didn't know that she's had other affairs."

"I think it would. You see, dearest, Primrose hasn't either loved me, or even *thought* that she loved me. She's very realistic. It's one of the things I admire about her."

Valentine meditated.

"Do you know, I believe that I do too? It's hurt me often, that realism of hers, but I do admire it."

"You've got it too, in a different form. You're honest with yourself."

Valentine felt tears rising into her eyes, partly because she found his words moving and reassuring, and partly at the remembrance of the immense gulf between herself and her daughter that neither admiration nor realism nor courage could ever bridge. She told Lonergan of her conversation with Jess, and of how Jess had said: "What *do* individual people matter?"

"She said it in such complete sincerity, Rory. Jess doesn't ever pose. She truly sees it like that."

"I know," he answered. "It's a point of view that's

inherent in her generation. It isn't in ours, and we shan't ever acquire it. At least, people like you and me won't."

"I suppose not."

"The conflict of individual souls *does* matter," he insisted. "It matters immensely. I see it as you do, Val."

And, looking at her, he repeated her own words of a few minutes earlier:

"You and I ought always to have been together— ever since the days when we were young and fell in love with one another, and had to let them separate us."

Lonergan drove Valentine back to Coombe just before the hour of her Red Cross meeting. As the ancient car bucketed over the ruts and pot-holes of the drive, they passed two girls riding bicycles, and a little way further on, a straggling procession of elderly and middle-aged women plodding along sedately and in silence.

Valentine waved to them, and they smiled and nodded at her in return.

"Is that your work-party?"

"Yes. They're mostly farmers' wives, and one or two of the tradespeople. The two girls on bicycles are the doctor's daughters. They come very regularly, although they're terribly busy, both of them."

"Any others?"

"A neighbour of ours, Lady Fields, who lives in rather a nice house on the other side of the hill. She's got a P.G. with her, now—a Mrs. Dalwood whose husband is abroad—and she generally brings her."

"It's good of you to have them."

It seemed to Valentine that Lonergan was purposely seeking to keep any inflection out of his deep and musical voice, and the thought brought with it the conviction that he felt bewildered, and out of sympathy with the limited and parochial futilities that made up so much of her life.

"Do you think it's all very useless?" she suggested rather timidly.

"Darling, no. It's not that. It's just that I don't understand. I've never seen that kind of life. It's one of the things that frightens me—all these interests and responsibilities that you've built up for yourself in the years. Will I ever be able to understand them?"

"Won't you, Rory?"

"Ah, I will. You'll make me understand everything. We've got to be together, always, for whatever time may be left to us. We'll find a way."

The warmth and colour had come back to his voice again, and his eyes smiled at her.

Her love flamed within her, responding to his mercurial ardour. But the parting words that they exchanged on the steps of Coombe, although they chimed like bells in her consciousness all the afternoon, could only partly drown the echo of his earlier words:

"It's just that I don't understand. I've never seen that kind of life. It's one of the things that frighten me. . . ."

The cutting-out, the stitching and folding, had all taken place to the customary accompaniment of disconnected conversation that always circled round the same topics: the war, news of those who were on active service, and domestic difficulties at home.

At four o'clock Madeleine brought in coffee and biscuits, and the workers, as usual, protested and exclaimed, and then praised the coffee that had, they knew, been made by Madeleine. They all exchanged experiences over the difficulty of obtaining this or that commodity.

Presently they were all gone.

Valentine went round the house to see whether the black-out had been properly done. In Lonergan's room she paused for an instant.

He had brought scarcely any personal possessions, and she felt sure that he owned very few. There were no photographs and only two or three books, all of them old and shabby-looking, neatly stacked on the bedside table.

Shall we ever share an intimate, everyday life together? thought Valentine.

She went away, to the other rooms, with the question still unanswered in her mind.

He's an artist, she thought, and a man of forty-eight who's lived his own sort of life always. He's afraid that I should want him to adapt himself to mine. And yet he's afraid, too, that I could never fit into his. Perhaps I never could. But I love him so. I'd give up anything in the world for him. Only that isn't any good. A true companionship can't be founded on a one-sided relinquishment. Not the kind of companionship that Rory and I were meant to have. He said, "We'll find a way." How can we?

The Red Room had been got ready. There was even a coal fire burning in the grate, and Jess had placed chrysanthemums on the dressing-table.

With the two officers' rooms already filled, only a very small bedroom that faced north had been available for Venetia's Hughie Spurway.

All the rooms in the house would be occupied, thought Valentine.

It was past six o'clock when the sound of a motor horn roused the two dogs to frenzied barking, the General to shouted maledictions at them both, and Jess to striding, slamming activity at the front door.

Valentine, already in her soft, shabby, ageless black dress, waited by the fire. Her slim fingers automatically disentangled the long silken fringes of the Chinese shawl caught in the back of her chair.

She already felt faintly nervous. Venetia's flawless armour of self-confidence, her complete non-recognition of any standards other than her own, had always frightened Valentine. Humphrey, neither liking nor disliking his only sister, had never minded them in the least. He had, indeed, had something of the same impenetrable complacency in his own character but in him it had been tempered by more kindliness and less astuteness.

But, as usual, when Venetia came into the hall and was greeted by her sister-in-law, Valentine was primarily struck by her beauty.

Impossible to say of Venetia Rockingham at fifty-one: She is *still* a pretty woman. Hers was the timeless beauty ensured by small and perfectly-formed bones, brilliant and deeply-set dark eyes beneath a broad, white brow, and a shapely nose and mouth that recalled certain portraits of the Umbrian school of painting in their mingling of sensuality, warmth and an arrogance that yet contrived to be dignified.

The pale-gold of her hair showed no trace of artifice, and if the golden gloss that Valentine had admired twenty-five years earlier had long since faded, the soft, unlustrous waves now framing the clearly-moulded, classically-spaced features only served to emphasize Venetia's ageless loveliness.

The slim lines of her figure possessed all the fluidity and grace that suggest youth, whilst actually far more often achieved by the poise of maturity and the assurance derived from wealth, beautiful clothes and the ability to wear them without self-consciousness.

She was followed into the hall by Hughie Spurway.

At a first glance, it was possible only to note that he undoubtedly belonged to the group so often and so angrily defined before the war by General Levallois as "Venetia's pansies". He was large-eyed, haggard, good-looking, in spite of prematurely thinning dark hair, but with all the nervous and agitating mannerisms of the neurotic.

"Darling, it's too angelic of you to have us like this," Lady Rockingham cried. "How are you? Reggie—lovely to see you again. Where's darling Primrose? Hughie, you know Primrose of course. This is her mother, Lady Arbell, who was a friend of *your* mother's somewhere in the dark ages when they were infants and I was already an elderly married woman. Reggie, this is Hughie Spurway—General Levallois."

Her manner and vocabulary were, strangely, still those of the Edwardian hostess.

Valentine always felt that it was really that elaborate social artificiality of Venetia's that, unknown to herself, and in spite of the almost transatlantic modernity with which she conducted the machinery of existence, divorced her irrevocably from youth.

Jess was looking at her aunt with candid and evident appraisement of her dark, swinging furs, her double row of pearls, the R.A.F. diamond and platinum badge pinned onto her slim-lined black coat, her sheer, palest grey silk stockings, and squared, low-heeled suède shoes.

Hughie Spurway, his black brows knotted into a frown of distress, stooped to pat the spaniel. Sally immediately bared her teeth and growled.

"Shut up, Sally," said the General, pushing her with his foot.

"She's frightfully old," Jess explained, "but she isn't bad-tempered as a rule. Do you like dogs?"

"Yes. Yes. Very much," said the young man unconvincingly. "At least, I don't really know frightfully much about them. I know more about cats."

"Cats are all right," said Jess encouragingly, if without much enthusiasm.

The General said that cats were selfish, sneaking, unfriendly creatures—you never knew where to have them —and that the stupidest dog on earth had more brains than any cat that ever walked the tiles.

At this, Hughie Spurway looked more distressed than ever, as though convicted of having said the wrong thing.

Valentine smiled at him, asked him to sit down, and said that she, too, was very fond of cats and didn't at all agree with her brother's estimate of them.

Relaxing very slightly, the young man took his seat beside her and, clinging to the topic as to a spar in a tempestuous sea, talked about cats.

Valentine felt that any attempt to start a fresh theme would at once throw him off his balance again and she continued the interchange long after it seemed to her that the last possible word about cats had been said.

Part of her attention was free to focus itself on Venetia, giving General Levallois an account of the afternoon's meeting in Bristol, of which all the implications served to prove that it would have been of a wholly disastrous tepidity but for the galvanizing effect of Venetia's own speech.

"What did you talk about?" Jess enquired.

Venetia said that she had talked about the progress of the war.

"Oh," said Jess. "When's it going to end?"

She seemed to be making the enquiry quite without irony.

149

"Rubbish," said the General.

"Darling, if one knew that, one would be the most popular speaker on any platform in England, not excepting Winston," declared Lady Rockingham. "Instead of having to address three old ladies and a couple of centenarians in a draughty parish hall, as too, too often happens to one. Charlie simply can't bear it, when I tell him about some of my meetings, but I feel these provincial places simply *must* have speakers, and it's the *one* thing I can do, don't you know what I mean?"

"You sit on millions of committees," Jess pointed out—but with a coldness in her voice that Valentine recognized. "How are Michael and Nicky, aunt Venetia?"

At the mention of the two young Service men, Venetia's sons, the tenuous thread of composure that the conversation about cats had spun round Valentine and Hughie Spurway seemed to quiver and then break altogether.

He looked round, faltered in the midst of his halting eulogy of Siamese kittens, and the look of misery in his haunted dark eyes deepened.

Valentine had to remind herself, from sheer compassion, that he probably, and fortunately, had no idea of the far too great expressiveness of his own face.

"Michael is still at Windsor, one's thankful to say, and gets up to London quite often, don't you know what I mean. Nicky can't tell us exactly where he is but one's sure it's Palestine. He dropped some terribly broad hint in a letter to Charlie about being able to see the Mount of Olives from where he was writing. He and Charlie's cousin, the Eric Camerons' boy, met the other day, and we all think it was in Jerusalem."

"What's Eric Cameron doing nowadays?" enquired the General, interested.

This was the kind of conversation, Valentine remembered, that he liked and understood, and to which he had once been accustomed. Conversation into which entered names that he knew, and references that he could identify without having to think about it. The slang, elliptical interchange of assertion and counter-assertion between the young irritated and puzzled him, and he only cared to speak of politics, either national or international, with men whose views coincided with his own. Nowadays, he seldom indeed met with such men.

Venetia, with Debrett at her fingers' ends and in-innumerable pieces of inside information to impart about the conduct of the war, the state of Germany and the opinions of President Roosevelt, was suiting him exactly.

Valentine wondered, as she had wondered all day at intervals, what Rory would feel about Venetia and Venetia's fluency, that took so much for granted in her listeners.

She presently heard Jess announce, as though in extension of her thought:

"You know we've got two officers billeted here? A Colonel and a Captain. The Colonel is Irish, his name is Lonergan, and he's an absolute smasher. Quite old, but terribly glamorous still. You'll simply adore him. He says 'will' instead of 'shall' every single time. I've noticed it particularly, and it's definitely rather wizard."

Valentine and Lady Rockingham both laughed, and the General said: "He's not a bad chap, except for being Irish. I hope I'm not a man who's in any way prejudiced, but I'm bound to say I've very little use for the Irish. You never know where to have them."

"Is the other one Irish too?"

"Oh no," said Jess. "He's frightfully good value, too. We're really awfully lucky. His name is Charles and he's got red hair, which I loathe personally, but I must say he gets away with it."

Valentine waited for her sister-in-law to ask:

"Charles *who*?"

She did so.

"Sedgewick, but no link anywhere so far as I know," said the General rather gloomily. "It's a North Country name, but this lad is a Londoner pure and simple."

"When are we going to see them?" Lady Rockingham asked lightly. "And where's darling Primrose?"

"Primrose has been in a most filthy temper all day, I don't know why, and she's been soaking in the bath ever since tea because the water happens to be boiling hot, and

I suppose," Jess said, "there won't be a drop left for any-body else."

"Good God!" said General Levallois.

Valentine stood up.

"Wouldn't you like to see your room, Venetia? Mr. Spurway, I hope you won't mind rather cramped quarters, but, with Colonel Lonergan and Captain Sedge-wick here and Primrose at home, we've only got two spare rooms available."

"I'm afraid I'm a frightful nuisance," said Hughie Spurway resentfully.

"Indeed you're not."

She led the way upstairs.

They met Primrose coming down, wearing her long periwinkle-blue house-coat.

Valentine was immediately conscious that a violent psychic disturbance had assailed Hughie Spurway, and she hoped that Primrose would greet him with some kindness.

Venetia exclaimed: "Darling, it's simply ages since I saw you! What an amusing way of doing your hair! New, isn't it?"

Primrose averted her face as far as possible from the contact imposed upon her by her aunt's embrace and said something indistinct.

She looked neither at Venetia nor at her mother, but her eyes rested for an instant coldly and appraisingly on Hughie Spurway.

"Look who's here," she drawled.

He put out his hand, but she seemed not to see it.

He said, "Hallo, my dear, how are you?" very faintly.

Primrose had already turned aside and was walking downstairs.

Valentine opened the door of the Red Room and said:

"You know where you are, Venetia. I'll show Mr. Spurway his room, and then come and see if you've got everything you need."

XII

IN the spring of nineteen hundred and forty-one—nearly a year earlier—Hughie Spurway had for a few weeks been Primrose's lover. Time out of mind he had asked himself, as he was asking himself now, why he could not forget her, or hate her for her cruelty, and fall in love with someone who might be kind and gentle and might even love him in return.

Then he reminded himself, with a savage pleasure in self-torture, that it was scarcely probable that any woman would ever love him. The thought had been familiar to him ever since the terrifying day in his twelfth year when he had seen his mother's white, sick face turned towards him after reading a letter from his headmaster. She had told him, then, why she had left his father.

She had two other boys, to make up to her for Hughie. He had sought refuge in thought even at twelve years old, and even in the blind despair and self-disgust that had driven him into lying continuously to her and to the grave, compassionate priests and doctors to whom she had sent him. None of them had, it seemed to him, done much to help him. None of them had given any real answer to his question: Why, *why* should it be me? My brothers are not like this. Why am I different?

He had crawled, like something with a mortal wound, through the years of adolescence, its normal pains intensified, deprived of its normal joys. In the end, he had come to take a kind of pleasure in feeling himself an outcast, in deliberately permitting his loss of self-respect to encroach further and further into his life.

Later on, there had been brief unrelated periods of a feverish happiness that he now qualified as illusory. They had ended, all of them, with more or less of violence and, exaggerating his own inadequacies, he told himself that it was only his perpetual fears and jealousies and suspicions that had brought about these ruptures.

He had fallen in love with Primrose at a party when he had taken too much to drink and found himself sufficiently released to talk with freedom about himself and his miseries, and she had listened and had seemed to him kind. He had found the courage to ask her if she would come back to his flat with him that night and she had, without demur, agreed.

The brief period that followed had seemed to Hughie like the opening of a new life, but when he asked Primrose if she would marry him she had unhesitatingly said no and he had passed almost at once into the old familiar region of nightmare jealousies and scenes of frenzied appeals and demands and reproaches.

It was always he who had forced them upon Primrose in the very teeth of his own agonized knowledge that they served only to antagonize her and cause her to despise him.

One day she told him, with a deliberate calm that carried instant conviction, that she had only listened to him and allowed him to take her home at their first meeting because she, too, had been drinking and had not really known what she was doing. It had meant nothing at all to her.

Hughie heard her with a sense of doom that found its only expression in hysterical threats of suicide that she, as well as he, knew to be theatrical and unreal.

Even his passion for Primrose was, he sometimes thought, unreal—although it dominated his days and his nights and throve insanely under the lash of her open contempt for his manifestations of it.

Yet she continued to see him, to make use of him and occasionally to throw him a word of mock tenderness.

He cursed himself now, because he had manœuvred for this way of seeing her again, knowing that Lady Rockingham was amused and would make a good story out of it, and that Primrose would despise him more than ever. Would she even give him a chance of talking to her alone? She had been on her way downstairs when they met—perhaps he could find her by herself now, if he made haste.

Hughie tore the things out of his suitcase, scattering

them about the room and cursing viciously below his breath, mechanically emitting schoolboy blasphemies and indecencies whenever his own nervous, frenzied fumblings impeded his movements.

It was characteristic of him that when he was ready and had dashed from the room, he came to a dead stop at the head of the stairs and then hesitated in an agony of indecision. Twice he turned back to his own room, fumbling with the door-handle as if to open it, and then moving away again.

At last, with the sweat shining on his forehead and upper lip, he went down the stairs and into the hall.

Primrose was slumped in a chair over the fire.

He was, as always, utterly disconcerted by her trick of neither moving nor looking round at him as he approached.

Striving to make his voice sound casual, Hughie said:

"You look terribly attractive in that colour, sweet. Have I seen it before?"

"No. It's warm, thank God, and one needs that in this dog-hole. See if you can do anything with the bellows, Hughie. My mama is the worst hand at running a house of any woman I've ever seen or heard of."

He thankfully knelt down and began to work the bellows.

She didn't sound angry, and she'd called him by his name. Mostly, nowadays, Primrose didn't call him anything.

"How did you and aunt Venetia get on coming down in the car?"

"Frightfully well," he lied. "She's quite amusing, isn't she?"

"D'you think so? I don't."

"I mean, in a period way," he amended hastily, "You don't mind my turning up like this, do you?"

"It's okay by me," Primrose answered indifferently. "If you like to sit through aunt Venetia's blatherings, on the platform and off it, why should *I* mind? By the way, what are the plans exactly? Are you driving her back to London or what?"

"I'm going on to Plymouth to-morrow, and she's going back to London by train on Wednesday. But I thought you and I could go back by car any day you say, after Wednesday. I could come and get you from here or meet you anywhere you like."

"Why not let's take aunt Venetia? She wouldn't mind staying on here an extra day."

"My God! no. I *must* talk to you, Primrose. I simply can't go on like this."

With terror, he heard in his own voice the note of hysteria that he knew she hated.

"You fool. I'm only pulling your leg. I'd die sooner than listen to that woman yattering all the way to London. Look, Hughie, I'll let you know. I'm in a bit of a jam, and I can't make up my mind."

"Can you tell me?" he ventured.

Warm, excited visions rushed through his mind of himself listening with wide, generous understanding whilst Primrose confided in him and realized suddenly the extent of his devotion.

"Good God! no," said Primrose. "There isn't anything to tell, and if there were, I'm not the type that goes in for outpourings of the soul, as you ought to know by this time, my pet."

"As you say," he acquiesced.

Primrose lit a cigarette.

"You'll find this place a bit of a madhouse, as Jess says. I expect you'll loathe it. Most people do."

He dared not say that, so long as he could see her, he minded nothing. At any moment her mood of unusual loquacity and friendliness might alter.

"Who's here? Besides your family, I mean."

"A soldier chap called Charles Sedgewick, whom you'll see at dinner, and Rory Lonergan."

"What's Sedgewick like?"

"Like a fox."

"It sounds a bit intriguing."

"He isn't, particularly."

"The Irish chap is, I suppose. He fell for you at that party in London, didn't he?"

Instinctive jealousy had prompted the question. Hughie had not really noticed Lonergan very specially at the Bloomsbury party.

He felt as though he had received a violent blow in the midriff when Primrose signed assent with an arrogant movement of the head.

"That's right, my poppet. He's quite a fast little worker, too. Witness his getting himself billeted here."

"Primrose, you're not in love with him, are you? For God's sake——"

"Cut it out," advised Primrose. "I loathe melo-dramatics, as you know, and I don't discuss my private affairs with anyone."

"Will he be here this evening?"

"After dinner."

Jess and her mother came down at the same moment, and Captain Sedgewick made a hasty appearance in the hall, asked Lady Arbell not to wait for him and dashed up the stairs three steps at a time.

Hughie thought how much at ease he seemed, and how completely sure of himself. He thought, also, that the young officer must have wondered why he wasn't in uniform. No one really believed in all the talk of "reserved occupation" and "essential war work"—at least in the case of young men of Hughie's age and appearance.

They just thought one a damned coward and shirker, as one was.

General Levallois shuffled in just before the gong rang and then they had to wait for Lady Rockingham.

Sedgewick had come down again before she appeared. As they sat round the table in the chilly dining-room Hughie, shivering slightly as much from nervousness as from cold, listened to Lady Rockingham's anecdotes about well-known people, that were obviously amusing the General, and to the brisk interchange of personalities between Jess and Charles Sedgewick.

He noticed that Primrose scarcely spoke at all and that whenever her mother addressed her, which was seldom, she looked away and replied as briefly as possible.

He knew that Primrose disliked her mother intensely: she had always said so.

Hughie, without much interest, wondered why. Lady Arbell seemed to him gentle and uninteresting, and he felt rather grateful to her because she was taking the trouble to talk to him. He answered her, and joined from time to time in the laughter that Lady Rockingham always seemed to wait for after each one of her stories, and he looked continually at Primrose, remembering with agony the times that he most longed to forget: times when her graceful body had lain sprawled against him, when he had twisted his fingers in and out of the stiff flaxen rings of hair that stood out round her head, unrebuked. Was Lonergan her lover now? He felt certain that he would know once he saw them together and the age-old delusion, that from bitter experience he well knew to be delusion, possessed him once again: truth would hurt less than uncertainty.

Hughie tried to remember what the Irishman looked like, and could not. He must be a great deal older than Primrose and perhaps what she had implied was not true. She was capable of having said it on purpose to make him jealous.

The nine o'clock time-signal had just sounded and the General was imperatively holding up his hand to silence Lady Rockingham when Jess, sitting on the floor by aunt Sophy, scrambled to her feet.

"Here's the Colonel," she remarked confidently. "He's early—that's wizard. I'll go and let him in."

The announcer's voice came over the air, and no one made any comment. Hughie, with his eyes fixed on Primrose, saw no change in her face.

Jess and her prancing dog preceded Lonergan into the half-circle round the fire, and Lady Arbell murmured introductions, acknowledged by everyone, in deference to the General's warning frowns and hisses, with apologetic smiles only, and in silence.

Hughie glanced surreptitiously at Lonergan, who had taken his seat beside Lady Arbell.

He at once told himself that this was a man who would always be attractive to women. His dark face was sensitive and intelligent, his eyes of dark, deep blue showed lines at the corners springing fanwise out onto the broad temples, that would, one saw, easily and agreeably deepen with amusement.

Large-boned and rather heavily built, his movements were deliberate but never indecisive.

Mature, confident and intensely vital, the Irishman seemed to Hughie, eyeing him with a jealous, analytical attention, to be the very antithesis of himself. He felt sick with despair and rage—a rage that was directed against himself far more than against Lonergan.

He glanced at Primrose but she, with her mouth all drawn down on one side, was examining the points of her finger-nails.

Lonergan was not looking at Primrose.

He was looking at her mother, and Hughie saw him smile at her, and saw that there was great charm in his way of smiling and that it mingled humour with a possible hint of underlying, unhurtful irony that held kindliness.

Lady Rockingham's clear, *maniérés* tones cut across the room.

"But darling Reggie, isn't that enough? We've heard all that matters and I *can't* see why we should all continue to sit in this death-like trance."

Everybody laughed, even the General, and Jess turned off the wireless.

"Gosh, mummie! Do you know what day it is? D'you know what you've forgotten?"

"No?" said Lady Arbell enquiringly.

"The First-Aid class in the village!" crowed Jess.

Lady Rockingham uttered her tinkling, unmirthful laugh and Primrose made a sound that might equally have stood for amusement or derision.

"Really, Val," said the General, looking at her reproachfully.

"If it's frightfully important, could I go down with a message or ring up anyone?" said Sedgewick.

"It's too late, thank you. I ought to have been there at half-past seven. I haven't any excuse at all. I simply forgot."

"Darling, it isn't going to lose us the war," Lady Rockingham pointed out. "And I suppose they can do whatever it is, bandaging and what-not, without you."

"Yes," said Lady Arbell rather helplessly. "But you see, they're very bad about attending the classes, really, and I've tried to urge it on them and always to be there myself, and now——"

"Good God!" Primrose said, "as if it mattered whether this village meets to make tourniquets or doesn't. If they can't take the initiative for themselves, they aren't going to be of the slightest use anyway. We might as well be living in Victorian days when nobody did anything unless the gentry were gracious enough to allow it and come and show them how."

"Don't talk such damned Bolshevik nonsense, Primrose," said the General. "These people are slack enough already without our making things worse by leaving them to their own devices. If you couldn't go down to the village, Val, why on earth didn't you warn them and tell someone to preside for you?"

"I'm afraid I forgot all about it."

The General looked thunderstruck.

"Forgot all about it!" he echoed.

"In the name of Heaven, will you tell me what all this means?" Lonergan asked his hostess, half laughing.

He spoke low and only to her, but the deep, clear notes of his voice carried, and Hughie Spurway heard the question, and Lady Arbell's softly-spoken reply.

"I always do go to these classes and I think Reggie is right—it does perhaps encourage busier women than myself to attend. I just forgot, to-day."

"Won't the doctor's daughters that we saw this afternoon be there, or that Lady Someone?"

"Lady Fields? She gets asthma, and never goes out in the evenings. The Dickinson girls may have gone, if they hadn't anything else arranged—but they both do A.R.P. work and a good many other things."

"My God!" ejaculated Lonergan. "Wouldn't the villagers be able to carry on without worrying the life out of you to be there week in and week out?"

"They ought, I know."

"Madeleine ought to have reminded you. Did she forget, too? What's the matter with you all?" enquired General Levallois.

"Madeleine didn't forget!" cried Jess. "At least, she said something about me going down there when I saw her before dinner, and I said Not on your life, and she said, *Ah, votre pauvre maman,* or something."

"She ought to have reminded you," the General repeated.

"I bet she thought mummie needed a rest and didn't remind her on purpose," Jess remarked. "Anyway, it's all over now, we can't do a thing."

"No telephoning?" suggested Sedgewick once more.

Hughie Spurway was watching Primrose now, and saw the contemptuous twist of her mouth. She was bored with all this unnecessary fuss about an affair of the parish pump. Odd, in a way, because she'd been brought up in this atmosphere, that took such trivialities with a mortal and humourless seriousness. So indeed had everyone present, excepting the two soldiers.

Charles Sedgewick was showing a polite readiness to be of any assistance but Hughie guessed that his mind was not really on the question at all. He was probably thinking of something quite else, whilst uttering his obliging offers.

Lonergan's reaction was different. For some reason, he was really interested and concerned. He was puzzled, too. Hughie could see his eyes—eyes that were very un-English in their expressiveness—turning from one speaker to another.

I suppose, thought Hughie, that if he's in love with Primrose he wants to understand the sort of background she's been used to—though God knows it won't be there much longer, and anyway she loathes it all and only wants to get away. Perhaps she means to marry this man.

A shaft of pain and fury shot through him—pain that was not only mental but sharply physical, so that he moved quickly and involuntarily in his seat, seeking relief in a change of position.

They were still going on talking about the class in the village that Lady Arbell had forgotten, and whether or not she should telephone to someone or other.

"God!" said Primrose suddenly, "do we have to go on about this all night?"

She reared up her length from the low stool on which she had sat hunched together.

161

6

"Let's do something," Jess cried zealously. "Charles, why not let's dance? Can you dance?"

"Certainly. Got a gramophone?"

"It's in the schoolroom. You wouldn't like to go and get it, would you?"

Hughie dared not look at Primrose. It would be Heaven to dance with her, and hold her in his arms—but if she saw his eagerness, she might refuse.

"Okay, come on," she said. "It'll warm us, if it does nothing else. In the drawing-room, I suppose?"

"I must see if the black-out is all right," said Lady Arbell.

"Will I roll up the carpet or something?" Lonergan asked, rising also.

"It's up already," she answered, smiling.

He followed her out of the hall and into the shrouded drawing-room.

General Levallois made his inevitable comment, as the heavily-stressed, limping rhythm of the dance-music reached the hall through the open doorway of the big cold drawing-room.

"Personally, I adore swing-music," said Venetia Rockingham, "but with quite a different compartment of my mind, don't you know what I mean, Reggie. There's nothing like music—of course I adore classical music—and yet I can absolutely see the fascination of this present-day stuff. I can dance to it quite as well as any *débutante*, though I say it as shouldn't. Nicky and Michael both tell me so."

The General was not interested in Venetia's personal triumphs.

He made a small, polite sound and changed the conversation.

"What kind of Spurway is this chap? Lincolnshire?"

"Yes. His father was a younger son, killed in the last war. His mother was Dorothy Herbert-MacDowell of Aeres, a sister of the present man. She's got two other boys. Hughie is the eldest."

"I don't much care for the looks of him, to be frank with you," said the General. "Why isn't he in uniform?"

"Too tragic, my dear. He's really terribly clever but he's neurasthenic and too fearfully highly-strung and he'd certainly go completely bats if he was forced into the war. He went through some of the London blitzes last winter and had *the* most fearful breakdown and had to be sent right into the country for weeks, don't you know what I mean. The doctors all agreed that he was simply hopelessly unfit for service and mercifully he's got this marvellous job with the B.B.C."

"What sort of job?"

"You must get him to tell you all about it. I know they think him *quite* indispensable," Venetia asserted glibly. "Of course, poor Dorothy has always been one of these insanely over-anxious mothers. Such a pity she never married again."

"Herbert-MacDowell," said the General thoughtfully. "Haven't they got rather a lot of money?"

"My dear, yes. These boys will all be well-off, and the second one has married marmalade and they're rolling in wealth, or would be if it wasn't for taxation. You do realize that poor Hughie is completely crazy about Primrose?"

"Lots of fellers are, I'm told. I can't see why. A dam' disagreeable girl with bad manners, if you ask me. I grant you she's got good legs, but so has young Jess— and a nice-tempered, well-behaved child into the bargain."

"They're both of them too sweet," Venetia asserted unconvincingly. "I wish darling Valentine understood them better, but I suppose daughters *are* impossible with their mother. The boys and I are *such* friends, don't you know what I mean. I'm sometimes afraid they'll never fall in love and marry, they *both* say they'd rather do things with me than with any of their girls."

"Jess gets on perfectly with her mother. Val manages her very well."

"I couldn't agree more than I do, Reggie. And of course Primrose will marry. Personally, I hope she'll have Hughie. I think she'd be good for him, and really, I may be a snob, Reggie, but it *is* rather a relief when these young things marry somebody one does know something about. Look at the poor Camerons! Their girl has just insisted on marrying somebody from the Australian backwoods, whom she met at an Army dance. All glamour and good looks, I admit, and they say he's doing brilliantly—but what I want to know is, *who is he?* Naturally, nobody can tell one."

"I don't see what else anybody can expect, in war-time. It's always the same thing. These girls go dashing about all over the place, and meet every sort and kind, and think they're in love, and they're so damned independent nobody can stop them doing anything they please."

"Too right," murmured Lady Rockingham. "It's propinquity, don't you know what I mean. If you're going to have officers billeted here, Reggie, it's quite a good thing that Jess is joining up."

"Ah," said the General.

He appeared to ponder for a moment.

Venetia Rockingham's large and lovely eyes rested upon him thoughtfully.

"What's Colonel Lonergan like?" she asked presently. "The other one—the young one—is quite a bore, isn't he, but I thought Lonergan was an interesting type, don't you know what I mean. Very Irish of course."

The General's reply was indirect.

"Has Val told you that she knew him years ago, when my father was at the Embassy in Rome?"

"She did say something—Reggie *darling*! Don't tell me he's the one there was the fuss about!"

The General nodded.

"But that one was a music teacher, or an art student, or something."

"Well, it's the same chap. He draws pictures and gets paid for them in peace-time—but I'm bound to say he strikes me as being a good soldier."

"Is he married?"

"Not that I know of. In fact, my dear, between you and me and the gate-post, I'm not perfectly certain that he isn't after Val now. He was by way of being a pal of Primrose's, which might have meant anything or nothing with a girl like her—but if you ask me, he's much more inclined to play the ass about Val."

Venetia's eyes glittered with interest and amusement.

"How too intriguing. Of course I won't say a word to a soul—anything to do with the family is always *sacred* to me, as you know. And I've always been so terribly fond of darling Val. But just tell me one thing, Reggie—how long has he been here?"

"Since Saturday."

"But this is only Monday night, and he's been out all to-day."

"She met him at the Victoria Hotel for luncheon. Not," said the General, "that there's the slightest reason why she shouldn't, but it isn't like Val. Not at all like her. And there's been a most extraordinary amount of sitting over the fire and talking. What she can have to say to a chap like that, whom she's only known for two days, beats me."

"Of course, if they knew each other before——"

"Twenty-five years ago!" broke in the General.

"Valentine's at the sort of age when women want to take a last fling, don't you know what I mean. The girls are grown-up, and it's her last chance of having any fun, especially living down here, poor pet."

"Fun! What on earth does she want with fun? She isn't a girl of twenty."

"If she was, it wouldn't be half so dangerous. I must say, I've always rather wondered why she never married again."

They both glanced up at Humphrey's portrait as though seeking an explanation there.

"She'd never marry a chap of Lonergan's sort," said General Levallois. "What on earth have they got in common?"

"Women like Val are so terribly romantic," sighed her sister-in-law. "The kind that always remembers her first love, and I suppose he *was* her first love."

"Dam' nonsense," said the General angrily.

The music in the drawing-room had stopped and they could hear Jessica's voice directing the changing of a record.

"Where the devil is Val now?" suddenly demanded the General. "Don't tell me she and Lonergan are foxtrotting, or whatever they call it, with the rest of them in there."

165

Venetia stood up.

"I'll see what's going on," she said, "and come back and tell you."

She moved over to the open doorway and, herself in shadow, stood gazing into the lighted drawing-room.

The gramophone—a very old one—was stridently giving forth the opening bars of a waltz.

"Hallo, aunt Venetia! Come and dance," shouted Jess. "I'll work the gramophone, and you can have Hughie."

"No thanks, Jess darling."

Venetia's gaze, unhurried, swept the room. It looked strange and ghostly, with its bare boards and isolated clumps of white-sheeted furniture under the glittering chandelier hanging from the centre of the ceiling.

Primrose was dancing with Charles Sedgewick and Venetia had leisure for a passing reflection: Good Heavens, he dances exactly like a professional.

Hughie Spurway stood with Jess beside the gramophone.

Her dog lay curled up on the shrouded seat of an armchair.

At the far end of the long room, the door that opened into the little breakfast-room was closed. From beneath it, a bar of warm red light was plainly visible.

"Come on, Hughie," said Jess.

As they began to dance Lady Rockingham turned away and went back to where General Levallois sat over the fire.

XIII

"SWEETHEART, when are you going to marry me?" asked Lonergan.

He had drawn Valentine into his arms and her head was resting against his shoulder.

The shuffling feet of the dancers and the raucous blare of the gramophone next door went on, unheeded by either of them.

She did not answer immediately and he asked quickly:
"Do you still want to marry me?"

"More than anything on earth, Rory."

"Dearest love. I get frightened, you know, from time to time."

She looked up at him and smiled, but he saw that her eyes were wet.

"So do I."

"I know, love." He stooped and kissed her eyelids.

"Not about anything fundamental, Rory. Not about us. But about Primrose—partly—and other things. Silly things. Unimportant, really."

"I know," he repeated. "It's the same with me. The thought of the adjustments we'll both have to make—and your family—they're not going to take this lying down, I'd have you know."

"There's your family, too. I mean Arlette."

"True for you, as we say in Ireland. But all those problems we'll face together, darling. There's really only one thing that matters now."

"I know."

The music stopped, and they heard Jessica and the two young men arguing and laughing, and Jess's flying feet rushing across the room.

"Val, my beloved, there's only one thing for it. We haven't a lot of time anyway and I may be sent off anywhere at any minute. Will you marry me as soon as I can get a special licence?"

"You know I will."

"It's Primrose that's distressing you."

"Yes. It would be difficult to tell her anyhow but now——"

"Would it be any better if I did it?"

Valentine shook her head.

"You can talk to her, of course. I don't know about that—you must judge. But I must tell her—and Jess and Reggie too."

"Will you do that to-morrow, love?"

"Yes."

"God bless you!"

He kissed her, holding her closely against him.

"I'm happy," said Valentine below her breath, her shining eyes looking into his. "I'm madly happy. You've made the whole of life quite different."

They were together until a sudden startling and violent crash against the communicating door caused them to move quickly apart.

"In the name of heaven!" ejaculated Lonergan.

He opened the door.

Jess, on the floor, was screaming with laughter.

"Aunt Sophy got under my feet and I simply skidded," she shrieked happily. "My legs just shot away from under me. It was too funny for anything!"

Lonergan pulled her to her feet.

"Have you hurt yourself?" Valentine asked.

"Gosh, yes. I shall be black and blue to-morrow, I should think. I bet I shan't be able to sit down for a week."

"What's happened?" called Venetia Rockingham's voice from the hall.

"Only Jess making a forced landing," said Charles Sedgewick. "No harm done."

"That's all you know about it," Jess protested. "I'm not sure I can walk, even."

"I'll carry you."

She screamed and laughed as Sedgewick picked her up, her long legs kicking, and carried her into the hall.

"Take aunt Sophy, Hughie!" shrieked Jess.

Hughie Spurway made a grab at the dog, which eluded him with ungainly caperings.

Primrose gave her scoffing laugh.

"What for would a great old dog like that one need carrying at all?" demanded Lonergan. "Get on with you, aunt Sophy!"

He gently shoved the dog with his foot.

Aunt Sophy, delighted, plunged along beside him.

Hughie's face was drawn and his eyes looked miserable.

All of them went back to the fire in the hall.

"Well, a nice row you've been kicking up in there," said the General leniently. "Good God, Jessica, what do you think you're doing?"

Sedgewick, laughing and out of breath, deposited his struggling burden on a broad sofa.

She gave voluble vent to her mock indignation.

The fringes of Valentine's shawl were caught in a chair-back and she mechanically began to disentangle them.

Primrose took out a cigarette.

Hughie went up to her and offered her his lighter.

They moved away from the circle, Primrose saying something inaudible between her teeth.

"Colonel Lonergan, do tell me if you're any relation to a most entertaining creature called Willie Lonergan who used to hunt with the Quorn, years and years ago."

"I am not, so far as I know."

By an almost imperceptible gesture Venetia invited him to come and sit beside her, and Lonergan, smiling, went.

"He knew everything there was to know about a horse—like most Irishmen—but I can't remember what part of Ireland he came from. He married a girl called Patsy Berresford and they went to live in the Shires somewhere and then one somehow lost sight of them, don't you know what I mean. But I'm sure he was Irish."

"Probably, if he was called Lonergan. There are quite a few of them, but whether I'm related to all or any of them, I couldn't tell you."

"Which Berresford was that?" asked General Levallois.

Venetia told him. She gave genealogical details and the General, interested, supplemented them.

They talked about people—people who were nearly all related to one another, and bore names well known within very narrow limits.

Lonergan, falling silent, idly pencilled outlines on the back of an envelope. His eyes were narrowed and his long upper lip pressing firmly down upon the full lower one.

Presently Lady Rockingham engaged him in conversation once more, this time talking about pictures.

It was impossible to say that she knew nothing about art: on the contrary, she had a good deal of information, both about art and about artists, that went considerably

169

beyond the usual range of the amateur's stock phrases. Her judgments, glibly uttered as they were, were founded on premises that commanded respect, even from a listener as critical, and as nearly hostile, as Lonergan just then was —for her personality antagonized him and he resented her evident determination to draw him out.

Their conversation continued.

The General withdrew behind a newspaper, and Valentine, the fringes of the shawl released once more, leant back in an armchair and from time to time spoke, when appealed to by her sister-in-law.

Sedgewick, Primrose, Jess and Hughie had retreated from the hall altogether.

Jess and her dog reappeared just when Lady Rockingham had declared that she really must go to bed.

"What are you all doing?" she asked her niece.

"Nothing. Just sitting about. I was wishing I had some sweets," candidly remarked Jess.

"Too bad, you poor pet. But at least it's good for one's figure to go without."

"One thing abou tbeing in the W.A.A.F., I suppose there'll be a N.A.A.F.I. or something where one can get chocolate. 'Smatter of fact, Charles thinks he can get me some to-morrow. He's going to try."

Lady Rockingham laughed indulgently as she turned to go upstairs.

"I'll come and see if you've got all you want," said Valentine. "I'm afraid Esther is a very inexperienced housemaid, Venetia."

"Darling, too marvellous of you to have anyone. I can't imagine how we're all going to live when every single domestic in the country has left us, don't you know what I mean. Good-night, Reggie. Good-night, Colonel Lonergan."

"Good-night, Lady Rockingham."

Lonergan looked straight at his hostess.

"Are you coming down again?"

"Yes, in a few minutes."

The General heaved himself to his feet.

"I'll turn out the lights, Val. No need for you to bother."

"It's all right, thank you, dear," she said gently. "I want to come down for a little while."

The General gazed at her, then, seeming to realize that there was nothing more to be said, dropped slowly back into his chair again.

"I've some writing to do," Lonergan announced. "So I'll be off to the office. Jess, where can I get hold of Charles?"

"I'll send him. We were all in the schoolroom. You aren't going to make him do any work *to-night*, are you?"

"I am. Not for long, though."

"Gosh! Fancy you being so strict. You're like my old headmistress was."

"I am not like any headmistress that ever lived, you bold brat."

Jess laughed as she went off.

Valentine and her sister-in-law laughed also, as they went upstairs together and, in Venetia's bedroom, she began at once to speak of the Irishman.

"What an attractive creature he is, my dear. Such a pity he's from *South* Ireland, Reggie tells me."

"I don't think it makes a lot of difference. He doesn't agree that Eire should be neutral. He's lived too much abroad to have any very nationalistic, hard-and-fast point of view, I think."

"Oh, one quite feels that. Darling, do tell me, *is* he the artist you flirted with years and years ago in Rome and there was such a ridiculous fuss about?"

"We were both very young, then," said Valentine, smiling.

"Good heavens, how too extraordinary his turning up again. Well, I think he's a charmer and must have been too devastating as a penniless art student. Just like something in one of Mrs. Humphry Ward's novels. Of course, girls of our date—though I'm *years* older than you are— were never allowed to marry their first love, were they? One lives to be thankful, I suppose."

"Do you think that many girls marry their first love nowadays?"

"Darling, I trust not. It's nearly always disastrous.

Do just imagine yourself, wedded to an artist, and an Irishman—and I suppose he's an R.C.?"

"Yes."

"And as Bohemian as possible. Artistic temperament, and all that."

"No, I don't think so. And Bohemianism is rather out of date, Venetia, isn't it? Anyway, I'm sure Bohemians don't make good soldiers."

"I suppose he's married?"

"No."

"Don't let him start anything with Primrose, darling," Lady Rockingham suavely advised. "I should think he quite easily might—I saw him look at her once or twice, don't you know what I mean—and I want her for poor darling Hughie."

"Oh no, Venetia."

"My dear, it would be the very best thing in the world for both of them. He's absolutely crackers about her, and he'd be in Heaven if she accepted him and that would get him and his wretched nerves all calmed down, don't you know what I mean. That's absolutely all that's wrong with him—simply nerves. And, being frankly a thoroughly worldly woman, as you know, I'm all for a good match. One knows who he is, and there's quite a lot of money. A girl like Primrose is much more likely to make a success of marriage if there's money, so that they can get away from one another when they want to."

"I quite agree. But I don't think she'd marry a man so much weaker than she is. I hope she wouldn't."

"Well, my dear, whatever she does you may be sure she won't consult you or me about it. Boys may confide in their mothers, but girls certainly never do. I hear the most amazing stories about darling Primrose and the second-rate people she *will* go about with in London, and I think it would be the greatest relief to know she was safely married."

Valentine moved a small chair nearer to the fire.

"I do hope you've got everything you want and won't be cold. I suppose she's filled your hot-water bottle?"

"Darling, don't try to snub me. I simply won't be snubbed."

"It's only that Primrose is capable of managing her own life, Venetia, and she'd very much resent my discussing it with anybody."

"You're just the same little adorable prig that you always were, darling. Well, all I've got to say is, let Hughie have a fair chance, and keep your Irish friend where he belongs. I shouldn't be in the least surprised to hear that he'd made one pass at you and another one at Primrose. He looks to me *capable de tout*, don't you know what I mean."

Lady Rockingham sat down before the dressing-table and began to strip her slim fingers of their glittering sapphire and diamond rings.

She had raised her hands to unfasten the clasp of her pearl necklace when Valentine, still standing by the fire, began to speak. Venetia could see her reflected in the mirror, but Valentine's face was turned away and her eyes fixed upon the fire.

"Rory Lonergan is in love with me, Venetia, and he's told me so. I shouldn't have said this at all, if I wasn't rather afraid of you. I've always been rather afraid of you, because you can hurt people and I don't think you mind hurting them. Humphrey could be like that too, sometimes, and Primrose.

"Please don't talk to me about Rory any more. You know nothing about him and I know a great deal."

"My dear!" The silken, mannered voice suddenly assumed the character of a squeal. Derision, vexation and a vulgar curiosity were all discernible in the sound.

"Is this the Soul's Awakening or Love's Young Dream or *what*? Are you trying to tell me that you're just starting a *grande passion*, or that he is? My dear, do forgive me if there's really something in it. I simply hadn't the slightest idea, or naturally I shouldn't have said a word. You know I adore you."

Valentine turned round then, so as to face her sister-in-law. She looked tired and pale, her eyes, distressed but no longer bewildered, fixed upon Lady Rockingham's vivid, beautiful face, all alight with a kind of shallow, mischievous enjoyment of the situation.

"It's difficult to tell you anything," said Valentine,

"because we've never understood one another, have we, all these years. It's been partly my fault, I've never—never since I married Humphrey—been my real self. I think I've been more nearly my real self in the last two days than I ever have, since I was nineteen. That's why I'm talking to you like this now, I suppose. I've somehow got to make you realize, Venetia, that I know what I want at last and that I'm going to have it."

There was a second of silence, while Lady Rockingham's eyebrows slowly lifted, giving to her face an expression of disapproving and rather contemptuous astonishment.

"Darling, you *don't* mean you're thinking of marrying this man?"

"Yes."

"Well, you're old enough to know your own mind. I suppose you realize that you've only known him two days, and another thing—too hateful of me to say it, I know, but if I don't who will—that you're at *exactly* the age when women do these insane things and simply live to regret them ever afterwards?"

"I know all that. I know that a great many people will say that."

"My pet, all of them, I should imagine. I can only implore you to give yourself time, and think of the girls. Do they know, by the way?"

"No, not yet. Nor Reggie. I was going to tell them to-morrow."

"Take my advice, and don't tell a soul. I don't suppose you mean to do anything utterly drastic this very minute, do you?"

"I don't know. We're at war, and Rory may be sent off at a moment's notice. Anyhow," said Valentine, smiling faintly, "we haven't, either of us, a very great deal of time left, have we?"

"Well, darling, I assure you it's utter madness to dash into marriage with a man you haven't known three days and with whom you can't possibly have a thing in common —and one simply can't imagine how it could ever work out, don't you know what I mean—but of course you're your own mistress."

Venetia rose from her seat and came over to where Valentine stood.

"You mustn't think me too odious and unsympathetic, darling," she said lightly. "I know your life has been a perfect hell of dullness, poked away down here, and God knows I don't grudge you a last fling—only I do feel it's *too* fatal if you're going to do anything as final as marrying this man. Reggie, of course, will simply have an apoplectic fit, don't you know what I mean."

She put her arm round Valentine's shoulders and deposited a butterfly kiss on her cheek.

"You poor darling! You look like a tragedy queen, standing there, and to think the whole thing is simply the damned old C. of L.!"

Valentine disengaged herself. She had coloured deeply.

Venetia laughed.

"I wish you'd tell me the whole story from beginning to end. You know that I'm a well of discretion, and I swear not to give you any more advice now that I've said my say. Sit down and talk to me."

Valentine shook her head.

"No thank you, Venetia. I'm going now. Good-night."

Lady Rockingham shrugged her shoulders.

"As you like, my dear, of course."

She turned back to the mirror as Valentine went out of the room.

In the passage Valentine met Charles Sedgewick.

"Good-night, Lady Arbell," he said politely.

"Are you going down to work?"

"The Colonel wants to see me. I don't think it'll take long."

"I hope not. Good-night."

She went on to the schoolroom, hoping to find Jess there. It would be easier to tell Jess first, and she knew that because she had, on an impulse, spoken to Venetia Rockingham of her engagement to marry Rory Lonergan, she must not delay at all in speaking of it to the two girls and to her brother. Venetia was not what she called herself: a well of discretion. She was a mischievous and relentless talker—a *mauvaise langue*.

Giving herself no time to think, Valentine went into the schoolroom.

Primrose was sitting on the old and shabby fender-seat, the folds of her long gown swathed round her and a tweed coat flung over her shoulders. She was smoking a cigarette and looking at the carpet.

Hughie Spurway stood in front of her and Valentine saw, with horror but with little sense of surprise, that he was crying. His face was twisted, like that of a weeping child, and the tears were pouring down it.

Primrose lifted her eyes as the door opened and she, too, raised her eyebrows as Venetia had done.

"Hughie, for God's sake, clear out," said Primrose. "It's the middle of the night or something—I may as well say it first—and children ought to be asleep. I quite agree, for once."

A terrible sound of sobbing broke from Hughie as he made some effort to say good-night and then pushed blindly to the door.

"Good-night," said Valentine in very gentle tones, and she turned her eyes away from the wretched young man.

The door-handle slipped from his indeterminate grasp and the door banged-to behind him.

Valentine faced her daughter.

"I didn't come to disturb you, Primrose."

"As a matter of fact, I'm dam' glad to get rid of him. He was throwing an act, as you perceived, and going all hysterical on me."

"I feel so sorry for him."

"Why?" drawled Primrose.

She got up.

"I don't know why aunt Venetia either turned up herself, or brought the pansy-boy. If she thinks I can cope, she was never more utterly mistaken in her life, and that's saying plenty."

She went to the door.

"Primrose, I came to find you. It's about Rory Lonergan, and it's about me too."

Valentine heard her own voice wavering and she took a long breath and steadied it.

"He wants me to marry him."

She could not look at Primrose.

The ticking of the old cuckoo-clock on the wall above the schoolroom piano sounded like the giant, irregular blows of a hammer jerkily wielded in the silence.

"The hell he does," said Primrose, and her voice held no hint of any kind of emotion. "The hell he does. You've only known him about two days."

"I know. But he and I were in love, all those years ago, in Rome."

"Are you going to marry him?"

"Yes."

"Well," said Primrose slowly, "it's okay by me. I mean, it doesn't matter to me one way or the other, does it? I'm not living at home, anyway."

Valentine raised her eyes now and met those of Primrose.

"Doesn't it matter to you?" she said. "I'd better tell you, Primrose. I know he's been in love with you."

Primrose stared at her. The hostility in her eyes seemed slowly to lessen.

"That's about the first realistic thing you've ever said to me, isn't it?" she remarked detachedly. "No, as a matter of fact, I don't mind particularly. Of course I think it's utter nonsense, in two people of your age, and I don't suppose you've the least idea what Rory's really like—but that's your funeral, isn't it? I'm quite glad you told me."

In her overwhelming relief, Valentine drove her teeth into her trembling lower lip to keep from the tears that would infuriate Primrose.

"Thank you," was all that she found to say.

"What for? Rory's a free agent, and he and I weren't all out for a special licence or anything. He told me he'd fallen for somebody else, and I thought it might be you when Jess told me about your going off to lunch with him like that. Is Jess to be told about this, incidentally?"

"Yes, Jess is to be told, and uncle Reggie and everyone, I suppose. Because I had to tell Venetia."

"Good God, all this talking and discussing," said Primrose, her tone wearily contemptuous. "I should have thought it was your own show and not anybody else's."

Valentine, in her mingled confusion and relief, felt unable to reply.

She thought that it was not possible for her, at her age and with the involved responsibilities of a lifetime behind her, to break all her chains and take her own way.

Primrose would have denied that scornfully.

Perhaps, even, Primrose was right.

Rory will know, thought Valentine, and the feeling that she could trust him as she had never been able to trust anybody yet, gave her courage.

"I'd like to tell Jess to-night," she said.

"She's only fooling about in Madeleine's sitting-room," Primrose said.

She went to the door and Valentine heard her calling up the short flight of stairs that led to Madeleine's little room.

"Hallo!" shouted Jess in return.

I ought to tell them not to make so much noise, thought Valentine, but she said nothing, and presently Jess clattered down the stairs and came into the schoolroom.

"D'you want me, mummie?"

There was something that hinted, so faintly as to be scarcely perceptible, at suspicion in her tone. Valentine wondered what she expected to hear.

Primrose opened her cigarette-case, found it empty and swore—coldly and unemphatically.

She glanced obliquely at Jess, standing by the door in her short printed silk frock that was both too short and too tight, her light flaxen hair tousled as though she had been romping, her hands on her hips in an attitude that vaguely suggested defiance.

"What's up?" she demanded in abrupt, childlike phraseology.

"God, let's not make a thing out of it," Primrose said. "It'll be all the same a hundred years hence, anyway."

"What?"

Primrose shrugged her shoulders and looked at Valentine. With that inescapable, unerring intuition that brings only pain where love is completely one-sided, Valentine knew that Primrose would have told Jess the truth then and there if she could have brought herself to refer to her mother directly. She was inhibited from doing so because there was no name by which she could endure to call her.

"Jess, Colonel Lonergan has asked me to marry him. I've said I will."

"Oh," said Jess.

It was no exclamation of surprise. It held reflectiveness, and a certain hard young disapproval. After a moment's pause she added:

"How frightfully funny. I mean funny-peculiar."

"Shall you—you won't mind, will you?" Valentine asked.

The vitality that had moved her in Venetia's room was ebbing from her so rapidly that she could scarcely choose her own words. They seemed to fall from her, weak and unmeaning, of their own accord.

Jess replied almost as Primrose had done.

"Why should I? It isn't anything to do with me, anyway. I'll be gone any day now and after the war I'm going to get a job. It's entirely your own show, mummie. Uncle Reggie will be in a rage, though, won't he?"

"Perhaps. I don't know."

"Gosh, I bet he will. He loathes Irish people, doesn't he? When will you get married?"

"I think very soon," Valentine answered, but the words as she spoke them carried no conviction to her at all.

"Gosh!" Jess repeated.

"Let's not go on," Primrose suggested. "All this talking things over."

"I'm just going," Valentine said.

She stood up and found that her knees were shaking and that she was very cold. She felt suddenly afraid of fainting.

Jess was looking at her, without unkindness and without kindness. Her fresh, open face wore merely a rather thoughtful expression, as though she were impersonally pondering a new idea of no great essential significance.

Primrose was examining the tips of her fingers and there was an air of faint distaste about the arrogant lines of her mouth, and her narrowed eyes.

They had nothing more to say to her, and there was nothing more that Valentine could say to them.

She moved slowly to the door, resisting the impulse to steady herself against the shabby pieces of furniture. "Good-night," she said, and her voice sounded forlorn and unreal through the strange buzzing noises in her ears.

"'Night," said Jess, with relief in her tone.

Primrose said nothing.

Valentine went out of the room, and shut the door, then stood quite still in the passage, unwilling for the moment to move further.

When her senses cleared again, she slowly went along the passage, uncertain where she wanted to go.

"It's all right," said Lonergan's voice. "It's all right, it's all *right*."

He was, miraculously, beside her—his hand grasping her cold ones and his arm steadying her.

"What is it, dearest? What have they been doing to you, to make you look like that?"

Valentine's breast lifted in a short sob of pure relief. "It's nothing, now I'm with you again. I had to tell Primrose and Jess, Rory, about us."

"Why did you have to, darling?"

"Because Venetia knows and she'd have done it if I hadn't."

"The bitch," said Lonergan coolly. "What has it to do with her, I'd like to know. Were the girls not kind to you, love?"

Valentine smiled.

"Primrose said it was the first time I'd ever said anything realistic to her—when I told her that I knew you and she had been lovers. It somehow made her kinder than I'd expected her to be."

"I understand that. There's a sort of nobility about

180

Primrose, the way she'll accept anything provided it's a really true thing. It's what one likes best in her. Was Jess all right?"

"I think she felt embarrassed."

Lonergan laughed indulgently.

"She'll get over it, the nice, poor child! I suppose she feels we've each got one foot in the grave, the pair of us, and should be thinking about making a holy death and nothing else besides. She'll get over it."

"They both said that it had nothing to do with them, because they wouldn't be living here any more."

"Neither will we."

He spoke the words casually and matter-of-factly, but Valentine was startled by them and a profound feeling of dismay invaded her.

She instinctively and at once checked her first impulse to speak of this and stood quite still, leaning against him.

"What is it?" he asked.

"It's nothing. Nothing that I can tell you about now."

"Then you'll tell me another time. We're not going to have anything that can't be said between us, darling. Will you be coming downstairs again later, or are you too tired? I came to get some papers I want Sedgewick to look at—we'll be through with them in about twenty minutes. Would you be able to come to the little office then?"

"Yes."

"Thank God," said Lonergan with a grave simplicity that gave to the words a quality of reverence.

"Rory, is Reggie still downstairs?"

"He is."

"I think I'll speak to him at once. Now that Venetia knows, and the children."

"If you think so, sweetheart. You know best. I suppose they've all got to be told, the way you'd think it was any of their dam' business instead of being simply yours and mine. Tell me, will there be a lot of old talk about this—everyone telling you what to do, or not to do, and giving you all sorts of advice?"

"Perhaps. It won't make any difference."

181

"It's a pity you wouldn't be allowed to live your own life your own way," he said. "I'll never understand all this kind of nonsense. Interference and all that."

"That's one of the reasons why you haven't ever married, isn't it? Because it almost always means interference."

"It does," he agreed. "But all the interference in the world isn't going to stop me now. Darling, I've to leave you while I get this done. I won't be long. You'll come to me downstairs?"

"I'll come," repeated Valentine.

She saw him dash into his room and out again with his handful of papers.

As he passed her, Lonergan, pausing for an instant, looked straight at her, unsmiling, and then he went on down the stairs.

Valentine, thinking of all that her lover's eyes had said to her and unaware of anything else, slowly drew the fringes of her Chinese silk shawl away from the banister rails.

On her way down she passed Venetia's closed door. There was a thin line of light beneath it.

The grandfather clock on the landing showed it to be a quarter to twelve.

But that isn't really very late, Valentine thought, although she felt as though many hours must have gone by since she had come upstairs with her sister-in-law.

For how many years had she assumed that all evenings came to an end before midnight!

In the wider world, outside Coombe and houses like it—in the world to which Rory Lonergan belonged—no such routine existed.

His world would be less unfamiliar to her than hers to him. And not only would Rory find her tiny world unfamiliar: Valentine knew that its conventions would always, to the artist and the Irishman, seem unendurable. He would never see in them anything worthy of respect or of toleration so far as his own conduct was concerned and he would never conform to standards that he saw as meaningless and unreal. What he had said of Primrose was equally true of himself: She'll accept anything provided it's a really true thing.

Rory wouldn't feel the pattern of life at Coombe to be a really true thing. He would, for all his intelligence and his insight and his sympathy, find himself for ever unable to view seriously the traditional and long-since out-moded forms of existence that to Valentine still seemed natural.

It's I who'll change, she thought. Not Rory.

She felt a swift lightening of her spirit within her and knew a long-forgotten sense of exhilaration.

She would be glad to change, to abandon at last the personality that marriage, and the years, and the children, had gradually manufactured for Valentine Arbell, for the protection of the true self of Valentine Levallois.

XIV

WHEN Hughie Spurway, gulping and grimacing, had left the schoolroom and regained his own room the always-tenuous thread that bound him to sanity snapped temporarily.

He lost all control, throwing himself on the bed, gnashing his teeth and weeping, swearing and sobbing under his breath.

"She needn't have been like that—she *needn't* have been," he repeated over and over again, saying the words aloud.

Primrose had danced with Charles Sedgewick in the drawing-room until Jess had clamoured for a change of partners and Sedgewick himself had said:

"Okay. Let's change over."

Jess had giggled and said apologetically: "Of course, you're terrifically good, Charles, and I'm not. But I don't mind if you don't."

They'd laughed about it.

Hughie wasn't as good a dancer as Charles Sedgewick either, and, unlike Jess, he did mind. He had been afraid lest Primrose should comment on his inadequacy.

But she had said nothing at all—only pressed herself against him as they moved and given herself up completely to his guidance. And a measure of self-confidence had come back to him on that account.

"Darling, this is marvellous for me," he'd ventured to say.

Primrose had replied with her favourite monosyllable. "Why?"

"You know I'm crazy about you."

Hughie had tried to make the words, in themselves so banal, sound casual.

"Idiotic."

"Sweet, it isn't. I swear it's not. Oh, Primrose, can't things go back to what they used to be? We were so terribly happy a year ago."

"Were we? I don't know what you were—you often looked to me pretty miserable—but I can assure you that I was bored stiff more than half the time."

"For God's sake, don't take everything away from me. At least let me be able to remember that it *was* heaven once, even if it's been hell ever since."

"Aren't you the complete neurotic hero of a pre-war novel! Going all tense and embittered and tragic."

He'd tried to laugh, then, in the middle of the torture, thinking that perhaps if he followed her mood she might be placated and stop being cruel to him.

"It did sound a bit that way, I admit. But honestly, Primrose, I do simply adore you. There's no other woman in the world, and never has been."

"Good reason why."

He'd driven straight on, crashing through his own agonies of pain and humiliation.

"That's all over. You know as well as I do that there's nothing and no one in my life now except you. Why can't you be kind to me again?"

"Don't be such a fool, Hughie. Can't you see that when a thing's over, it's over?"

"Then don't you care for me at all any more?"

It was the question that had burned in his heart and on his lips for months past and that he had sworn to himself never to ask, lest he should have to hear the answer.

Even as he did ask it, Hughie had known an additional twist of self-contempt at his lack of resolution.

Failed—once more.

The punishment had come very swiftly and surely.

"I'm afraid I don't, Hughie. Since you ask me. Anyway, it wasn't ever very much of a thing. I'm not much of a one for what the poets call Lâhve—as I've always told you."

"You've had lovers?"

"Naturally. But I've never pretended to them, or to myself or anybody, that there was going to be any question of fidelity. For God's sake, don't grip my arm like that. You're hurting like hell."

"I'm frightfully sorry. I didn't mean to. Look, Primrose, I accept all that. I do know how you feel, about fidelity. I don't care. Will you marry me just the same?"

"No, of course I won't."

"Are you going to marry somebody else? That Irishman—who's old enough to be your father?"

"He isn't—and I'm not."

"I believe you're in love with him."

"Believe anything you dam' well please. If I didn't think you practically barking mad, Hughie, I'd quite definitely hit you in the face for that."

"Why? Why are you so angry? It's because you're in love with him. I've known it all along. You're having an affair with him. That's why you're treating me like this."

"I'll say it is! I'm treating you like this, as you call it, because I loathe scenes and you do nothing but make them, and because you're just as neurotic as they come and you make me sick."

The gramophone had run down and Primrose had stopped dead, and detached herself from his arms.

The evening hadn't been over, even after that. There had been more dancing, and Jessica had put on records of popular songs, and Venetia Rockingham had come in. But all that Hughie clearly remembered was that fragment of dialogue.

It had gone on and on, repeating itself in his ears.

It had driven him, after they had all gone upstairs, to follow Primrose—like a whining cur, he said to himself savagely—to the schoolroom and plead with her to unsay what he knew that she never would unsay.

He had pleaded, had debased himself, had even made a wild attempt that to himself seemed theatrical and false to act the virile lover and force her into his arms, and the thing had finished when Primrose, her mouth all pulled down on one side and her eyes dark with furious contempt, had said:

"Get this. *You've had it.* I couldn't be more through with you than I am, Hughie. I ought to have known better than ever to take up with a hysterical degenerate. Not my cup of tea at all."

It was then that the final humiliation had descended upon him and, sputtering threats of suicide, he had felt tears and sobs contorting his face down which the sweat was already streaming and shaking uncontrollably all over, had stumbled from the room as Lady Arbell came into it.

"I'll kill myself, I'll kill myself, I'll kill myself. She needn't have been like that."

He raved and moaned and suffered until the fit had passed and left him sick with exhaustion and self-pity.

He wanted to drink himself blind, so that he could attain oblivion, for although Hughie disliked the taste of spirits as a child dislikes it, he had recourse to them whenever his nerves had passed entirely beyond his control.

He emptied his brandy-flask, but there was very little in it and he knew that it would have no real effect.

There must surely be some drink downstairs, though they'd had precious little at dinner. Perhaps he could find someone and say that he was ill. He felt ill and he crawled to the mirror and gazed at himself to see whether he looked it.

His appearance was ghastly.

It gave him a sort of self-loathing satisfaction to see the stained pallor of his face, his black-ringed, starting eyes and pinched nostrils. At the same time Primrose's

description came back to him: A hysterical degenerate—
and he writhed again.

Either he must obliterate misery by getting drunk, or
he'd kill himself.

Hughie, for whom self-discipline held no meaning,
knew of no other alternatives, and the second one, he was
aware in the depths of his heart, would never be his.

He went to the door and opened it. He had no idea
of the time, but it could not be very late. Lights were
still burning in the passage and at the head of the stairs.
He moved with no particular attempt at silence. The
subconscious craving of the introvert to be observed, and
questioned, so that he could talk about himself and his
wretchedness, was strong in him and he started eagerly,
and then stopped dead, when he thought he heard a
sound behind Lady Rockingham's closed door.

But no one came out and Hughie went on, down into
the hall.

The General was in his armchair, his head back and
his mouth slightly open—asleep. The sheets of *The
Times* lay scattered on the floor beside him, and his
spectacles were still precariously grasped between his
knotted fingers as though sleep had overtaken him recently
and held him lightly.

Hughie had no wish to awaken General Levallois.
He saw that the door of Colonel Lonergan's office was
open and that the room was lit and he went towards it.

The damned Irishman— But he'd have some drink
there, for a certainty, and Hughie thought he'd only to
show himself and he'd be offered one.

Sedgewick was alone in the room, writing rapidly at
a small marquetry table that was loaded with files and
papers.

He looked up sharply at Hughie standing in the doorway.

"Yes?"

"Are you frightfully busy?" stuttered Hughie. "The
fact is, I—I've had a queer sort of turn. Got a chill or
something. And it's so damned cold upstairs, and the old
gentleman's asleep by the fire in the hall—it's nearly
out, anyway."

He looked at the blazing fire on which logs had been heaped prodigally.

"I'll say it's cold upstairs, all right," Sedgewick assented. "The Colonel's going to give me a spot of work to do—he's gone to fetch it. Come and sit down till he's back, and get warm."

His bright, alert eyes travelled curiously over Hughie, who crouched, shivering, before the fire.

"You look like hell," Sedgewick commented dispassionately. "Are you feeling rotten?"

Hughie nodded.

"I'd sell my soul for a stiff drink. It's the only thing to pull one together."

Sedgewick raised his eyebrows.

"I couldn't disagree more. I'm no faddist, but in my opinion it's absolutely fatal to let yourself depend on drink. It simply means that when you can't get one you go to pieces."

"Don't you ever drink?"

"Only at weddings," said Sedgewick firmly.

"Do you despise everyone who does?"

"Don't be an ass. Why should I care what anybody else does? I'm not interested."

Hughie gazed at the soldier—younger than himself by several years but so much harder and more poised, and with a calm self-assurance that Hughie envied more than anything else.

"As a matter of fact," Segdewick conceded, "if the Colonel comes down and sees you looking like a sick cat, he'll probably hand you a stiff brandy straight away. He's about the most generous chap, and the kindest one, I've ever met in my life."

"Is he?"

"I'll say he is," Sedgewick answered briefly. "You ask any of the men what they think of the Colonel."

"Why isn't he with an Irish regiment?"

"Better ask him."

Hughie knew that Sedgewick intended to snub him, and he winced again.

"God, I'm cold," he muttered in order to break the silence.

"Well, it's warm enough in here. D'you mind if I go on with what I'm doing? I want to get it finished."

"Of course."

Sedgewick, who had availed himself of the permission some seconds before it was granted, wrote on without looking round.

Presently they heard Lonergan's rapid tread and he came in carrying his papers.

Both the young men stood up.

Lonergan looked first at Hughie Spurway, giving him the friendly, intelligent smile that made faint lines spread out fanwise at the corners of his eyes.

"Were you wanting a decent fire? I thought you'd all got warm dancing in the drawing-room, the way you were after dinner. But you look frozen."

"I've caught a chill, or something," Hughie muttered again in the schoolboy formula that he had used before.

"That's bad luck."

The Colonel was looking at him not at all as Sedgewick had looked—coldly, and with a faint hint of dislike—but as though he really felt rather interested in him.

"Could you do with a drink?"

"Thanks frightfully, sir."

"Get out that whiskey, Charles. Sorry we've no soda-water, Spurway, but I daresay you can manage it neat."

Sedgewick went to a corner cupboard, opened it and took out a decanter and glasses. Imperturbably he placed them on the corner of Colonel Lonergan's desk.

Lonergan poured out two stiff drinks.

"Nothing doing with you, Charles, I suppose?"

"No, thanks, sir."

"Ah, you're a good boy—but mistaken."

He handed the longer of the two drinks to Hughie.

"Knock that one back."

Hughie obeyed eagerly.

"It's a cold night, and this isn't the warmest house in the world," observed Colonel Lonergan.

He disposed of his own drink slowly.

"Thanks very much, sir," Hughie said.

Already he could feel the edges of his misery becoming slightly blurred. He had a weak head, and drink acting

189

on the state of nervous exhaustion in which he found himself now would, he well knew, rapidly produce in him that blunting of feeling and perception that was the nearest he could ever attain to peace of mind:

"That's done you good," said Lonergan kindly. "You look done in. What about bed?"

"It's so cold, upstairs."

"Ask for a hot-water bottle and a pair of bed socks," suggested Sedgewick.

His tone was not agreeable and, to Hughie's ears, contained unspoken reference to young men who were not, in war-time, serving in the Forces but complained of being cold in their beds.

Hughie wanted to explain, immediately, that he had been through the worst of the London air raids, had been bombed and shell-shocked, and was doing work of great national importance.

Lonergan laughed.

"Ah, you!" he said to Sedgewick. "No Englishman has any real understanding of what it's like to feel cold. They're brought up to it, God help them!"

"That's right, sir," Sedgewick agreed, unmoved.

He placed a file in front of his Colonel.

"Are you ready for these now, sir?"

"I suppose I am."

Hughie saw that he must go.

He moved reluctantly away from the fire.

"Good-night," said Lonergan. "I hope you'll be feeling better by to-morrow."

"Good-night, sir. Thank you very much."

As he closed the door behind him, some curious intuition told him of Lonergan's probable comment on his appearance: What on earth's the matter with that chap?

He wondered what Sedgewick's reply would be, and was glad that he would never know.

He felt better, thanks to the whiskey, and wished that he had been offered a second drink. He wasn't nearly drunk enough, and the slight haze that was now mercifully enveloping his senses wouldn't last.

"Hallo!" said the General, from his armchair.

He gazed at Hughie as though not quite certain whom he might be. Then he said:

"I say, d'you mind ringing the bell, like a good chap. Ring twice. Madeleine knows what that means. She'll bring the whiskey. I don't often touch it, nowadays, but I feel like a drink to-night. I hope you'll have one with me. Sorry we couldn't offer you anything at dinner, but there it is. Times aren't what they were."

Hughie rang the bell twice. In a slightly maudlin way, he felt touched by this old man who was apologizing to him for what he viewed as a lack of hospitality.

"I never miss the stuff, sir, and nobody's got much of it nowadays. But I'd be delighted to have a drink with you now."

"Sit down," directed the General. "I suppose the other chap—young What's-his-name—isn't anywhere about?"

"Sedgewick? He's in the office with the Colonel, sir, doing a job of work. But he tells me he practically never touches wine or spirits at all."

"Ah," said the General. And he added thoughtfully: "I believe a lot of these young chaps who go into the Services nowadays are like that. Quite right, of course. It's the way they're brought up, no doubt."

"Sedgewick has a widowed mother, I fancy."

"So have you," said General Levallois sharply. "But she hasn't made you into a chap who can't tell good port from bad claret, I'll be bound. Tell me something about your mother—I remember her before she came out, and her elder sister, too. Edith. What's happened to Edith?"

Hughie obediently embarked upon a recital of marriages, deaths and divorces amongst the older generation of his relations.

Madeleine brought in a tray with a whiskey decanter, glasses and a jug of water.

The General's knotted and twisted hands dealt with these things whilst he listened and interposed questions. It gave him evident pleasure to recall memories of that long-since broken circle in which he himself, young and uncrippled, had once held a place.

He prided himself on remembering names and family connections.

It was easy enough to listen to him and make such answers as were required. Hughie drank whiskey and felt thankful.

As usual, alcohol was giving him false courage and false optimism. He even began to wonder whether he couldn't mak eanother appeal to Primrose. Surely she'd be kinder to him this time—more like what she used to be.

Perhaps he'd go to her room later on—or she might still be sitting in the schoolroom.

His heart began to beat faster at the thought. He had forgotten that he had seen Primrose's mother in the schoolroom with her. He imagined her alone, sitting on the fender-seat with a half-smoked cigarette between her lips, and he tried hard to believe that she might be glad to see him.

The General, pleased with the conversation, went on with his questions and reminiscences and poured out more whiskey.

Charles Sedgewick came out of the office, was offered and refused a drink, said good-night and went upstairs.

Soon afterwards Lady Arbell came down.

"Not gone to bed yet, Val?" said her brother, frowning.

"Not yet, Reggie. Please don't move, Mr. Spurway—unless you're going upstairs?"

Hughie, aware that he was pleasantly drunk, told himself that he must be careful and at the same time inwardly applauded himself for what he felt certain was his masterly self-command.

"I think perhaps I will go up, now. Good-night, sir. Good-night, Lady Arbell."

He hadn't any difficulty with his speech, and his mind, he felt convinced, must be absolutely clear since he had so quickly realized that last time he'd seen Lady Arbell she'd been in the schoolroom with Primrose. Now, she was down here—so Primrose must be alone.

As usual, the drink would make it a little bit difficult for him to control his motor reactions. Drink always did that to him, whilst leaving his mind as clear as possible. If it wasn't as clear as possible, Hughie told himself, he couldn't possibly be thinking all this now, so logically and lucidly.

He heard their good-nights as from a distance, and concentrated his faculties on crossing the hall, avoiding the large chairs and small tables, and reaching the staircase.

Then he grasped the banister rail.

Now he'd be all right.

The wild misery of an hour before had receded. He knew, dimly, that it was still there waiting to attack him again—but for the moment he was freed from it. His present condition of semi-intoxication was really sharpening all his senses, he felt. He had distinctly heard what Lady Arbell had said, down in the hall, when he was already half-way up the stairs.

"I want to tell you something, Reggie," she'd said. What on earth could she want to tell the General in the middle of the night? Perhaps it was something about Primrose.

Actually, thought Hughie, pausing on the stairs and wiping his forehead which was suddenly wet—although he was not hot—*actually*, that was the way in which people announced an engagement. Perhaps Primrose was engaged all the time and had told her mother about it in the schoolroom.

At the thought, he felt sick.

It appeared to him imperative that he should find Primrose at once and ask her whether this was true. He'd make her understand that he couldn't go on like this. The words, that he had so often used to her before, seemed to speak themselves aloud: "I can't go on like this."

As though in ironic commentary on his own phrase, Hughie stumbled on the top step. He lunged forward, trying to regain his balance, caught at the air and then found himself clutching at some piece of furniture on the landing. The next instant he had pulled it over, an avalanche of books was falling about his ears and he had crashed onto his knees.

Terrified of being seen and found ludicrous Hughie scrambled up from the floor, trembling.

193

He was surrounded by the disordered books—there seemed to be enormous numbers of old-fashioned yellow-backed novels—and some half-dozen of them were still bouncing off the top step, down the stairs. The little circular bookcase lay on its side.

Someone came along the passage and at the same moment Lady Rockingham's door flew open and the light from her bedroom illuminated the disordered landing plainly.

"Good heavens, I thought a bomb had dropped on the house!" she said in mock-dramatic tones, standing framed in the doorway, a pale silk dressing-gown wrapped round her and her lovely hair loose and wavy on her shoulders.

"I'm frightfully sorry," he stammered weakly.

To his horror he saw that it was Primrose who had come along the passage, from the schoolroom.

She stood a few feet away from him, one hand on her hip and the other one holding a cigarette, saying nothing.

"Of course, Hughie darling, there's all the difference in the world between being drunk and being happy," said Lady Rockingham suavely, "but one would rather like to know what you think you're doing, don't you know what I mean."

"I'm frightfully sorry——"

"But you said that before. Do pick up those frightful books. Primrose will help you."

"Help him my elbow,". Primrose said. "What a fool you look, Hughie!"

Humiliated, furious with himself, and now very drunk indeed, Hughie suddenly turned on her.

"I came up to find you. I'm not going on like this any longer," he cried shrilly. "I shall leave here to-night."

"I hope you'll enjoy walking four miles to the station in the black-out carrying your luggage," scoffed Primrose.

"Hughie, are you quite mad?" said Lady Rockingham.

There was nothing dramatic about the tone of the enquiry. She sounded merely impatient, and a little bit amused.

None of them, *none* of them understood what he was

suffering, Hughie told himself on a fresh wave of agonized self-pity.

"You're bats," Primrose remarked. "Or else plastered, though I don't know what there is to get plastered on in this house. Unless Rory's been fool enough to give you some drink, not knowing that you've got a head that can't take it."

Lady Rockingham bent down and picked up two of the nearest books.

"*'Folle Farine,'* " she read aloud, in a voice of mildly incredulous amusement. "Why on earth doesn't darling Valentine send all this rubbish for salvage? I really must talk to her. Salvage *is* so important."

Hughie stared and stared at Primrose.

Somehow, he must force her to see him as significant—a real person whom, if she would not love, she must hate or fear.

"Lonergan is a great deal too good for you," he enunciated with careful and conscious distinctness. "I know you think you're going to marry him. I heard your mother telling the Gel—General about it. And I can only say I'm damned sorry for him, marrying a bitch like you. Lonergan's a decent fellow. A frightfully decent fellow. He's kind. He's *frightfully* kind."

He suddenly wanted to weep, moved by the thought of Lonergan's kindness.

The two women were quite silent.

Then Lady Rockingham, in a small, queer voice, read out mechanically:

"*'Verbena Camellia Stephanotis,'* by Walter Besant—I *ask* you!"

She raised her eyes and looked at Primrose.

"He's quite, quite drunk, darling. He must be. Hadn't we better get him to his room?"

"He can go to hell, for all of me. He's nothing in my young life," Primrose remarked.

Hughie, shaking all over and afraid of bursting into tears, leant against the wall.

"That isn't true," he said loudly, addressing Primrose. "You know perfectly well it isn't true. I meant a very great deal in your life—not so very long ago either.

You let me make love to you, and then all of a sudden you changed, but you wouldn't let me go. Not you! You played with me like a cat with a mouse. You're cruel and heartless and you're pro—promiscuous, too. Everybody knows you are. Now you're playing the same game with Lonergan, aren't you? But he isn't such a fool as I've been. He'll——"

Lady Rockingham put her hands on his shoulders and gave him a foolish, half-hearted, woman-like little shake.

"For Heaven's sake, shut up. You don't know what you're saying. You're drunk. Go to bed and sleep it off, Hughie, like a good boy, and we'll forget it."

"No," said Hughie finding release and even pleasure in the scene. "You ought to know what she's really like, all of you. If no one else has the guts to tell you, I have."

He could hear his own voice, shouting.

"Be quiet! Do you want to have the whole house up here? Primrose—we shall have to get a man to deal with him. Can't you fetch someone?"

Hughie emitted a sound that he characterized to himself as a reckless laugh.

He saw Primrose move swiftly through the open door of the bedroom and remained with his mouth only half closed, wondering what she was doing and whether he'd frightened her.

But he wouldn't hurt her. He wouldn't hurt *Primrose*. Only he'd felt obliged to let her know that he saw through her.

He decided that he must explain—reassure her.

He wanted to go after her, but all those damned books were in the way. He kicked at them unsteadily and then, as he seemed to have missed his aim, kicked again more viciously.

He heard Lady Rockingham shriek faintly and saw her rush to the other side of the landing.

Primrose stood in the doorway, holding in both hands a large, old-fashioned ewer patterned with red roses.

"You've got it coming to you," she said, and dashed the ice-cold water full into his face and over his head and shoulders.

It was minutes before Hughie, choked, blinded and drenched, could see or hear anything at all.

When he could, he was conscious of nothing but extreme bodily discomfort and of the fact that he had been insanely drunk and was now sobered.

He saw Primrose's face, her mouth pulled down on one side, her blue-green eyes contemptuous and unwavering, water splashed all down the front of her periwinkle-coloured dress, the empty jug rolling gently on its side at her feet, wiping her hands on a handkerchief.

Stumbling over the soaked and scattered books that strewed the floor in wild disorder, Hughie, his teeth chattering with cold, found his way to his own room.

XV

VENETIA ROCKINGHAM was laughing rather unconvincingly.

"Darling, *too* uncivilized altogether. Of course the little horror was completely blotto—but really—! He'll probably get pneumonia now, and die on you."

"It'll be okay by me if he does. But he won't."

"And, my dear, look at the mess!"

The thin, shabby carpet was wet through and so were most of the yellow-backed books. The circular pedestal bookcase that had contained them lay on its side, slowly spilling more volumes into the wet pools on the floor, and the rose-patterned water-jug had rolled against the jamb of the door.

"*Too* like the morning after an air raid, don't you know what I mean. I wish I'd never brought him here, but I hadn't the slightest idea he was that way inclined. It's really too bad. Darling, was he quite mad, about Colonel Lonergan, or is there something in it? I needn't tell you I'm the most broad-minded woman that God ever created—it's being so tremendously one with my boys, I think, so that I simply, absolutely, *see* youth's point of view—but I just couldn't bear you to make any sort of mistake. And I do feel there's something you ought to know."

"I know it already, thanks frightfully. If you mean that Rory's thinking of becoming my step-papa."

Lady Rockingham glanced sharply at the smooth young face, expressionless beneath its heavy mask of make-up.

"Darling, let's hope it doesn't come to that. And now what *are* we going to do with this deluge that you've created?"

"Leave it. The sluts can see to it in the morning."

"Nonsense. All this wet—it'll drip through the ceiling into the hall."

"Will it?" said Primrose indifferently. "Oh, God! It has already—or something. They're coming up."

She leant back against the wall as her mother reached the top of the stairs.

They could hear the sound of the General's two sticks further down on the lower steps.

Valentine held two or three of the yellow-backs in her hand.

She looked at the confusion on the landing and then at Primrose and Venetia.

"We haven't been throwing the books at one another's heads, darling, though I do admit it looks too like it for words. But the whole bookcase, as you perceive, has been turned over. What a frightful collection of rubbish, darling!"

Primrose laughed shortly.

"You'd better explain the tidal wave, aunt Venetia, hadn't you? He's *your* boy friend, you know, not mine."

"It's too late for explanations, my sweet. Your mother ought to be in bed, she looks tired to death. In one word, Val, poor Hughie has been a very naughty boy and having no head whatsoever has obviously been drinking and managed to crash into the furniture on his way to bed. Hence all this."

"But where is he?" Valentine asked.

She bent and picked up one of the books and then let it fall again.

"Why is it all wet?" Her eyes fell on the water-jug. "Have you been emptying the water-jug over him?"

she enquired in a tone that held enquiry rather than surprise.

"That's right," Primrose acquiesced. "Blast, here's uncle Reggie. I've had enough fun and games for to-night. I'm going to bed."

"Darling, you can't do that to us," Venetia cried, a little shrilly. "It's really your row, don't you know what I mean, and you simply must stay and face it."

The General reached the landing.

"What the devil's been happening? Books don't fly downstairs all by themselves, I suppose. And what on earth——"

A trickle of water, taking some freakish course over the uneven flooring, had reached his slippers.

"I'll get a cloth," Valentine said. "The bookcase got overturned, Reggie, and some water has been spilt. There's no harm done."

She turned towards the housemaid's cupboard further along the passage.

Primrose said icily:

"Let's not be so frightfully suave and polite and mysterious, shall we? Hughie Spurway somehow got hold of some drink—for which he has no head whatever and never has had ever since I've known him—and he's roaring drunk. At least he was, until I sobered him up a bit by chucking some cold water at him."

"Good God!" said the General. "Has everybody in this house gone mad? Mop up that disgraceful mess, for heaven's sake."

Valentine returned with two worn and discoloured floor-cloths and knelt down.

"Here," said the General, and he indicated the over-turned and now empty water-jug with one stick.

Primrose, holding her long skirts up with one hand, set it erect.

"Where's that damned young fool?"

"In his room, Reggie—so *much* the best place for him, don't you feel? One is simply covered in blushes for ever having brought him down here, and of course I shall tell him exactly what I think of him in the morning. I heard him crashing up the stairs—but literally *crashing*, my dears—and naturally came out, and there were all these dreadful railway novels—Heavens! how it dates one to call them that—clattering down in every direction, and Hughie sputtering and stumbling in the midst, so that one knew only too well what was the matter, don't you know what I mean."

"He had a couple of whiskeys downstairs with me," said General Levallois—("Primrose, why in God's name are you standing there without lifting a finger to help your mother?")—"but not enough to fuddle a child, I shouldn't have thought. Unless he'd been drinking earlier in the evening."

"Probably had," Primrose said.

She had taken no other notice of the General's admonition.

The General turned on her.

"And may I ask where you come into it? Chucking water about like some damned washerwoman. You don't condescend to come home more than once in a blue moon, and then it's only because of some man or other, and you behave about as badly as any young woman can do. I suppose you've made a fool of this unfortunate young idiot, and he lost his head."

General Levallois had raised his voice until it had become a shout. His habitual manner of carping discontent had given place to one of indignant wrath.

"Reggie, please don't," said his sister.

She wrung out the cloth into the empty jug and straightened herself.

"Let's leave it all, for to-night. He's leaving the house to-morrow, anyway."

"I'm not thinking about him," said the General loudly. "I don't give a twopenny damn for him, one way or the other, except that I think he's practically off his rocker—and it's your daughter who's to blame. Carrying on with first one and then another chap, and then half a dozen of them at once. Three days ago it was the Irishman——"

He stopped abruptly, recollection seizing him, and glared at Valentine.

Venetia Rockingham sank onto a hard, uncomfortable blackwood chair in a corner of the landing.

"Darlings," she wailed, in the thinnest and most affected of voices, "one simply feels *too* like something in the middle act of some terribly Edwardian triangle play. *Who* is in love with the Lonergan person, and *why*, and *how* many people in this house has he been making love to?"

There was a dead silence when she stopped speaking.

Primrose turned on her a look of such concentrated, venomous hatred that her eyes seemed to recede into her head above the discoloured patches that suddenly stained her face.

Valentine, also, changed colour.

She had become white.

It was she who first found words with which to reply to Venetia and they were spoken with firmness and clarity.

"You're unpardonable. There are things that can't be said—and you say them. It was you who forced me to tell you that Rory Lonergan and I are going to be married. Primrose knows it already and so does Reggie."

"You can't marry the fellow," said the General, in a sort of sullen aside. "Idiotic thing to do."

Not one of the three women paid the slightest attention to him.

Valentine was facing her daughter.

"You've got a great deal to forgive me, Primrose," she said. "I don't know where I went wrong with you, but I know that I did—somewhere. I've destroyed the relationship between us. But about this, when you might so easily have hated me—I think we've understood one another."

"That's right," said Primrose, and for the first time in many months her eyes—dense blue-green—met those of her mother, so identical in colour with her own.

There was no softness in the gaze of Primrose, but it held a kind of thoughtful appraisement, as though mentally she was readjusting some earlier, harsher judgment.

"Then everything in the garden is lovely," Venetia Rockingham said with deliberate flippancy. "Quite, quite beyond me, darlings, all these givings and takings, don't you know what I mean. I suppose poor Hughie was really too far gone to know what he was talking about —but I do feel we ought all to realize that Primrose, poor darling, has got the reputation of being a terribly bad little girl with her dreadful little Communist friends, and that if Hughie says nasty things in a naughty temper, there's a very good chance of their being believed. I know you don't mind what anyone thinks of you, Primrose darling, but if this Lonergan of yours is *too* mixed up in it all, isn't it going to make it all very difficult for everybody?"

"No," said Valentine, still with the new note of cold decision in her voice. "No, Venetia. Not for me. I know what there is to know, and anything that Primrose has to say can be said to me. It concerns nobody else."

"I couldn't agree more than I do," Primrose drawled, addressing her words to Lady Rockingham—who made a fluttering, rather absurd, little movement with her hands.

"What the devil are you all talking about?" the General asked. He looked angrily and suspiciously at each of them, and underneath the anger in his voice there was also a dull fear.

"What *is* all this?" he muttered. "What's Val talking about, eh, Venetia? Do you understand her? She says she's going to marry this fellow and at the same time she talks as though he and Primrose——" He stopped, his clouded, puzzled eyes fixed on Venetia Rockingham.

He had always admired her, as a beautiful woman and a successful one, and a woman of the world, and it was to her that he turned now, instinctively feeling that only from her would he get an explanation in terms that he could reconcile to his own deeply-rooted sense of social and ethical values.

"What is it they mean, eh, Venetia?" he repeated.

Lady Rockingham laughed softly—a gentle little spiteful sound, with no mirth in it but with unmistakable enjoyment.

"My poor old Reggie! You're like me—quite, quite at a loss in these *too* extraordinary mix-ups, that I suppose means we're all becoming exactly like the Russians, and going to live as promiscuously as we please. Though I must say, I'm quite as shattered as you can be, to see darling Val, of all people, turning Bolshevik."

"Bolshie? Val?" was all that General Levallois found in reply.

"Bloody nonsense," Primrose ejaculated, with cold detachment.

She turned her eyes on the General.

"She's about as likely to turn Bolshevik as you are, or old Sallie. That's just a label and a dam' silly one at that, the way aunt Venetia uses it. She doesn't so much as know what the word means."

"Need you be rude, darling?" murmured Lady Rockingham. "And I think I *must* have a cigarette, if we're really going on sitting in this quite icy spot indefinitely."

It was the General who fumbled in the pocket of his old velveteen coat and extracted a crumpled packet of cheap cigarettes and handed it to her.

Primrose continued to look at him and address herself to him.

"Get this, uncle Reggie, and don't have a fit if you can help it because the thing's finished and over anyway, and ac'chally it's nobody's bloody business, now. I'm only telling you so as to spike that dam' woman's guns. Rory Lonergan and I have had an affair together, and we did go the whole hog, and it's through and over, and no bones broken. He's welcome to turn his attention elsewhere, for all of me, and the fact that it should be my mama just doesn't mean a thing. And now for God's sake let's all go and get some sleep."

General Levallois made an indistinct sound, his tired face became suffused with a deep crimson and he swung round on his sticks to face Valentine.

"If that's true, she's utterly corrupt. But I don't believe it."

"Reggie, you do believe it—but you don't understand it. Primrose is not corrupt," said Valentine. "She has standards that our generation doesn't know about, and she's faced all the facts and she's made me face them. It's quite true that she and Rory have been lovers and that I'm not going to let it make any difference to what I feel about him. I don't expect you, or anybody else, to understand. There's no reason why you should."

"That's right," said Primrose detachedly.

A rapid step came up the stairs, and before they knew it Charles Sedgewick was in their midst.

Lady Rockingham broke into edgy laughter. She rose and went into her room.

"Let me pick up some of these books," said Captain Sedgewick with calm politeness.

He had given them all one quick look and then stooped down to gather up the books.

"Wizard idea," muttered Primrose.

The General slowly turned away.

One of the sticks slipped and Valentine picked it up and then gave him her arm.

Primrose watched Sedgewick neatly piling up the wet and disordered yellow-backs.

"Tidy, aren't you?" she said in a tone of not unfriendly mockery.

"Quite," replied Sedgewick imperturbably. "Why don't you give me a hand?"

His red-brown eyes looked up at her.

Primrose sat down on the floor beside him, pulled a book or two towards her, and then suddenly began to laugh.

"It's all so bloody silly and dramatic. And your marvellous discretion is the last straw."

"Fancy a book being called *Ready-Money Mortiboy*!" said Sedgewick.

Side by side in the midst of the chaos they looked at one another, laughing.

XVI

"IN heaven's name," said General Levallois. He was muttering and gasping, stamping on the floor with one of his sticks.

Valentine, with quite unwonted decision, turned when they had reached the door of his bedroom.

"I'm going to send Madeleine to you," she said. "Go in, Reggie, and sit down. Madeleine will look after you."

"What the devil has Madeleine to do with any of all this? I tell you, I've never been so upset in all my life."

"I know. I'm sorry. Madeleine can make you one of her *tisanes* and it'll help you to sleep."

"If you think I can sleep, after the things I've been hearing to-night—! Do you realize, Valentine, that you, and that precious daughter of yours, and the whole world, has gone simply raving mad?"

The General looked distraught, and exhausted and suddenly like an old man. It was evident that he scarcely knew what he was saying.

Valentine opened the door of his bedroom and turned on the light.

"I'll send Madeleine," she repeated and, her heart wrung with compassion, pushed his favourite old shabby armchair forward. He lowered himself into it, groaning.

"It's knocked me out," he muttered. "Completely knocked me out. But if you think we're going to leave it at that, old girl, you were never more mistaken in your life. You and I are going to have this out to-morrow morning."

"You can say anything you like to me to-morrow, Reggie. It won't make any difference, but I'll hear anything you want to say," Valentine answered.

She went to Madeleine's little room.

The Frenchwoman's light was, as usual, burning late, and she sat at her needlework.

She stood up when Valentine came in. Her brown eyes, shrewd and kindly, showed no surprise.

"Will you go down to *monsieur le général*, Madeleine, please? He is in his room, very tired, and I think you could give him something hot to drink that might help to make him sleep."

"Naturally, madame. And shall I bring some to madame's room also? It is she who has need of sleep, it seems to me."

"I'm all right, Madeleine, but we've all been upset. I daresay you heard——"

Madeleine nodded and threw up her hands.

"Yes, indeed. These family scenes. Terrible, but inevitable. Mademoiselle Jess, fortunately, had gone to bed and heard nothing, through the snores of her miserable dog. Mademoiselle Primrose can take care of herself, and it is only on your account, madame, that I feel distressed."

"You needn't, Madeleine. I'll talk to you to-morrow. But try and calm the General."

"Leave him to me, madame."

Madeleine folded up her work and went to the corner cupboard on the wall in which she kept a number of private commodities. She fiddled amongst small bottles, little packets of herbs, a saucepan and battered silver spoons.

With her back turned to Valentine, she spoke.

"Madame will allow me to speak, out of my great affection for her? It is more than time—I permit myself to say this—that madame should consider her own happiness. If one is given a second chance in life, it is ingratitude to God to refuse it."

A rush of emotion so moved Valentine that tears came into her eyes.

She could say nothing.

Madeleine turned round and placed her little saucepan and a cup and saucer on the table.

"Ah, madame!" she said, with great gentleness and affection in her voice. "Madame will forgive me, but I have so long been in her service, and seen and thought so much. And this brave officer—this kind and distinguished Colonel Lonergan—one looks at him, and one knows that he understands what a woman means by love. Believe me, madame, he is a heart of gold. And there are not so many of those."

"Madeleine!" Valentine smiled, but there were tears in her eyes. "You know everything."

"But naturally, madame. All good servants know everything and repeat nothing," Madeleine remarked simply. "I am in the old tradition, as madame well

206

knows. And when I saw *monsieur le colonel*, and heard him speak, and listened to all that Miss Jess told me of his charm and his kindness, I thought: Here is a gentleman —an Irish Catholic—a man of the world—and he knew madame long years ago in the old days, and he loved her then. He has been sent in answer to my prayers for madame."

"Madeleine, you are very kind and very good," Valentine said, and bidding Madeleine good-night, she kissed her.

Then she went downstairs again, to find Lonergan.

There was no one now on the landing and the books had been stacked anyhow in the bookcase.

Venetia's door was shut and no light owshed beneath it.

What an evening, thought Valentine, and felt strangely inclined to laugh at the recollection of such unaccustomed drama at Coombe.

When she went into Lonergan's office he was sitting by the fire, staring into the embers and doing nothing.

"Did you think I was never coming?"

He stood up and drew her into his arms.

"I knew you'd come when you could. What's been happening? I'd a feeling young Spurway was up to no good, out there colloguing with the General—and then I heard your voice, and then the two of you going up together. I knew you'd send for me if there was anything I could do. Sit down, love—you're tired."

He put her gently into the armchair by the fire.

"I've told Reggie about us and tried to make him understand that I know what I'm doing. He didn't take it terribly well, I'm afraid. And then there was a disturbance upstairs, and the bookcase on the landing was upset and some of the books fell half-way down and so I went up, and Reggie came too."

She told him what had followed.

"God Almighty!" Lonergan ejaculated. "What a frightful scene for you to have to go through by yourself, my Val. I ought to have been there with you."

He paused, thinking over what she had just told him.

"Well, it's come to a crisis, and all the cards are on

the table. That's so much to the good, in my opinion. And from now on, love, I've the right to take care of you and you'll not be facing these things alone."

She looked at him, her eyes wet, her hands held in his.

"I love you, Rory."

"I love you, my darling."

Presently Lonergan uttered aloud a further comment.

"I'm sorry for that unfortunate Hugo, making a holy show of himself like that. Primrose has something to answer for, the way she's played cat and mouse with him. But isn't it true, the way I told you, that she's capable of certain nobilities? She *did* play up when it came to a show-down between you and her."

"Yes. I think," Valentine said, with a sudden colour flooding her face, "that Primrose has more generosity than I have."

"Why do you say that?"

Valentine hesitated for a long while and then spoke with some difficulty.

"I took something away from her. She's young and I'm not—and in spite of that, a man who'd made love to her, in the end wanted me. I know it hasn't broken her heart, but it's hurt her, and it's been a humiliation. She could have made capital out of that situation, Rory—there's almost no one who wouldn't feel that she had a right to. But it's as you said—Primrose is completely realistic and, whatever her standards may be, she has courage enough to abide by them openly. To-night, I thought we came nearer together than we'd been for years. Just for a minute. It won't last, but it was . . . something."

Her voice faltered—failed altogether.

After a minute she lifted her head and smiled.

"One always remembers the times when they were children, and it was all different. The summer holidays, and reading aloud to them in the evenings, and their little excited faces looking up at one before a Christmas tree, or a morning's cubbing. . . . There must be so many mothers, all over the world, who can't bear to look back on all that now, Rory."

"Ah, God help them!"

208

They were both silent for a little while.

Then she said:

"I'll have to go. It must be very late."

" It's only just after one."

She laughed.

"Just after one is very late for me to be sitting here talking to you, at Coombe."

"There's a very great deal to be said, my darling, and perhaps only a very little while in which to say it."

Valentine leant back in her great chair again.

She remembered thoughts that had come to here arlier in the evening.

"I shall have to readjust in so many ways, Rory—alter so many habits that I've formed and lived with ever since I married Humphrey and came here."

His dark-blue eyes looked keenly at her.

"You're afraid, aren't you?"

"A little bit, sometimes."

"Well, so am I."

"Are you, Rory?"

"Yes. I'm afraid of being clumsy,—of hurting you— of not being able to understand, always. I don't mean of not understanding you. I know we'll understand one another in the end. But any two people, finding one another so late in life and coming from such entirely different backgrounds, with such different traditions behind them, are bound to fail in understanding certain things, sometimes."

"Like when you asked what it all meant, because I was upset at having forgotten the First-Aid class in the village?"

"I was thinking of that," he admitted. "And of your feeling of responsibility towards all those local meetings, and people. I don't even understand why you go to church when it's clear that religion—in the church-going sense of the word—doesn't mean anything to you."

"Do you want me to become a Catholic, Rory?"

He shook his head, laughing.

"I do not. I'm not so set on converts, anyway—God forgive me for saying such a thing. I'm not a good

Catholic, Val, at all. But I was born in the Faith and brought up by priests—it's in my blood. I couldn't ever be anything else. If you and I had a child I'd want it to be a Catholic, the same as Arlette."

"Arlette— When shall I see her? I'd like to have her here, Rory."

"I know you would, love. You've the most generous, loving heart in the world."

Valentine could not have put into words, even to herself, any reason for the pain that assailed her: a fear, not amounting to conviction—a sense of some subtle and infinitesimal withdrawal of his spirit from hers.

Arlette was the child of Laurence.

Jealousy flared, instantly and insanely, within her.

Characteristically, she said very gently:

"You mustn't ever let me come between you and Arlette. I want never to."

"Dearest."

His eyes fixed on the fire, Lonergan spoke with sudden impetus.

"I can't see how I can ever make you understand about Arlette."

Valentine gave no sign that the words hurt her profoundly.

"Try. Please try," was all she said.

"Arlette stands for everything that's been real, and true, in my life. It doesn't matter that she's not in the least like Laurence—never was and never will be. It's not any question of a sentimental recalling of Laurence. It's something that's complete in itself. Hard. Fundamental. A sort of crystallization of my whole life with Laurence. I can't explain any better than that. Arlette is the only responsibility I've ever willingly accepted and it's something I can't ever fail in, even though I fail in everything else. It's something I owe to Laurence."

Valentine thought that she could have endured it better if he had said that it was something he owed to Arlette, herself.

"Tell me what you're thinking," he urged, his voice anxious.

"I can't."

"Ah—you can. I've hurt you?"

"It's all right. Only there's so much—so much in your past that I can never really know, and that I can never share in. The things that, as you've said, Arlette stands for."

"You have children, too," he reminded her gently.

"I didn't love their father as you love Laurence," Valentine said. "It's Laurence, and your life with her, that you see in Arlette. It's still a living thing to you."

Lonergan bent his black head in silent assent.

After a moment he said:

"Val, you're right. It's a great thing I'm asking of you, in asking you to accept it. I've had many loves, God forgive me, and some of them have been lively and happy, and good relationships—and most of them have been false and ephemeral—ending in pain and disappointment and humiliation for others besides myself. But my relationship with Laurence was—cast-iron. It had integrity. If ever I denied that, or forgot it, I believe I'd damn my own soul for all eternity."

The words, and the force with which Lonergan spoke them, carried inescapable conviction to Valentine.

She knew that she could never reply to them, and never forget them. They must be part of her acceptance of the new life for evermore. She must bear the pain of them always, but she might hope that one day, if they both lived, she would be enabled to accept it less blindly, with a braver, because more realistic, understanding through her love of Rory Lonergan.

As though in reply to her thought he said softly:

"We've found one another late, Val. It makes it hard, for both of us."

"The first time," she said, "was too soon."

Lonergan's smile—so expressive of all his kindness, intelligence and profound penetration—answered her.

"Too soon, perhaps. Not, thank God, too late."

Valentine, last to seek her own room at Coombe, was also the first to come down into the pervasive chill of the dining-room the following morning.

Lonergan's servant informed her that the Colonel,

211

accompanied by Captain Sedgewick, had gone out and that neither would be back before evening.

Venetia Rockingham always breakfasted upstairs, and Madeleine had already told Valentine that the General— *d'une humeur de chien, madame, je me permets de vous le dire*— had said that he would not be coming down until later in the morning.

The temperature had fallen and through the long windows Valentine could see a grey, leaden sky and the intricate pattern of the bare, bleak branches of the elms and the chestnut trees interlaced against it. Over the fields, from which thin spirals of mist were still curling upwards, sea-gulls were circling and swooping wildly.

Valentine made the coffee.

She tried to brace herself against the nervous, devitalizing shivering that always assailed her in very cold weather, but her hands were almost numb and she fumbled and clattered with the cups and saucers. It was a trick that had always exasperated Humphrey.

Jess, very pink and fresh, came in and said at once: "It's as cold as hell, isn't it? Morning, mummie. What was all the row last night?"

"Hughie Spurway knocked over a lot of books out of the bookcase on the landing. Some of them fell half-way downstairs."

"But who spilt what?" demanded Jess. "There are damp patches all over the carpet. Aunt Sophy tried to lick some of them up."

"It was unlucky, and very silly. He—Hughie Spurway—took too much to drink and didn't quite know what he was doing. He made all this noise on the landing, and disturbed everybody and then he had a scene with Primrose."

"Gosh! I do think some people are lucky. I wish I'd been there. But I'd just got into bed and begun to get warm, and I hadn't the courage to get out. I would of, though, if I'd known there was all that excitement going on. Were you there, mummie?"

"I came up soon afterwards."

"What happened to Hughie?"

"He went to his own room."

"I bet he feels a fool this morning. D'you think he'll turn up for breakfast?"

"I've been wondering myself," Valentine admitted.

"Shall I go and see?" Jess volunteered, ladling oatmeal porridge into her old and battered silver christening-bowl.

"I don't think so, thank you, darling. He'll probably turn up presently. You can stay and pour out some coffee for him, if you will. I think he'd much rather see you than see me, probably."

"Or Primrose," Jess suggested shrewdly. "I think she was pretty foul to him, yesterday. I must say Primrose has a terrific nerve, really. She treats all her men as if she didn't care whether they walked out on her or not. I suppose really she doesn't, because she can always get others. I bet I'm never like that. If anyone ever does fall for me, I shall hold on to him like grim death and absolutely *make* him marry me."

Valentine laughed.

"I don't suppose it'll be as difficult as all that, Jess. And you've still got plenty of time ahead of you."

"Seventeen and a half," said Jess gloomily. "About eight years, at the very outside, I should think."

Her expression altered.

"Good Gosh, you've got engaged yourself, haven't you? I forgot all about that. You know, mummie, I definitely think it's a good thing. I didn't really take it in yesterday, but the more I think of it, the more okay I think it is."

"I'm glad."

"You won't have to go and live in Ireland or anything, will you?"

"Certainly not as long as the war lasts."

"Oh, the war. I can't imagine that's *ever* coming to an end. I think it'll go on for ever and ever. Sit, aunt Sophy. *Sit!*"

Jess tried to balance pieces of bread on her dog's nose, held her up by the fore-paws, and laughed at her own want of success.

Then she took Valentine aback by suddenly returning to a former topic.

"You never told me what was spilt on the landing. Hughie wasn't sick or anything awful, was he?"

"No, no, he wasn't."

Hughie Spurway came in.

He looked neither sallower nor more unhappy than he had looked on the previous day, and his morning greetings were no more nervously uttered.

Valentine reflected that he had probably failed to realize that she knew anything about what had happened.

She expected him to say that he couldn't stay on but must leave Coombe that day, and purposely left the room when she saw the postman bicycling up the drive, so that he could make a decent pretence of having received a summons by post.

She had opened her own letters and was answering them at her desk in the hall when Venetia Rockingham appeared, wearing her smartly-tailored thick tweeds and a pale-blue angora-wool jumper against which gleamed her pearl necklace.

"Well, my sweet," she said to Valentine. " Isn't this cold too filthy? What about another log or two? *So* lovely to be able to burn wood, don't you know what I mean. They say next winter we shall have no coal, no electricity, no gas, no nothing, if the war goes on. Are you most terribly busy?"

"Not specially."

Valentine laid down her pen.

"Don't look so alarmed, darling." Venetia's soft, artificial-sounding laugh bridged the pause between her words and her installation of herself in the armchair nearest to the fire.

She began quickly and competently to knit, the khaki-coloured wool slipping swiftly between her slim white fingers.

Valentine noticed, as often before, that whatever the temperature Venetia's lovely hands never turned red or mottled from the cold.

"I want, if I may, to talk to you quite, quite frankly, darling Val."

To her own surprise Valentine replied:

"But I'd so much rather that you didn't, Venetia."

214

Lady Rockingham, seeming also surprised, for an instant stopped the rapid wielding of her knitting-needles.

Then she said lightly:

"Val, don't be unkind to me or I shall burst into floods of tears. I do so want you to feel I'm a *real* friend, darling, and able to enter into it all, don't you know what I mean. After all, nobody realises better than I do that Humphrey, poor pet, wasn't one of the great romantic lovers of the world, whatever else he may have been. I've often said why on *earth* didn't you marry again, and when dear old Reggie came and planted himself down here I remember telling Charlie at the time, you might marry any day and Reggie couldn't possibly count on staying at Coombe for ever."

"We can none of us count on staying at Coombe for ever now, Venetia."

"Darling, Primrose wouldn't live down here in the wilds if you paid her to do it. I doubt whether even Jess would. They'll make their own lives, like all these young things. And poor old Reggie won't really mind where he is, will he, so long as Madeleine is there too, to give him his little hot drinks and darn his socks. I'm much more interested in you than in all of them put together and I do really think I can help, perhaps, if you'll tell me your plans, and trust me."

Her lovely eyes were turned pleadingly on Valentine. Her smile was of the quality that is sometimes called disarming.

But Valentine was not disarmed.

"She's false," she thought. "Unreal and unkind."

Aloud, she said:

"You know all that I have to tell, Venetia. I don't think that you can possibly help me, in any way."

"But, my sweet, you do realize that all the family is going to be startled out of its senses if you suddenly announce that you mean to marry this Irishman, Lonergan?"

"There's no one to be startled, really, Venetia. Reggie and I are the only two left of our own generation, since the last war, and the aunts and uncle are much too old to care."

"That's the Levallois side of it, isn't it? But the Arbells *do* exist, my dear, and we've all been so fond of you always, and so interested about the girls, wanting them to marry decently and so on, don't you know what I mean. This is going to shatter Charlie, as well as me."

"Why?"

Lady Rockingham looked down at her knitting and murmured with deliberation:

"Seventeen—eighteen—nineteen—do forgive me, darling—just one minute. And twenty. For one thing, he's not at all one of us, is he? Not that I suppose it matters—I'm the most democratic woman in the world, as you know—but Charlie's terribl old-fashioned. Then there's his religion. One hates even the shadow of narrow-mindedness, and naturally, there are good people in every sect, and personally, I always say what does it matter whether we go to church or not, so long as we all do our best? Still, the family's always rather steered clear of Roman Catholics, don't you know what I mean."

"I'm not a young girl," Valentine said. "Nothing that you've said can have any possible application to a woman of my age, even if those things were important in themselves."

"Slip one . . . Yes, darling, you've learnt it all off too beautifully—I can *hear* your Lonergan saying it, in that rather endearing brogue of his that always sounds *too* like something on the stage, don't you know what I mean. Dear me, how I do dislike knitting! But I suppose one has to. Shall we come down to brass tacks, Val? Did I dream it last night, or did that little neurotic horror of a Hughie really start something, talking about Primrose, and did she own up to it without turning a hair?"

"I don't know what he may have said to Primrose, or about her, before I came up. You and I both know what Primrose said afterwards. I don't mean to discuss it."

"That's what's so *really* silly of you, darling, if I may be quite frank. You're like a dear little ostrich, just pushing your head in the sand and pretending the thing never happened. Now, Val, you know I'm not in the least censorious or narrow—the boys always say there's absolutely nothing they can't talk over with me quite,

quite freely—and I'm going to be absolutely straight with you. Primrose, whom I'm devoted to, has adopted this idiotic pose of having neither manners nor morals and saying every single thing that comes into her head. Is she going to stop at saying that she and her mother both fell for the same man, and that, after amusing himself with her, he decided to propose to you, and you, my poor lamb, immediately accepted him? I ask you, my dear. . . ."

The low, clipped tones went on.

Valentine realized suddenly that, although she heard the words, she was not listening to them. Venetia's words had become wholly unimportant.

They had less significance even than the staccato utterances of Hughie Spurway.

He had come into the hall, with Jessica and the dogs.

"Good-morning, Hughie," said Lady Rockingham, just glancing up from her murmured calculations over the knitting, and then immediately resuming them again.

"Ten—eleven—knit two together . . . Jess, darling, are you a knitter?"

"No," said Jess baldly. "Not if I can help it. I say, mummie, Hughie's in a bit of a flat spin because he thinks he made a fool of himself last night and he wants to go away at once, but I said I thought that was rather a dim idea. You don't mind, do you?"

Valentine smiled at her and at Hughie.

"We'll forget about last night," she suggested. "But you must do just what suits you best, about going or staying."

"I can't possibly stay," said Hughie, his white face working. "It's very kind of you, but I—I can't possibly."

"Why not?" Jess enquired amiably. "Because you had a row with Primrose?"

Hughie made an inarticulate sound.

"Really, Jess, aren't you rather overdoing the *enfant terrible* pose?" Lady Rockingham enquired. "I know you weren't there last night, but it was all very rude and unpleasant and uncle Reggie, I may add, was furious."

She turned to Hughie.

"Personally, I agree that the best thing you can do

217

is to disappear. It'd be so much comfier for you, wouldn't it?"

"Aunt Venetia," Jess remarked clearly and coldly, "I think you're perfectly beastly. I do really. And anyway, it's mummie's house, isn't it?"

Valentine stood up.

"I think we've all said enough. Jess is quite right—it *is* my house, and I'm going to ask Reggie, and everybody else, to forget what happened last night. It was quite silly and unimportant. Jess, will you go and let out the hens for me?"

Jess gave her mother a long, surprised stare. Then she said: "Come on, aunt Sophy. Come on, Sally. Come on, Hughie," and sloped out to the double doors.

The dogs trotted off beside her, and after a moment's hesitation, Hughie Spurway, with an odd, nervous gesture of waving his hands about uncertainly, followed them.

Venetia Rockingham looked at her sister-in-law with almost as much surprise as Jessica had shown.

"I must say, my dear, your Irish admirer has given your inferiority complex its death-blow, don't you know what I mean. Too wonderful. But I don't think it's really going to help, to be so high-handed, when it comes to poor darling old Reggie and the relations."

She gathered up her knitting and stood up, and Valentine, as always, noted her grace and the fluid competence of every movement.

"It's *too* obvious that you don't want any help from me, darling, at the moment. But when you do, I'll be there, and really you might do worse. I've always been devoted to you, Val, and after all, one *does* know one's world and can make allowances."

Venetia bestowed her famous and lovely smile upon her sister-in-law as she went away, unhurried and self-assured.

Valentine thought: "I shan't ever be afraid of her again. Rory's done that for me, too. He's given me courage."

The sense of courage, still mingled with surprise, remained with her even while she told herself that it would, as Venetia had hinted, be more difficult to confront her brother than almost anybody else.

Reggie might be unreasonable, obtuse, violently prejudiced.

But his affection and solicitude for her were real in their degree and she knew that she must outrage them both.

XVII

IT was nearly midday when General Levallois came downstairs. He was wearing a heavy shapeless old Burberry over his tweed suit, and carried, wedged under one arm, the battered green felt hat that he always used on week-days.

"Morning, Val."

His friendly greeting seemed conciliatory, as she remembered the anger with which he had left her on the night before.

"Good-morning, Reggie. Are you going out?"

"Thought I'd take a stroll. You wouldn't care to come with me, would you, old girl? I daresay it's not as cold outside as it is indoors."

He glanced doubtfully out of the window at the iron-grey, lowering sky and the bare branches swaying to the north-east wind.

"Of course I will," Valentine said. "We'll take the dogs."

She pulled on her heavy coat, hanging in the lobby amongst all the other ancient and shabby coats and mackintoshes and disused school blazers, and was thankful to find a pair of woollen gloves in a pocket and to put them on.

They moved slowly out into the wintry cold, obliged to accommodate their rate of progress to the General's infirmity.

"The news wasn't any too good this morning, Val."

"I didn't listen. I'll hear it at one o'clock."

"I wish we had a man like Kitchener, in these days. Or old Redvers Buller."

He had often expressed the same wish before, but now he uttered it mechanically, his voice depressed and uneasy-sounding.

"The state the whole world's in," he muttered. "I hope I'm as progressive as anybody, but I must say, things are getting a bit beyond me. Look at the books people write nowadays!"

"The books?" echoed Valentine, surprised.

"Yes. I suppose a great many people take their ideas out of books, don't they? All these modern books that crack up immorality and bad behaviour, and tell you that religion doesn't matter a hoot and to hell with the Ten Commandments. And what's it all led to, tell me that. The complete turning upside-down of—of every law of decency. I tell you, Val, I was awake half the night thinking about that girl of yours, and the utter shameless-ness of the things she said. If poor Humphrey had been alive, he'd have sent her packing then and there, it's my belief. But that's been the trouble—no father to keep her in order. Mind you, I'm not blaming you, Val. You did the best you could, I've no doubt."

"Let's not talk about Primrose, Reggie. I've made mistakes with her—I don't think I've helped her at all, or really understood her. And it's too late now."

"I refuse to believe it," asserted the General, and dogmatic as the phrase was, Valentine knew that it was spoken perfunctorily and without conviction. He went on immediately:

"The less Jess sees of Primrose in future the better, in my opinion. I thought it was a bit of a mistake, letting her join up so young, but upon my word I'm glad of it now."

He stopped dead, leaning on his two sticks, and faced his sister.

"Better have the tennis-court dug up and planted, you know. No one's going to use it again in our time, eh?"

"Perhaps not."

"Still," said the General, "it's your place, not

mine. I don't want to go cramming my ideas down your throat."

"You've often helped me very much, Reggie. I'm not practical, and I don't think I could have managed this place at all by myself."

"Perhaps not," conceded the General. "It's a man's job, not a woman's. Pity you and Humphrey never had a son. Though if you had, come to think of it, I suppose he'd have been caught up in this damned war, like the rest of 'em."

He paused, and then came to his real point at last.

"Look here, old girl, it's none of my business if you like, but I wish you'd tell me what's in your mind about plans, and so on."

"I'm going to marry him, Reggie."

"Lonergan," said the General, as if marking time. "Lonergan. Well, I don't want to go off the deep end about this, in any possible way."

His hands clenched themselves upon his two sticks and he swallowed violently.

"I know you said so last night, before young Spurway made such an ass of himself and we went upstairs, but I didn't know if you—you might have thought better of it, since then."

"No, Reggie."

"Venetia's dead against it, and mind you, Venetia's not only devoted to you but she's a very clever woman. Very clever. She's got brains, and she knows the world, and she's a good judge of men. I wish you'd talk to Venetia before you make up your mind."

"It is made up."

"You realize you've only known this chap a few days? Upon my soul, Val, it's Tuesday now and the fellow only got here on Saturday night, and you say you've decided to marry him—it's unbelievable!"

His self-control was slipping from him and he was growing loud and angry.

"I'm not saying anything against him, except that he probably knows which side his bread is buttered as well as the next man, but it's utterly unsuitable. There's no *sense* in it. And if it's true that he's been carrying on with

Primrose, it's perfectly outrageous. Not that I believe it is true."

He fixed anxious, furious eyes upon her face.

"What do you propose to do, may I ask? Keep this chap at Coombe, or go off and live in some Irish bog in that damned disloyal country of his?"

"Rory is in the Army now, and will be until the war's over. I don't know what will happen afterwards. Who does?"

"Very well then. Don't do anything until the war's over," triumphantly barked the General. "Call yourself engaged to him privately, and leave it at that. That gives you a chance to think things over. There's a devil of a lot to take into account, Val, mind you. Marriage is a serious business. Have you the slightest idea what this man's family is like, where he comes from, what sort of chance he has of making a living after the war?"

"He has a profession."

"Drawing and painting," said the General doubtfully. "I suppose he's a Catholic?"

"Yes, he is."

"Venetia hates the idea. Personally, I don't know that it matters very much one way or the other. I'd rather a man had any religion than none. But frankly, Val, you've pitched on a man who isn't—isn't exactly in your own walk of life so to speak, and I think that's a mistake. I may be old-fashioned but all this levelling-up never has appealed to me. You'll find there are a lot of things you take for granted that he won't understand."

"He'll find that about me, too," Valentine said. "We've taken it all into account, Reggie. I know it seems to have happened very quickly—and indeed it has—but I know it's all right. I don't expect you to believe me."

The General groaned.

He began to move down the avenue again and Valentine walked slowly beside him, her head bent in a vain endeavour to find some protection from the piercing cold.

"How soon— When do you intend to announce this?"

"I think we shall marry immediately, Reggie. There'll be nothing else to announce."

"Well," said the General violently, "I've always been told that the later in life these infatuations take hold of people, the stronger they are. But I must say, I've always thought you were a sensible woman, Val. Not the kind to lose her head. Venetia says that's the sort that gets it worst—and upon my soul, it looks as though she was right. One's always hearing of middle-aged women running off with the chauffeur, or the leader of a dance-band or something, and sooner or later coming to smash—usually sooner. Infatuation, that's what it is."

Valentine made no reply.

As she had expected, the General in another moment offered a kind of grumbling apology.

"Not that I mean to say Lonergan's all one with somebody's chauffeur. He's a Colonel in the British Army, and a decent enough fellow, no doubt. I don't dislike him, in fact. What about turning back? Get the wind behind us."

Valentine turned obediently.

"I suppose you were in love with him when you were a girl?"

"Yes."

"Still, you haven't been keeping it up ever since."

"Oh no, Reggie. But I suppose that was one reason why it happened so quickly."

The General made a sound that might pass for a grudging assent.

They were nearing the house when he spoke again and his voice then had become mild and meditative.

"Extraordinary, the way things come round. I can remember mother writing to me from Rome about you and an affair with some Irish fellow that nobody knew anything about, and saying how pretty you'd grown."

"Did she?"

Valentine was surprised and touched. Her mother had loved her, possessively and emotionally, but she had never praised her. Valentine had grown up believing herself to be uninteresting and unattractive.

The General nodded.

"Yes, I remember her writing that. I was at Simla when I got the letter. I remember feeling a bit surprised at your being old enough for that kind of thing. I suppose I was still thinking of you as the kid in short frocks I'd seen on my last furlough. It's a funny thing, that chap's name coming back to me directly I heard it, Lonergan. Well—I always say I never forget a name."

They reached the double-doors of the house and General Levallois performed the difficult feat of balancing himself and his supporting sticks whilst carefully wiping his boots against the ancient iron scraper.

They went into the lobby and the General pushed open the glass swing-doors and they passed through them.

"I'm glad we've had this talk about it, old girl."

"So am I, Reggie."

"Think over it, before you go and do anything silly," the General advised her. "Have a talk with Venetia. She's a good sort, and she knows what's what."

He moved slowly towards the staircase.

"Nearly time for the One O'Clock News. I shall go up and listen to it in Madeleine's room. One can't hear oneself think when young Jess and that dog of hers are anywhere about. Besides, if Spurway gets in my light I shall want to give him a kick in the pants. Can't understand his mother having a boy like that. She was a Herbert-MacDowell of Acres. I remember her, and her sister Edith too. Pretty girl, Edith."

He shifted his sticks, grasped the banister rail and began to climb upwards.

Valentine, gazing after him, thought that she had little more to fear from Reggie. His anger had spent itself, and his inelastic mind would for ever refuse to admit the full implications of all that Primrose had tried to force upon his understanding.

Watching his slow, creeping progress up the stairs Valentine remembered, for a moment, her eldest brother as the ambitious and successful soldier that he once had been before illness had turned him prematurely into an old man.

Now there was nothing left for him, except the oddly trivial remembrances on which his mind for the most part dwelt, the creature comforts of which he could still avail himself, and the devotion and kindness of Madeleine.

Madeleine will always look after him, she thought gratefully and with confidence.

Hughie Spurway, following Jess about like a dog, stood at her heels as though seeking protection in her sturdy normality while she announced for him:

"Mummie, Hughie says he absolutely must and will go to Plymouth directly after lunch. I suppose that means aunt Venetia'll go back to London by train. I hope she's really leaving here to-morrow, like she said. She makes me sick. Fancy if I had to travel up to London with her! I might, you know. I could be called up any day now. They never give you more than about five minutes' notice."

Primrose came in.

Hughie turned a sallower, more evil colour than before at the sight of her and he picked up a book from the table beside him and looked fixedly into it without stirring whilst Jessica glibly repeated her announcement of his departure.

"So what?" said Primrose.

"I was thinking how awful it'd be if it just happened that I had to report to Victory House to-morrow and had to travel to London with aunt V. Except that I suppose she'd pay for me to get in first class with her, but even then it wouldn't be worth it."

Jess chattered on and Valentine wondered exactly how far she realized that she was helping them all through an embarrassing and even painful hour. Jessica might be naïve, but she was also shrewd, and the inherited sense of social responsibility that Primrose so violently and consciously repudiated had not passed her by. Knowingly or not, she recognized it as a part of human intercourse and conformed to it, on her own terms and in her own way.

Throughout luncheon Hughie hardly spoke at all, Primrose addressed her few, discontented comments on the cooking and serving of the food into space, and the conversation lay between Lady Rockingham, the General

225

and Valentine, Jess keeping up a running under-current of talk that seemed mostly to be concerned with the dogs.

As they left the table she suddenly enquired of Hughie Spurway:

"Could aunt Sophy and I come as far as the post-office with you in your car, and then be dropped? We'll walk back."

"Certainly," he answered, looking startled.

"I can call for the second post," Jess explained. "I've got a terrific feeling there may be a letter telling me to join up."

"I'll get the car round," Hughie muttered.

He looked, for the first time, at Primrose but she made no movement at all and he went upstairs.

"Are you going to forgive him before he goes?" Lady Rockingham asked lightly of her niece. "It's really all your own fault, darling, for upsetting the poor wretch so that he lost his head. He looks half dead with shame, this morning."

Primrose made no reply.

"When you do *that* with your mouth," Jess observed to her sister dispassionately, "you look exactly like a camel. I wish I could."

Primrose was still wearing the same expression when Hughie Spurway took his leave.

He stammered something inarticulate to Lady Rockingham, who laughed and waved her hand at him without touching his.

"Ring me up at the Dorchester one of these days, my dear. I can't promise I'll be there because one's so run off one's feet these days, don't you know what I mean, but we can but hope for the best. Don't forget."

Her little nod dismissed him as coldly and deliberately as had her unmeaning phrases.

Valentine moved forward in time to prevent Hughie from attempting whatever difficult speech he had prepared for her.

"I'll come with you to the door," she said. "I hope your bag has been taken down."

"It's in the car."

Valentine looked at Primrose.

She was lying back in an armchair in the furthest corner of the hall, a cigarette between her lips, her head bent over the crossword puzzle in the daily paper.

Jess spoke the words that Valentine had lacked the courage to utter.

"Hughie's just going."

Primrose lifted her yellow-curled head. Her long, narrow face was expressionless except for the curve of the ironically-arched thick eyebrows that so expressively suggested her arrogant contempt for her surroundings.

Hughie advanced, stood stock-still in front of her, and said in the unnaturally loud voice of one who has been afraid that he will not be able to speak at all:

"Well, goodbye. It's been grand, seeing you."

" 'Bye," said Primrose. The monosyllable seemed to drop from one corner of her mouth and she did not raise her eyes.

"Goodbye," repeated Hughie. "I'll be writing to you from Plymouth, I expect."

"I shouldn't bother," said Primrose.

Her pencil hovered over the paper, then filled in one of the little blank squares.

For the third time Hughie said goodbye and this time she made no answer.

He turned away and followed Valentine and Jess to where the car stood waiting beside the moss-grown stone pillars at the entrance.

"Fancy, someone's mended the chain," said Jess, and she put up her hand and pulled at the rusty iron links.

The chain immediately broke again.

"I bet it was Charles who did that and thought himself awfully clever," Jess remarked, unperturbed, as she pushed the broken length of chain into her coat-pocket. "I'll just show him that when he comes back to-night. Come on, aunt Sophy. You can sit on my knee."

She climbed into the car.

"Goodbye," said Valentine, and she held out her hand to Hughie, smiling. "Don't worry, please."

She felt that the words were very inadequate but his chilly fingers grasped hers in a painful effusion of gratitude.

"Thanks frightfully, Lady Arbell. I'm afraid it's—I've—oh, God, I can't say what I mean."

"Aren't you *coming*?" Jess called.

Valentine drew back and the young man turned his haggard stare away from her, took his place at the wheel and drove off down the winding avenue, away from Coombe.

A fleeting arrow of compassion shot through Valentine's mind, and the next instant she was giving herself up joyously and with profound excitement to the thought that her lover would be with her again that evening.

In a very little while—in a day or two—they would marry.

"Rory and I will belong to one another in every way there is," she thought, and for a little while she, whom the years had taught to be neither optimistic nor enterprising, gave herself up to the day-dreaming that had coloured all life for the girl, Valentine Levallois.

The ringing of the telephone bell sounded through the hall.

Certain that it was Lonergan, Valentine went to answer it and found her certainty justified.

"Yes?"

"Ah, thank God it's you, dearest. Listen, could you meet me the way you did before, at the Victoria Hotel? I've to talk to you."

"I'll come, Rory. What time?"

"As soon as you can, love."

She thought that she could detect hesitation in his voice.

"What is it? Has something happened?"

"You're terribly quick. Listen, love. I've got forty-eight hours' leave, from to-morrow. We all have."

Her heart seemed to stop, and then to race.

"Is it embarkation leave?"

"It is, my darling."

There was an instant of silence and then his deep, musical voice came over the air again with a note of great urgency.

"Val, my sweet, are you all right?"

"Yes. Tell me what you want me to do."

"I want you to come to the Victoria Hotel, now. We'll talk, then. I can take an hour, with any luck. We've everything to settle."

"You can't tell me anything . . .?"

"Nothing, love. Indeed, I know very little myself. By the way, Sedgewick is off to-night. He'll come back to fetch his things and catch the night train up to London. He asked me to let you know. He'll be up about six o'clock."

"I'll get his things ready for packing," Valentine answered mechanically. "Am I to say anything about this?"

"Ah, there's nothing private about it. The whole town knows already, and of course the boys themselves are lepping mad with excitement."

"I suppose so."

She felt as though she had been stunned and was incapable of thought or speech.

"I must go," said Lonergan's voice. "I've to book a call to Kilronan post-office, in County Roscommon, God help me, for Arlette. It'll be the work of the world to get hold of her, at that, for my sister Nellie's house isn't on the telephone."

The now familiar pang struck at her heart.

"Couldn't you telegraph beforehand and tell Arlette what time to be at the post-office and ring up then?"

"I have telegraphed, but I don't suppose there's a hope of it's getting delivered in time. I'll have to book the call now for some time this evening and take a chance on their getting hold of her. One thing, she's certain to be in after eight o'clock, the poor child. Nellie would see to that. Will it be all right for me to take the call at Coombe?"

"Of course."

"I knew it would be, God bless you. Listen, Val, will you be coming by the road?"

"I can. I think I'd better."

"I'll try and meet you, with the car. If I can't, will you wait for me at the Victoria? I'll anyway drive you back, though you may have to wait for me in the hotel a little while."

229

She assented.

"Then I'll be seeing you in less than an hour's time, my darling. Goodbye and take care of your sweet self."

"Goodbye, Rory. I'll start at once."

She replaced the receiver.

Embarkation leave, thought Valentine. That means foreign service. We must marry before he goes. He didn't say that. He said he must put a call through to Arlette. He's telegraphed to her already. That was the first thing he thought of. With the careful reasonableness that she brought always, instinctively and from long custom, to bear upon her own problems she reminded herself that Rory had known he would see her within the hour.

The habit of organization would impel him to deal first with the complexities and uncertainties of telephone communication in war-time between Devonshire and a remote village in South Ireland.

She found that, without being aware of having done so, she had returned to the hall where Venetia Rockingham still sat beside the fire, directing her bright, delicately-enunciated spate of faintly malicious conversation towards the General, and Primrose still sprawled, motionless, in her distant corner.

Still motionless and still looking down at the crossword puzzle, she enquired:

"Anything or nothing? The telephone, I mean."

"It was a message to say that Charles Sedgewick is coming back this evening to collect his things, and then going off by the late train. They're being moved."

"My God," remarked Primrose without expression. She filled in another clue.

"Being moved?" echoed the General. "Scandalous waste of the country's money, the way the Army is being pushed about from pillar to post, in my opinion. Are these chaps going abroad?"

"I think they are, Reggie. Charles Sedgewick is off to London on embarkation leave."

"My dear," exclaimed Venetia. "He hasn't got embarkation leave all to himself, I imagine. What about the Colonel?"

"Rory's got his embarkation leave too, Venetia."

"And what are you going to do?" Lady Rockingham asked, looking curiously at her sister-in-law. "Nothing desperate, darling, I do hope and trust. If you ask me, this gives everybody time to turn round—such a mercy, don't you know what I mean."

Valentine rang the bell without answering.

When Ivy appeared she said:

"Would you or Esther take Captain Sedgewick's suitcases to his room, if you please. He's going on leave tonight. Ask Mrs. Ditchley to send in dinner early. Seven o'clock."

"Yes, my lady."

The girl's face showed no surprise. Valentine surmised that she had heard the news already.

After Ivy had left the room Lady Rockingham remarked:

"I suppose Colonel Lonergan's batman looks after his packing—or isn't he going away?"

"I'm walking into the town now to meet him and talk over what we're going to do," Valentine replied.

It was only as she went out of the house by the garden door five minutes later that she realized, with surprise, that her announcement had met with no comment from anybody.

She walked as quickly as possible down the avenue and thought that it was growing colder every minute, although the wind had fallen. It had given place to a sullen, snow-laden stillness that enveloped the dark and leafless trees and the sodden-looking earth in a chilled immobility.

Valentine's exultation of an hour earlier had all left her. She felt despairing, apprehensive and forlorn.

"It will be all right when I see him," she told herself without conviction. Her mind dwelt upon the immediate present, unable to envisage the idea that Lonergan was going away, leaving England for a destination unknown, from which he might well never return again.

She had walked rapidly for a mile and a half or more when she saw a tall young figure swinging along the lane, coming towards her. It was Jess, with her dogs.

Aunt Sophy, recognizing Valentine, rushed wildly to

meet her, capering extravagantly and making short rushes backwards and forwards between her and Jess.

"Hallo!" Jess shouted, lengthening her stride. She was waving a paper above her head. "It's come! I was absolutely dead right, as usual. Wasn't it extraordinary, mummie, I just *knew* that letter would be at the post-office. And it was. I'm to report at Victory House at twelve noon on Thursday. Gosh! that's the day after to-morrow. I'll have to take the early train. Gosh! It's pretty marvellous, having to dash off all in a minute like that, like the Secret Service or something. Mummie, it *is* okay by you, isn't it? I mean, you don't **mind**, do you?"

"No, darling. Not if you're glad."

Valentine forced back the emotion that threatened to bring tears into her eyes.

"I'm dying to tell Madeleine. Gosh! won't she be thrilled! It'll make up for the battalion going. Mummie, they're being sent abroad and they don't know where, only they're being issued with tropical kit. They're getting embarkation leave, straight away now this minute. They'll all be gone by to-morrow. So'll I, by Thursday. I wonder what uncle Reggie will say. Mummie, you'll take care of aunt Sophy, won't you?"

"Indeed I will."

"And look, are you on your way to meet the Colonel? Because if you are, I saw him in the Square and he told me to tell you it was no good. He looked as sick as mud. He's got to see some old General or other and he told some chap to ring up Coombe in case he could catch you before you started, to say not to come."

Valentine's heart sank lower. She felt no surprise, only an overwhelming disappointment.

"He came dashing across the Square just as I came out of the post-office, and asked if I was going home and told me I'd prob'bly meet you on the road. Gosh, it's parky, isn't it? We hadn't better go on standing here freezing, had we?"

Valentine turned and walked beside her daughter in the direction of Coombe.

"It's a pity about Charles and the Colonel going,"

Jess observed. "And Buster and Jack and all the others. They were wizard. I suppose I won't be able to say goodbye to them now. I'll only see Charles. He's coming in at about six, and the Colonel as soon as he can make it. Earlier than six if he can, he said."

Jess whistled piercingly to her dog.

"Did you tell Colonel Lonergan that you were going to Victory House on Thursday?" asked Valentine, in order to break the silence that she felt unable to endure. "What did he say?"

"As a matter of fac', I didn't say anything about it. I thought," said Jess, elaborately off-hand, "that you might as well be the absolutely first person to be told about it."

XVIII

WITH his customary efficiency and detachment Charles Sedgewick looked round his bedroom at Coombe and ascertained that his belongings were packed, and his room left in order.

He took a last appraising look at the old-fashioned wallpaper, the dark, massive furniture, the steel engravings framed in narrow black and gold. It was pretty certainly the last time he'd ever stay in a house like Coombe, he reflected without any sentimental regret— indeed with a momentary relief in the recollection that his mother's little villa would be comfortably warmed throughout.

Well, thought Sedgewick, it had been interesting enough to see how these people, so unmistakably in the last ditch, conducted such life as they might be said to have left. Something to be said for the individual, perhaps—he grinned at the remembrance of Jessica, who was a nice kid, young enough and tough enough to find and keep a place in the new order.

He gave a fleeting thought to Lady Arbell, not because he considered her in any way significant but because his

Colonel apparently did. One can't ever tell, with people of that generation, was Sedgewick's mental summing-up of his passing surmise. And he added in his own mind: "Any more than they can with ours".

The people who might be liquidated with positive advantage to the community were, in Sedgewick's dispassionate view, the Rockingham woman, who was a bitch, Hughie Spurway, a degenerate and a pestilential bore, and the old Blimp, General Levallois.

Thus briefly, methodically, and without qualifying clauses did Charles Sedgewick classify his impressions of these people whom he had tabulated as "the real thing's on his first arrival at Coombe. There remained hi' awareness of Primrose, and hers of him.

Sedgewick glanced at his wrist-watch, noted that it was only twenty minutes past six, and with characteristic promptitude decided that he had plenty of time in which to discover whether or not Primrose was interested.

The non-committal phrase exactly expressed his own attitude of mind.

With no further backward look at his temporary lodging, Sedgewick tramped out of the room and down the dark, draughty passage to the schoolroom.

She was, as he had expected, sitting over the fire, smoking and with a copy of *The New Yorker* lying face-downwards on her lap.

"Hallo, Primrose."

"Hallo to you. So you're off."

"That is correct."

"Jess has got to go, too. Quite a break-up."

"Isn't it? What about you?"

"It's me for the first train to London to-morrow—so long as my poisonous aunt isn't in it."

"Travel up with me to-night. We'll be making Waterloo at twenty-four hours, if the train's punctual."

"Too much of a rush."

"As you say."

Primrose turned her head slightly towards him for the first time and gave him her queer, crooked smile.

"I might turn up to-morrow lunch-time at the bar of the Café Royal."

"I'll buy you a drink there."

"Okay."

His eyes held hers for a moment and then they both laughed,—brief, excited, mirthless laughter.

Sedgewick walked over to the armchair and pulled Primrose onto her feet.

"Mind my cigarette," she said.

"Chuck it away."

" 'Save to defend'," she mocked.

Then she threw the half-smoked cigarette, stained with her lip-stick, into the fire.

It was nearly nine o'clock before Lonergan returned to Coombe. A succession of telephone messages had announced one delay after another, and the last one had said that no dinner was to be kept for him.

Dinner at Coombe had been early, and immediately afterwards Primrose, offering no explanation to anyone, had gone in Sedgewick's taxi to the station and seen his train pull out from the darkened little country platform.

The taxi brought her back as far as the gates of the avenue and there she got out and prepared to walk to the house, swearing between her teeth at the cold that slashed through her belted leather jacket and thick skirt.

A car hooted behind her and she saw and recognized it preparing to take the entrance, travelling slowly.

Primrose flashed her torch onto the path ahead, swinging it backwards and forwards, and the car came to a noisy standstill.

Lonergan leant out and opened the door.

"It's me," Primrose said, and she climbed into the seat next the driver's.

"What in God's name are you doing, girl, catching pneumonia out here?"

"Pneumonia is right," said Primrose, and she leant back and dragged at the rug on the back seat.

"Here, wait a minute."

Lonergan switched off the engine and put the rug over her knees, tucking it round her.

"History repeating itself," Primrose remarked. "Remember driving me out from Exeter last Saturday?"

"I do," he answered gently.

"Go on. Start her up. You're driving me to the house, aren't you?"

"I am, of course."

He started the engine again and the car bumped away over the uneven surface between the dark clumps of the gorse bushes and the groups of leafless trees.

"You're late," Primrose said.

"Indeed I am. It's been one thing after another, all day. Has Sedgewick gone?"

"Yes. 'Smatter of fact, I've just been seeing him off."

"You have?"

After a pause, as though Lonergan had been silently taking in the implication of that statement, he said:

"So that's the way of it. Well, Sedgewick's a good lad, tough as they come, and he deserves a slice of luck. He'll be on the high seas a week from now."

"So'll you."

"I shall."

"I shan't be seeing you again. I'm going back to London to-morrow."

"So Sedgewick gets his slice of luck."

"If that's what you call it," she agreed.

"It is," said Lonergan, and in his voice was a smile that she could not see.

They were nearing the house.

"Primrose, you'll call this a lot of nonsense—but I want to tell you that there's a good deal that I'm terribly sorry about. Forgive me."

"Forget it," Primrose said, in her indifferent drawl.

The car jolted its way round the oval grass plot before the stone pillars. Primrose swayed deliberately to the movement and, as her whole slim length fell against him, she put her hand over Lonergan's on the gear-lever.

He slipped the clutch into neutral, and the car stopped.

For a moment they both remained motionless. Then Primrose pulled herself upright and opened the door of the car. She swung her long legs over the step.

"Good-night, Rory. Thanks for the lift."

"Good-night, my dear."

"Damn this black-out, I can't see a thing."

236

He saw the flash of her torch as she stumbled forward, under the lead-roofed portico.

"Are you all right, Primrose?"

"I'm okay."

The tiny light of the torch went out.

"In case I don't see you again, good luck and all that."

Her voice reached him through the darkness and the echo of it was immediately lost as the doors banged-to behind her.

As he walked into the hall Lonergan's eyes sought anxiously for Valentine.

He saw her at once, and that she looked pale and very tired. The others were there too—Lady Rockingham and the General and Jess—sitting in silence, whilst the voice of a B.B.C. announcer passionlessly enunciated the cheerless items of the Nine O'Clock News.

Lonergan began an apology for his lateness, but was immediately checked by an impatient gesture and portentous glare from the General.

He looked at Valentine with a despair born of fatigue, urgency and exasperation, and she got up and came towards him.

The telephone-bell cut shrilly into the careful silence, the General ejaculated angrily and Jess scrambled up from her seat on the floor.

"It'll be for me," said Lonergan. "I've a call to Roscommon."

He strode to the telephone, and Valentine sank back into her chair again.

Lonergan, pushing into the dark corner where the telephone so inconveniently stood on a bracket in an angle of the wall, fumbled for the electric-light switch, failed to find it, and cursed.

He was in a mood of acute nervous impatience that he knew well and had reason to dread.

The stereotyped phrases and unexplained delays to which the telephone operator subjected him did nothing to allay it.

He had three times repeated his own number and

explained his requirements before, through a variety of buzzing noises and fragmentary directions, the connection was made.

"Kilronan post-*office*," said the far-away voice, putting the authentic Irish stress on the last word.

Lonergan explained that his call was for the young French girl living at Miss Lonergan's house opposite. Could she be fetched at once, please?

"I'll ask me brother will he step over. Is it Miss Nellie you're wanting?"

"It is *not*. It's her niece, that's staying with her."

"The young foreign girl would that be?"

"It would. If you could have her fetched to the telephone, I'd be grateful. It's urgent. I'll hold on."

The disembodied voice ejaculated sympathetically and Lonergan was left to the strange, intermittent sounds that penetrated through the receiver into his right ear.

The time seemed endless.

He made another effort to find the light-switch with his disengaged hand and failed again.

"Have you finished?" enquired the thin English accents of the local operator.

"I have not. Don't cut me off, please. They've gone to fetch someone."

"Okay."

The three-minute signal sounded.

He was afraid the operator would cut him off, and his urgent request to her not to do so seemed to fall into space and met with no reply.

Lonergan began to rehearse what he would say to Arlette, as he had been doing at snatched intervals throughout the day.

She'd be distressed, the poor little thing, and she'd written that she so much wanted to see him. Nellie was the kindest creature in the world, but she was narrow-minded, provincial and inclined to domineer, and it was plain that Arlette wasn't happy with her.

And now this — she'd think it was her last hope gone.

Lonergan wished to God she'd come to the telephone quickly and reminded himself with dismay that Nellie, as likely as not, would come with her. But they'd talk in

238

French, anyway, and Nellie could make what she liked of it.

The time signal sounded again and Lonergan groaned.

A noise like that of an exploding cracker assaulted his hearing.

A voice spoke, but the words were indistinguishable.

"Arlette?"

Suddenly the voice became clearly audible.

It was the Irish operator in Kilronan post-office again.

"You're out of luck entirely, sir. Believe you me or believe you me not, that house is empty only for old Maggie Dolan."

"What?" said Lonergan blankly.

"They've gone into town for the St. Vincent de Paul Grand Concert and they'll not be home till all hours, says Maggie Dolan."

Lonergan thanked her mechanically.

It must be the only night in the whole year, he thought, that Nellie would be setting foot out of doors after dark and taking Arlette with her.

He slowly replaced the receiver, and found that his hand was shaking and his forehead damp.

"I'll try again to-morrow morning early," he told himself—but without any conviction.

His nerves were on edge and he was in the grip of that panic desolation of spirit that, in its degree, periodically assails all artists.

"Oh, God, I mustn't let myself go," he thought. "If only all these people would get to hell out of here and leave me alone with Val——"

Resolved to see her at once and alone, he went back into the hall.

Only Lady Rockingham still sat there, her hands idle in her lap, the wireless on the table now silenced.

She bestowed upon Lonergan a smile that held all the conscious grace in the world.

"I'm really rather waiting to ring up a London number but one hasn't got the courage to retire to that arctic spot, don't you know what I mean. Did you get through to Ireland?"

239

"I did, thank you."

He looked round.

"I suppose they haven't all gone to bed?"

"No, no. Val is in the little breakfast-room, where I'm sure she's waiting for you. Poor darling Val. She's looking quite shattered to-night and I hate leaving her in the midst of all this agitation, but alas, duty calls."

Lonergan hated her.

"I'll go in to her," he said curtly.

"Do, my dear. Too wretched for you both. She poured out the whole thing to me, of course—we've always been rather specially devoted to one another in spite of being in-laws, which I always think is such an odious expression. I just wanted to tell you that I'll do everything I can to calm down Reggie, poor old pet, and make the family behave itself. I hear you're off at once?"

"I've forty-eight hours' leave before I go," he answered with cold, deliberate significance.

Lady Rockingham seemed wholly unperturbed.

"Too nerve-racking, all these comings and goings," she murmured. "Still, things settle themselves, one always feels, and I did so want you to know that Valentine will have me behind her, poor lamb, whatever happens. I always say I'm the most broad-minded woman of my acquaintance."

Lonergan turned on her a furious look.

"I'd like to know, if I may, in what way it's become necessary for you to be broad-minded where Valentine is concerned. Would it be because she's promised to marry me?"

"My dear, she can promise to marry the crossing-sweeper if she likes. She's quite old enough to know her own mind, as I've told her. But, since we're talking so frankly, we do—all of *us*, I mean—feel that it will be a thousand pities if she rushes just now into any rather irrevocable affair like marriage, don't you know what I mean. One saw so much of that in the last war."

"Just what is the insuperable objection to Valentine's marrying me if she does me that honour? My nationality, or my religion, or my profession, or the class to which—I'm proud to say—I belong?"

Lady Rockingham got up from her seat, still smiling.

"I always think this sort of discussion is so embarrassing, don't you? Personally, I detest the word class but then I'm democratic. Practically a socialist. One only feels that poor darling Val, out of her setting, Devon and Coombe, and the family and all that—would be too utterly lost and wretched, don't you know what I mean. I mean, she's not really adaptable, is she—even if she was a younger woman. One's only thinking of her happiness, which I'm quite sure is all you're thinking of either."

She smiled at him again.

"Do forgive me. I must now wrestle with a trunk call. So impossible, nowadays. They always tell one the junctions are engaged, whatever that may mean, don't they?"

Lonergan gave her a long, level look of anger and dislike.

"You're right about one thing—which is as well, since you're wrong about everything else on earth. I want nothing but Valentine's happiness and I've the arrogance to be perfectly convinced that she'll find it with me, and that she's completely and entirely missed it with you and all the rest of her relations, God help her! It's well she's the courage to break away from the whole lot of you, and I'm going to see to it that she does so, the very first minute it can be done."

He walked into the breakfast-room and shut the door.

"Val! I've been almost out of my mind—not able to get next or near you all day. Forgive me, love. Did Jess meet you this afternoon?"

"Yes. I got all your messages."

She looked exhausted and distraught.

"I knew you'd understand how it was. There was everything in the world to do, and I'm not through yet. I've to go out again in an hour. Oh, God, Valentine, I'm not a free agent any more. I'm caught up in this machinery of war and now that I've found you, I can't stay with you."

He saw the wild look of pain in her eyes and it increased his sense of frenzied helplessness.

"When must you go, Rory?"

"My leave is up at nine o'clock on Friday morning."

"I mayn't even know where they're sending you, may I?"

"I don't actually know myself. But it doesn't follow we shall sail immediately, sweetheart. We may be kept hanging about for weeks at the port of embarkation. Or, of course, we may sail directly."

"I can't bear it," said Valentine, and she hid her face in her hands.

"What'll we do?" he asked desperately. "I've a special licence, Val, that'll be available to-morrow. We could be married before the Registrar immediately and have the next two days together. You might even join me for a while after that, if we're not to be sent off at once. God knows I never meant to rush you like this, though."

He knew, from her immobility, that he was hurting her, but the bitter anger and dismay that Venetia Rockingham's insinuations had roused in him drove him on.

"It's a mad thing, to have to take the decision of a lifetime in five minutes. It's asking you to go against all your family, and your tradition and theirs. It's asking you to take on something more or less blind, as things are now. How can I ask you to do that?"

"Rory——" she said entreatingly.

He went on recklessly, disregarding alike her suffering and his own.

"Dearest, dearest love—God knows I adore you, but the risk of it is so immense. I've been here, in your house, I've seen something of your life, of the people it's linked up with—and I've nothing, *nothing* in common with any of it. Supposing I get through the war and come back to you—what'll happen to us? What would we do? I could never live this kind of life, and what do you know of my kind? You'd be bewildered by my friends—riff-raff of the artist world, most of them—and my good, simple, middle-class Irish relations. And there's Arlette. I'm out of my mind about Arlette, now this minute. I couldn't get her on the telephone just now and when I do, what can I say? That I'm leaving her in a place where she obviously isn't happy, and that even if I come back after the war, I won't be having her to live with me in Paris the way she thinks I will."

"Arlette could come here," Valentine said in a very low voice.

"Ah, you don't understand. That isn't what would ever make her happy. She's used to an artist's life—the kind that Laurence and I led. Freedom, and every sort of mad contact—a whole lot of drinking even—and conversation that really means something. Not the chitter-chatter about who So-and-so was before she married somebody's first cousin from the next county. . . . Forgive me, Val!"

"Go on," she said.

"Why do you say 'Go on' when it's clear that every word I say is nearly killing you?"

The anger in his own voice horrified Lonergan as he heard it, even though it was not directed against her, and he strove to control it.

"You see, darling, I'm terrified—plain terrified—at the thought that we'd do this thing in a desperate hurry— as we must, if we're to do it all—and then not know how to make a success of it afterwards—if there's to be any afterwards. I'm afraid of myself. Life is too complex for people of our age—there are too many adjustments to make. If we'd come together as we ought to have done, when we loved one another in youth, we'd have made a go of it. But we've had to make our lives separately. You belong to Coombe, and to these people—who all think you'd be ruining yourself by marrying an Irishman like me—someone who just draws pictures. You've got your own responsibilities, that you take so seriously."

"Jess is the only responsibility that really counts. I could leave Coombe."

She looked at him with the extreme gravity of a gentle and sensitive child, seeking a formula in which to express her goodwill.

"I'd thought—but I see that it isn't any use—that perhaps, if it was only ourselves—and Jess and Arlette sometimes—you'd live at Coombe, Rory. You wouldn't, would you?"

"Ah, how can I answer that? You break my heart—

you're so gentle, so generous. But this place—it's the background of almost all your life—it holds all your memories. But what about mine? What about Rory Lonergan? If I lived here I'd be betraying myself, as a person. You don't understand"—he used the phrase that he had used before—"I'd continually need to get away from this way of living. It's all right for you and Coombe, I know, but it all means nothing, and less than nothing, to me. I couldn't stand these people. I'd miss my own raffish friends—all the goings-on that I've taken for granted—getting drunk—I'd lose my own soul. Oh, God, I'll never be able to make you see what I mean."

"I do see. You say that I don't understand, but I do."

She pushed back the silvery wave of hair from her forehead, still looking at him earnestly.

"Val—I'm out of my mind, going on like this. Dear God, what will we do? I love you so, and we're not free —we're being forced apart like this—we can't even take time to make a decision as important as this one."

Valentine drew his head to rest against her breast.

"Do you want not to marry me, Rory? For me to become your mistress?"

"Ah, no, not that, with you. I'd never want that."

"I'm glad."

Presently he said:

"Forgive me for what I've put you through, Val— you must forgive me. Sometimes I get these panics and I can't manage them. Laurence was the only person who could help me—she had great instinctive wisdom. But I hurt her many times, God forgive me, and now I've hurt you."

"It's all right, Rory."

"It is not," he answered sadly.

"You told me once that everything had to be made clear between us. You said that our relationship was far too important for anything else to be possible. It was quite true. The things that you've said to-night had to be faced by us both, hadn't they?"

"They had, but not in the wild, crack-pot state I'm in now. It's been a shattering day, and finding that I

244

couldn't get the child on the telephone to-night just about finished it. To-morrow I'll have sense, Val."

He rose to his feet and looked down at her, appalled by the shadowed pallor of her face and the dark stains beneath her eyes.

"If we had time—if only we had time!" he repeated helplessly.

As though in ironic comment, the clock outside chimed the hour.

"I'll have to go. It'll be to-morrow when I get back."

He took her in his arms and kissed the sorrowful line of her mouth.

"Will it be our wedding day, darling—darling?"

Valentine clung to him without speaking a word for a long moment.

Then she said:

"I don't know, Rory. I love you."

"And I love you," he echoed passionately.

XIX

SHE heard the heavy inner doors swing open and come together again, and then a more distant vibration that was the front door shutting behind Lonergan.

Valentine lay back in her chair, motionless. She was too much tired to move.

The frustrations and disappointments of the day, the news that Lonergan was to be sent overseas and, above all, his exposition of such deeply-rooted complexities of mind and temperament—so deeply rooted that they could temporarily take possession of his judgment and impinge upon his love—had left her desolate and exhausted.

She felt herself to be at last defeated, wholly and finally, in the long, inner conflict between her own romantic spirit and the reality of human relations.

Valentine had no falsely cynical comments to make upon this sense of disillusionment.

She knew still that life might have been otherwise. But defeat was natural to her. She felt it to be inevitable and she had no impulse of blame either towards herself or Lonergan, nor even towards those who had interfered in their affairs.

It was nothing outside himself that had caused her lover to speak the words that kept on repeating themselves over and again in her mind.

"I've seen something of your life . . . I've nothing, nothing in common with any of it. . . . And there's Arlette . . . she's used to an artist's life—the kind that Laurence and I led. . . ."

It came back to Laurence in the end, always. He had even said:

"I get these panics . . . Laurence was the only person who could help me. . . ."

His mad solicitude for Arlette, for whom he had had so little feeling throughout her childhood, was in reality an extension of his love for Arlette's mother.

Not seeking it, but unable to escape it, Valentine was obsessed by the remembrance of Lonergan's profound emotion when he had first told her about Laurence.

"Her forehead was lovely—I honestly can only think of one word that could ever describe the breadth and purity of it—and that's luminous. She had that quality, and it was all in that beautiful, wide brow."

And he'd said:

"We were crazy about one another. I'd decided long ago I wasn't ever going to marry. But I had to ask Laurence to marry me."

Laurence hadn't married him. She'd stood in the little *tonnelle* in the garden of the tall, pink house at Saumur, with the tears running down her face, and she'd offered to come and live with him in Paris.

"That was the thing about Laurence—she understood and accepted things that were quite outside her own tradition."

Lonergan's words, the deep, musical intonations that his voice had given to them, were as living to her as though she were listening as she had listened on the night of his arrival at Coombe. Indeed, they had returned to

246

her many times since then, always with that strange, agonizing pang made of jealousy, and of a deliberate acceptance of the inalienable truth.

He and she had found one another too soon, and too late.

In the years between their two encounters lay their separate lives.

Lonergan had met Laurence. He had loved her as he had not loved, before or since, any of the women who had roused his easy susceptibilities. There would always remain in him the profound desire to keep something of this one true and passionate union alive, in his preoccupation with Laurence's child.

Perhaps I could have borne that—I once thought that I could—Valentine told herself—but he won't share it with me. I can't make him feel that I accept it. He said: I'll never be able to make you see what I mean. . . . You don't understand. . . .

He'd said that more than once.

We ought to have spent our lives together, he and I, thought Valentine. I'd have been the person I was meant to be, then, and we should have felt safe with one another.

She heard a door slam and there was the indefinable sound that warned her of someone approaching.

Valentine put out her hand and turned off the light.

"Val, my dear! Where are you?"

It was Venetia Rockingham's voice.

Valentine made no movement and no reply, and she heard her sister-in-law, after pausing for a moment, go upstairs.

Next day Venetia would have left Coombe. Soon they would all have gone—the girls as well.

Valentine rose wearily. She had felt herself too tired to move, but the physical effort automatically became possible at the remembrance of Primrose and Jessica.

She would go upstairs and say good-night to Jess, even though she might not intrude upon her other and most-loved child.

When she came downstairs again, to extinguish the lights and make certain that the door was unbolted for

Lonergan's return in the early morning, it was nearly midnight and Valentine was startled by the sound of the telephone-bell.

There leapt instantly to her mind the wild hope that she might hear Rory Lonergan's voice, but it was a busy-sounding, impersonal tone that came through the receiver.

"I have a telegram for Colonel Lonergan. Will you take it?"

"I'll take it," said Valentine.

She drew towards her the little pad that swung against the wall and balanced it against the bracket on which stood the telephone. Her cold fingers found the blunt, small pencil that lay there in readiness. Her mind automatically registered, as it had done for years, a protest against the inconvenience of all these arrangements.

"Handed in at Kilronan at twenty-five minutes past four."

Valentine's pencil obediently wrote down: Kilronan 4.25. She waited while the male voice at the other end gave Lonergan's name and address.

The message followed:

"Please come or send for me flying quite possible want terribly to see you please telephone first I implore you come to Babette qui rit please.

"That's all. No signature. Shall I send a confirmation copy?"

"Yes, please."

"What is the postal address?"

Valentine gave it, and hung up the receiver.

She stood in the cold, mechanically smoothing out the paper on which she had taken down Arlette's message.

Babette qui rit.

Rory hadn't told her about that pet-name, the familiar household joke that must have survived from Arlette's baby days.

Poor, touching, frantic child, making use of it now to strengthen her appeal.

Valentine had no idea whether or not it would be possible for Lonergan to get to Ireland and back within

248

the forty-eight hours of his leave. She supposed that probably it would.

Or he could send for Arlette if there was the least chance that the battalion might not be sailing at once.

She returned to the hall, moving slowly and stiffly as if the intense cold that gripped her was slowly freezing her body into rigidity. Her thoughts worked, with careful impersonality, over the mechanics of the situation.

Lonergan had missed Arlette at the telephone but he said that he had telegraphed to her in the morning.

That message must have reached her quickly enough, or she couldn't have despatched her own telegram at twenty-five minutes past four.

Perhaps he hadn't told her what time he would ring up.

Perhaps the old aunt, whom it was so impossible to think of as Rory's sister, had decided that Arlette must attend the concert, and that another telephone call could be put through next day. But no—that wouldn't do. There'd have been a message left at Kilronan post-office in that case, surely.

Valentine decided that Lonergan, in his telegram, had announced the fact of his embarkation leave and had said that he would telephone, without specifying the day or the hour. How, indeed, could he have been certain of the hour at all?

Her meaningless speculations and calculations brought Valentine into her own room, the full onslaught of the pain that awaited her still held at bay.

The clock on the landing struck five. Valentine had heard the chiming of all the hours since one o'clock.

As the last reverberation died away, another sound, remote and carefully controlled, reached her. It was that of the hall door being cautiously opened and shut again.

She knew that Lonergan had returned.

Lying open-eyed in the dark, her senses acutely sharpened, she seemed to herself able to follow all his movements accurately.

Now he had passed through the swing-doors and stopped in the hall. Conspicuous on a table at the foot of the stairs lay her transcription of Arlette's telegram, where she had placed it, clearing everything off the little table so that he could not miss it.

He was reading it now.

There was no further sound.

She lay, expecting to hear him go down the hall again, to where the telephone was. But no movement of any kind reached her.

Valentine remained tense and motionless for what appeared to her a long while.

Presently she glanced at the illuminated face of the travelling clock, old and shabby and reliable—one of her wedding presents, she remembered—that stood in its faded blue-and-gilt folding frame next to her bedside.

Twenty minutes had gone by since she had heard the clock strike, and Rory Lonergan letting himself in at the door. The stillness was absolute.

At last it was broken.

She heard Lonergan's step on the stairs.

He was walking slowly and with care, as though anxious to make no noise.

At the door of his room he did not stop, nor did the faint, familiar click of the turning handle reach her. He was going straight on, past his own room, to the end of the schoolroom passage where the short flight of stairs led to the top storey.

Valentine waited, sad and bewildered, but she heard nothing more.

No explanation occurred to her. She was too weary to search for one, and presently she fell asleep.

Madeleine's knock at the door woke her.

Madeleine put down the small tea-tray by the bed and drew back the curtains. It was not quite dark, a chill dawn was breaking and a pearly grey light filtered into the room.

Valentine shivered and lay still.

Madeleine came and stood beside the bed.

"Madame," she said softly, "the world is all white. It has been snowing."

Old associations rushed into Valentine's mind instantly. Her own astonished pleasure, in childhood, at the still purity of the English countryside under snow . . . the excited delight of Primrose as a little girl building a snow-man on the lawn with Humphrey . . . the branches of the trees in the orchard sending up an occasional light flurry of white from snow-laden branches. All came and went in a flash and then she was fully awakened, caught into the realities of the present.

"Is it half-past seven?" she asked doubtfully.

There was a strange stillness over everything, as though Coombe had not yet emerged from the enveloping quiet of the night.

"Seven o'clock, madame—six, in reality," answered Madeleine. "It has been snowing hard since midnight."

She indicated the window by a gesture, but it was not yet light enough to see anything.

"It was *monsieur le colonel* who told me," Madeleine said, and she fixed her great brown eyes on Valentine's face with a compelling candour.

"*Monsieur le colonel* came to find me, madame, at five o'clock this morning and he gave me a letter for madame."

She laid it on the bed, and as Valentine took it and opened it Madeleine found a pale woollen wrap and placed it over her shoulders.

With astonishment Valentine realized that she had never seen Lonergan's handwriting before. It was heavy, as though he wrote with a thick-pointed nib, and it bore the appearance of being illegible. But she found that she could read easily the few lines that he had written.

"*My Love, my own darling—I'd come to you now but that it's the middle of the night and I mustn't make a scandal for you at Coombe. Will you come down to me in the office as soon as you get this? I've been out of my mind, since leaving you last night. Nothing matters at all, except that we belong to one another. I love you utterly.*"

He had signed it with his initial.

Madeleine stood at the foot of the bed.

"When madame is dressed, I will bring coffee to the little breakfast-room. It is better that everything should be arranged before anyone is downstairs. *Monsieur le colonel* will be there already, for I called him before coming in here. Madame will forgive me."

"Ah, Madeleine!" said Valentine, and she smiled although tears were falling from her eyes.

"Madame perceives that I know all. *Monsieur le colonel* did well, to come and find me so early this morning. He knew that I could help madame."

She paused for a moment, and then, choosing her words with delicacy and discretion, she said:

"I think madame will find that *monsieur le colonel* has his car at the door. Madame will need her fur coat, if she decides to go out with him. It is waiting in the hall."

The fur-lined grey tweed, shabby and shapeless, lay across the back of a chair when Valentine, a very few minutes later, went downstairs to find Rory Lonergan.

He was waiting for her at the foot of the stairs, his dark upturned face full of the strain and fatigue of the night.

As he saw her, all look of fatigue fled, leaving nothing but the defenceless look of love.

"Rory."

"Val. My darling. My Val."

As he bent his black head over hers, he said:

"I was mad yesterday. Forgive me. There's nothing and no one but you in the world. Marry me, Val, and let's make what we can of what's left to us."

"I'll do anything that you want me to do," she said, and joy rang in her voice.

"Ah, darling—darling!"

"Arlette—— Did you find Arlette's message?"'s he asked.

"I did, the little poor child! I'll talk to her on the telephone and see what can be done."

"Can you go to Ireland?"

"If I go to Ireland," he answered gravely, "it'll be with my wife. That's all that matters to me."

Madeleine passed through the red-baize door carrying a tray and took it into Lonergan's office.

"She's got some coffee for us."

"Come and drink it, love. You need it. Val, will we get away before anyone else comes down? Will you marry me this morning, as soon as the Registrar's office opens?"

"You know I will."

She poured out the hot coffee and handed him a cup.

The dream-like sensation that lay upon Valentine like a spell slowly lost its strength.

"Last night," she said, "I thought that we couldn't do it. We couldn't marry. And the things that you said then are still true, you know."

"They're true—but not the whole truth," he answered. "God forgive me for talking the way I did, darling, but I was fit to be tied, the way that sister-in-law of yours had been going on, and I got into a panic. And all the time, I knew very well I was behaving like a lunatic and that whatever the difficulties, we could surmount them together. Forgive me, Val. Forgive me."

"Anything in the world. Always. If there's anything to forgive, Rory."

"Ah, you know there is. There will be again, if we're allowed any sort of life together."

Their eyes met over the tragic implication of the words, and they were silent.

Presently Lonergan said:

"Love, you're quite right. The things I spoke of yesterday are still true—they'll always to a certain extent be true. I can't live your life, at Coombe. Can you live mine? Not the way it was before the war—that's over and done with—but perhaps in London, when I'll be doing my own job again, drawing."

"I can," she answered gently and steadily. "Coombe was for the children, and there are no children any more. Even Jess—she's going away and she won't ever live here again while the war lasts. And after that we none of us know what this war country will be like, do we? All we know is that our daughters won't be able to live at home, idle, in houses like Coombe, ever again."

She looked round the room, already made unfamiliar by the office equipment that had been installed for Lonergan.

She thought of the house and the garden, so closely associated with the whole of her married life and with the childhood of Primrose and Jess, so full of the memories of five and twenty years.

Then she looked again at Rory Lonergan.

No conscious recollection came to her of the young

253

Irish boy with whom she had once shared a true and ardent moment of emotion in youth. She saw in him simply her lover: the man who justified to herself her deepest beliefs for ever.

"You've made everything come true," she said, hardly knowing that she was speaking the words aloud.

"And you for me," he answered.

When they went out together through the double doors the pale light of the winter's day was dawning.

The slopes of the park were enveloped in snow, all traces of the winding road buried beneath its smooth and dazzling white.

The outline of every bush and tree was altered and rendered new and unfamiliar.

The strange hush that belongs to the fall of snow lay over everything.

For a moment they looked in silence.

Then Lonergan spoke, very softly :

"Ah, it's wonderful. What a day on which to find one another!"

"It was early summer, the first time," she said. "Do you remember?"

"I remember, love. My girl of the Pincio Gardens!"

His hand touched gently the silvery wave of her hair.

Made and printed in France.
7766-9-48. — Imp. CRÉTÉ, Corbeil. — C. O. L. 31-1631.

A LIST OF PAN BOOKS

GREAT PAN DOUBLE-VOLUMES

Alice's Adventures in Wonderland *with*
Through the Looking-Glass   LEWIS CARROLL

Including all the original 92 illustrations by Sir John Tenniel.

The Fountain   CHARLES MORGAN

World-famous love-story of passionate intensity, pitched on a high spiritual level.

Guide to Modern Thought   C. E. M. JOAD

Revised and enlarged edition. Explains and assesses contemporary views on physics, psychology, abnormal psychical phenomena, etc. By the famous broadcaster.

Fanny by Gaslight   MICHAEL SADLEIR

Well-known novel about the grim underworld of London high society in the 1870s.

Royal Dukes   ROGER FULFORD

Highly entertaining biography of Queen Victoria's father and "wicked uncles"—the eccentric sons of George III over whose lives a curtain of modesty used to be drawn.

The Years   VIRGINIA WOOLF

Exquisitely written "family" novel by the greatest English woman writer of her time, depicting the half-century from the 'eighties to the nineteen-thirties.

The Young Melbourne   LORD DAVID CECIL

Fascinating account of the early years of Queen Victoria's great Prime Minister, with the full story of his marriage to the wayward Lady Caroline Ponsonby and of her extraordinary love-affair with Byron. With 7 photogravure illustrations.

Escape with Me!   OSBERT SITWELL

Entrancing travel-book about the amazing ruined temples of Cambodia and the Forbidden City of Peking, by winner of the *Sunday Times'* 1947 Book Prize of £1,000.